Bigby Bear

THE EXPLORER

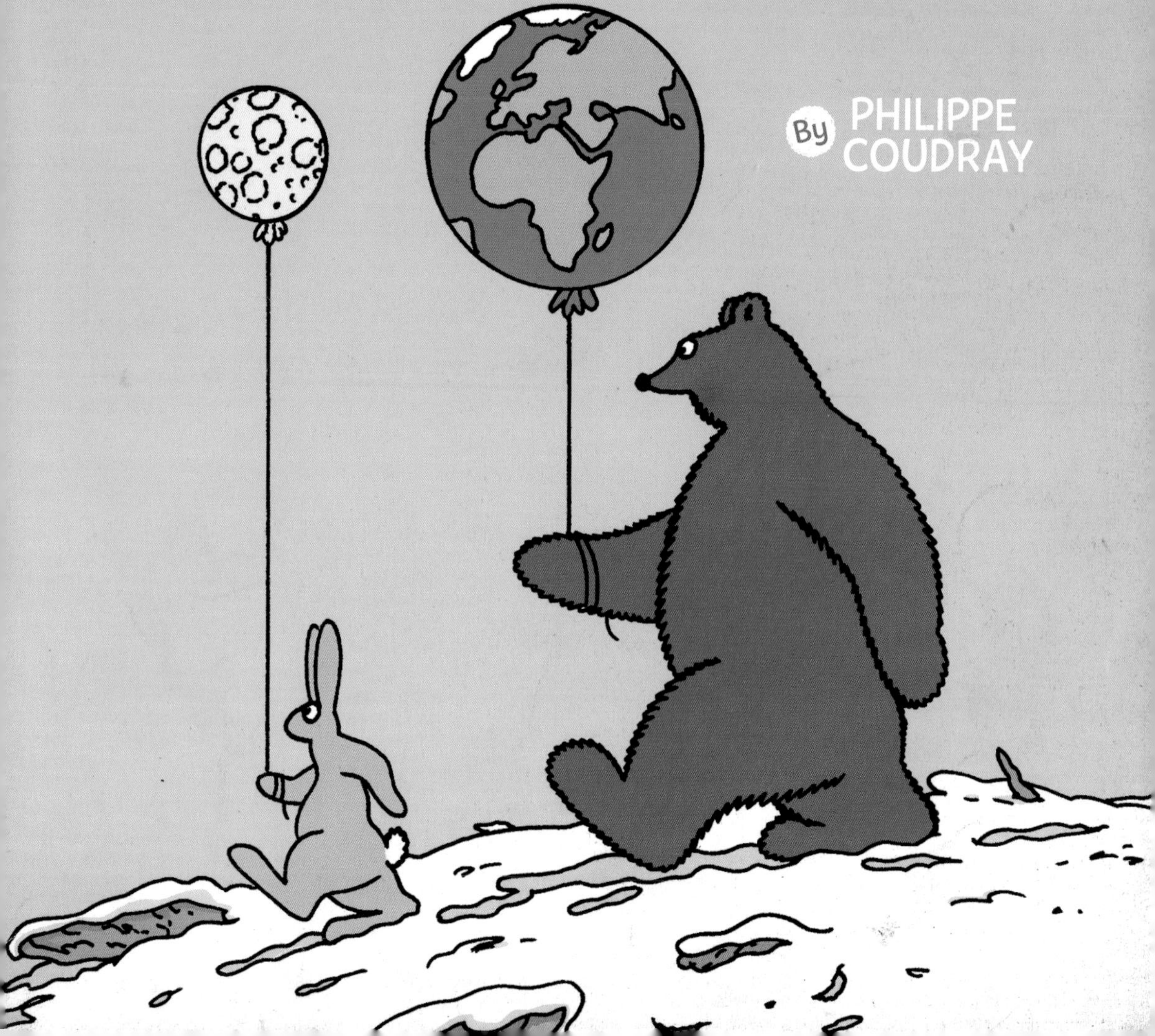

By PHILIPPE COUDRAY

Philippe Coudray
Story & Art

•

Miceal Beausang-O'Griafa
Translator

•

Fabrice Sapolsky
US Edition Editor

Amanda Lucido
Assistant Editor

Vincent Henry
Original Edition Editor

Jerry Frissen
Senior Art Director

Fabrice Giger
Publisher

Rights and Licensing - licensing@humanoids.com
Press and Social Media - pr@humanoids.com

BIGBY BEAR, BOOK 3: THE EXPLORER. This title is a publication of Humanoids, Inc. 8033 Sunset Blvd. #628, Los Angeles, CA 90046.
Copyright © 2020 Humanoids, Inc., Los Angeles (USA). All rights reserved. Humanoids and its logos are ® and © 2020 Humanoids, Inc.
Library of Congress Control Number: 2019914898

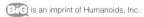 is an imprint of Humanoids, Inc.

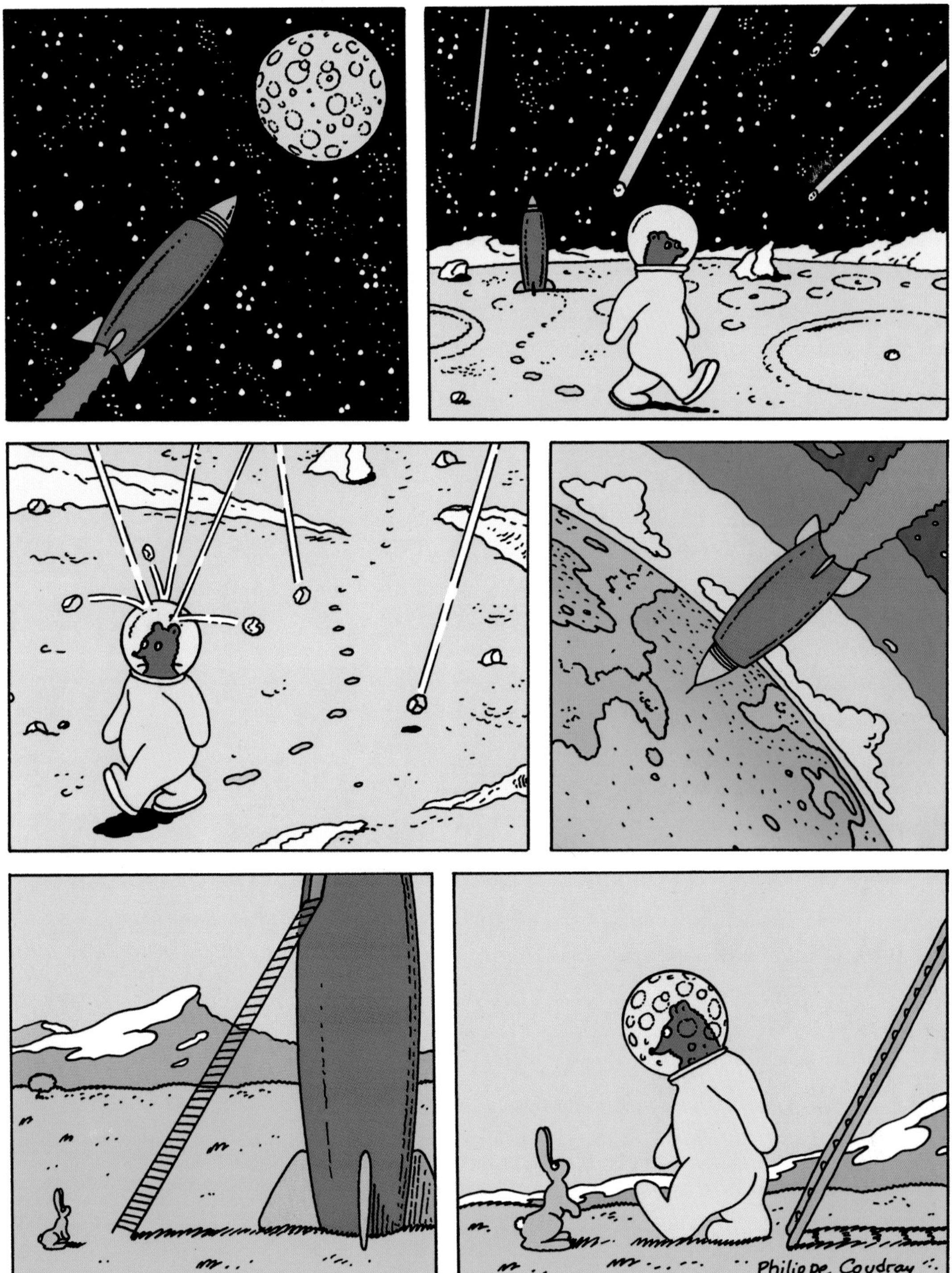
Philippe Coudray

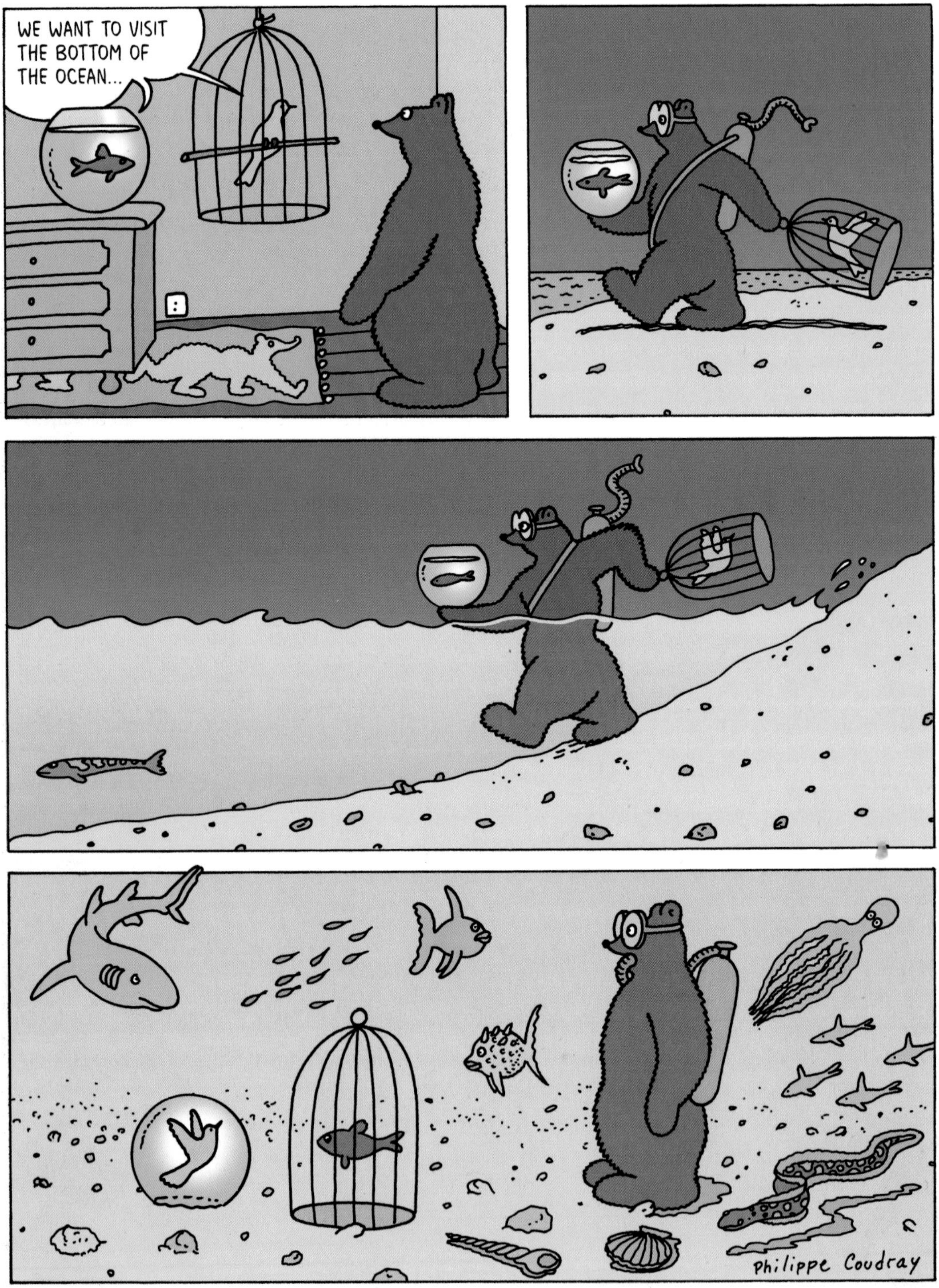
WE WANT TO VISIT THE BOTTOM OF THE OCEAN...
Philippe Coudray

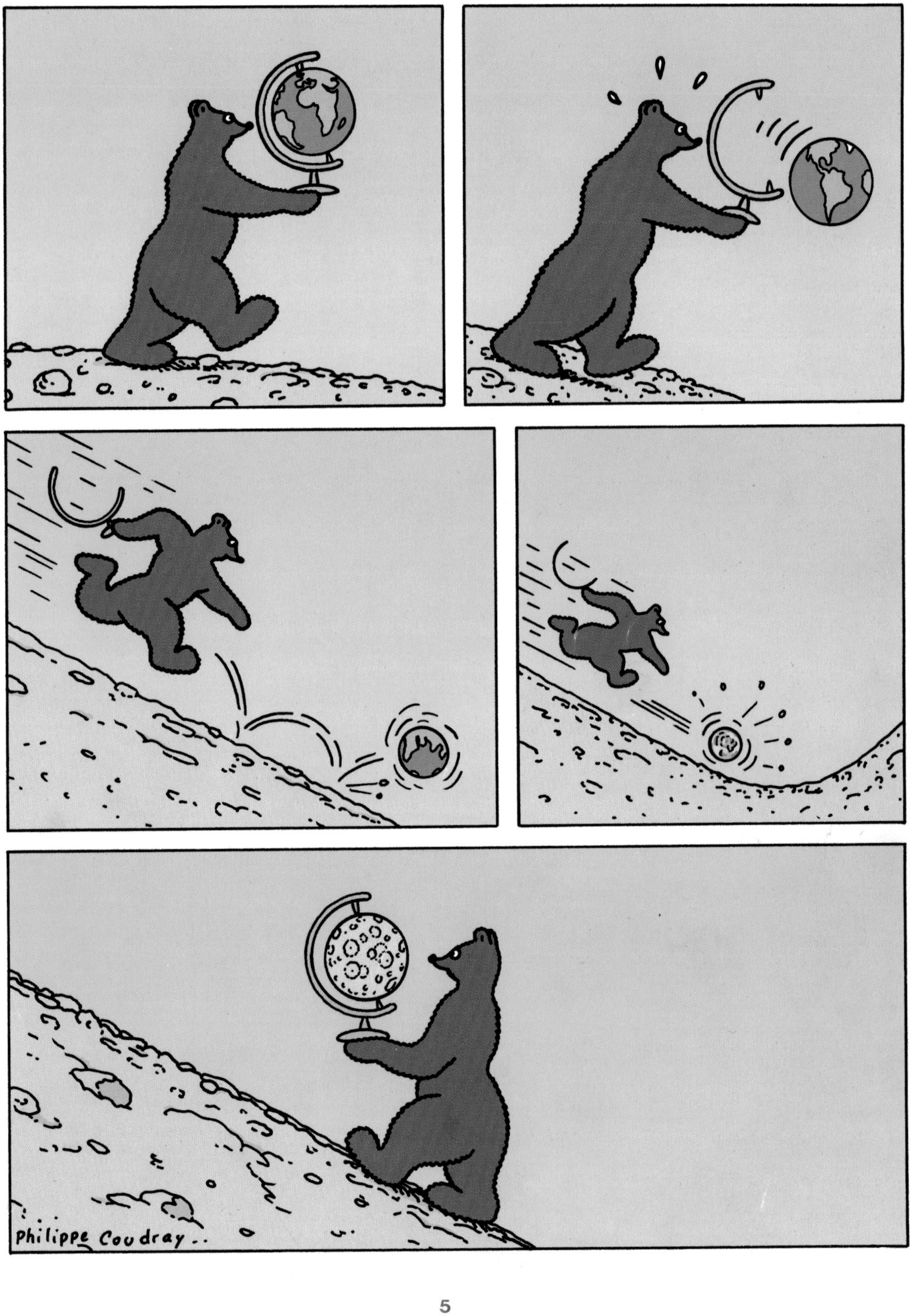
Philippe Coudray

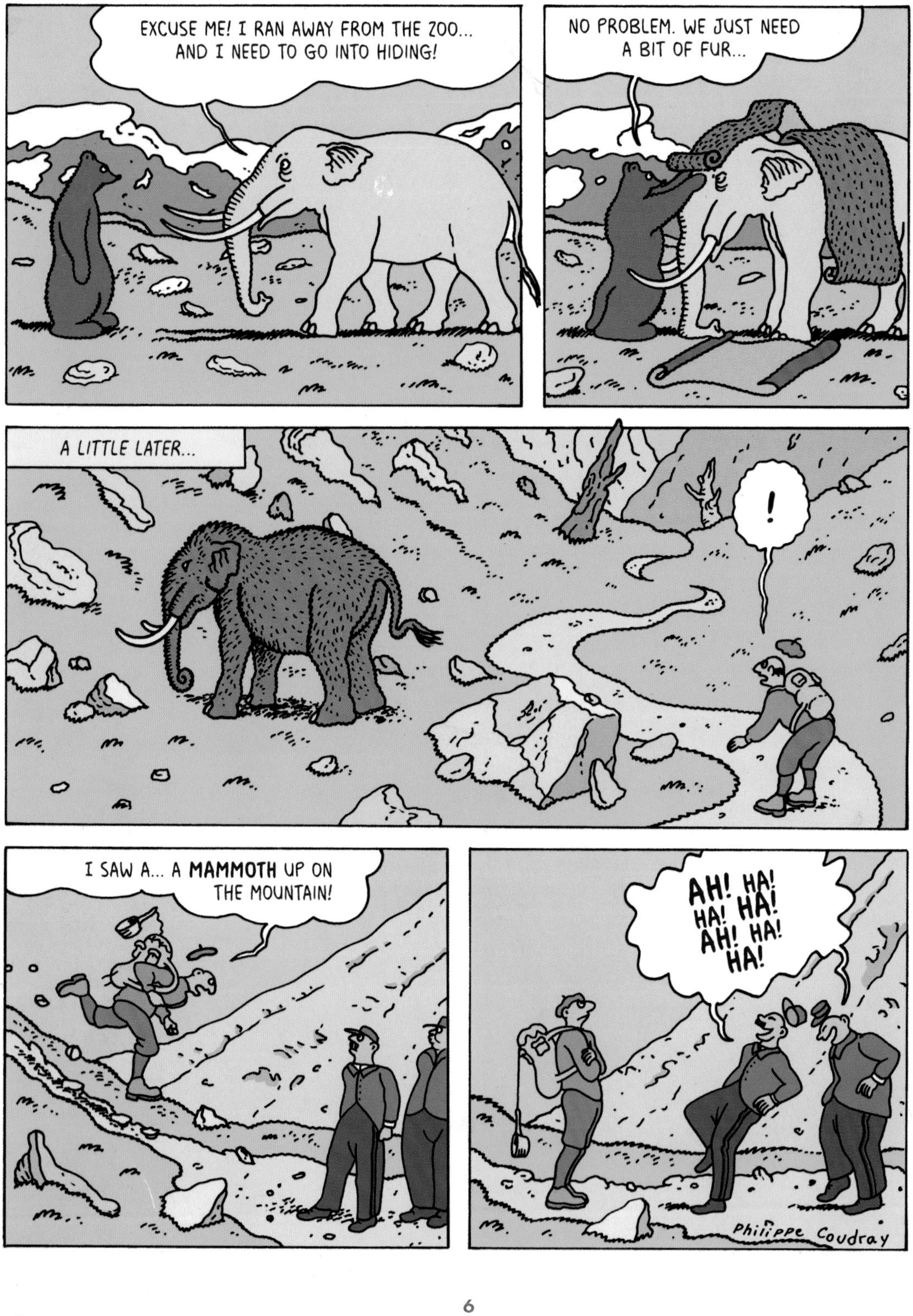
EXCUSE ME! I RAN AWAY FROM THE ZOO... AND I NEED TO GO INTO HIDING!
NO PROBLEM. WE JUST NEED A BIT OF FUR...
A LITTLE LATER...
!
I SAW A... A **MAMMOTH** UP ON THE MOUNTAIN!
AH! HA! HA! HA! AH! HA! HA!
Philippe Coudray

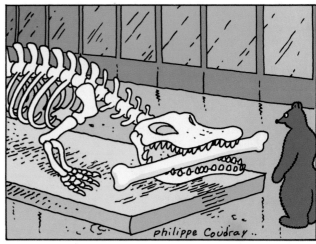

philippe Coudray

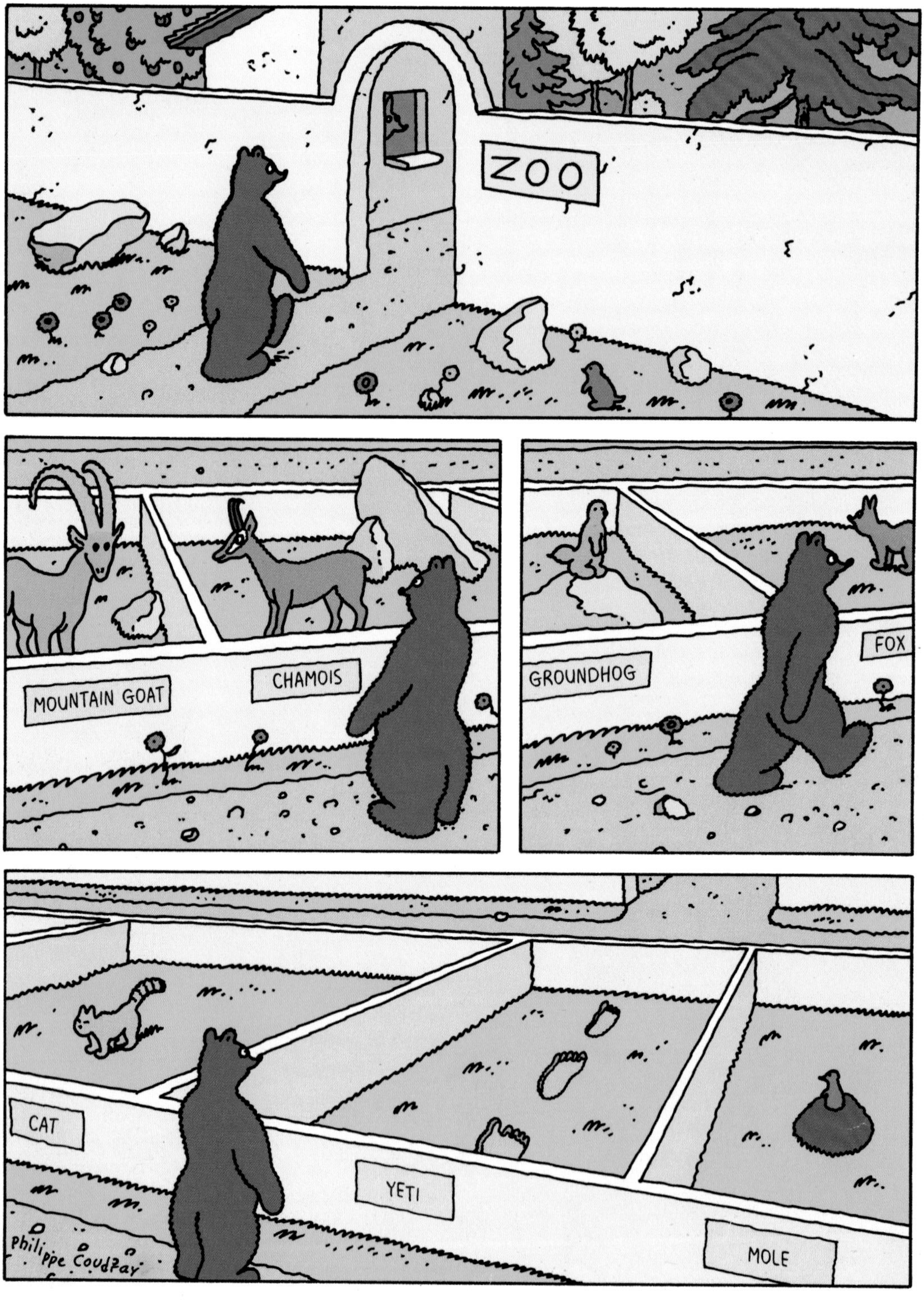
ZOO
MOUNTAIN GOAT
CHAMOIS
GROUNDHOG
FOX
CAT
YETI
MOLE
Philippe Coudray

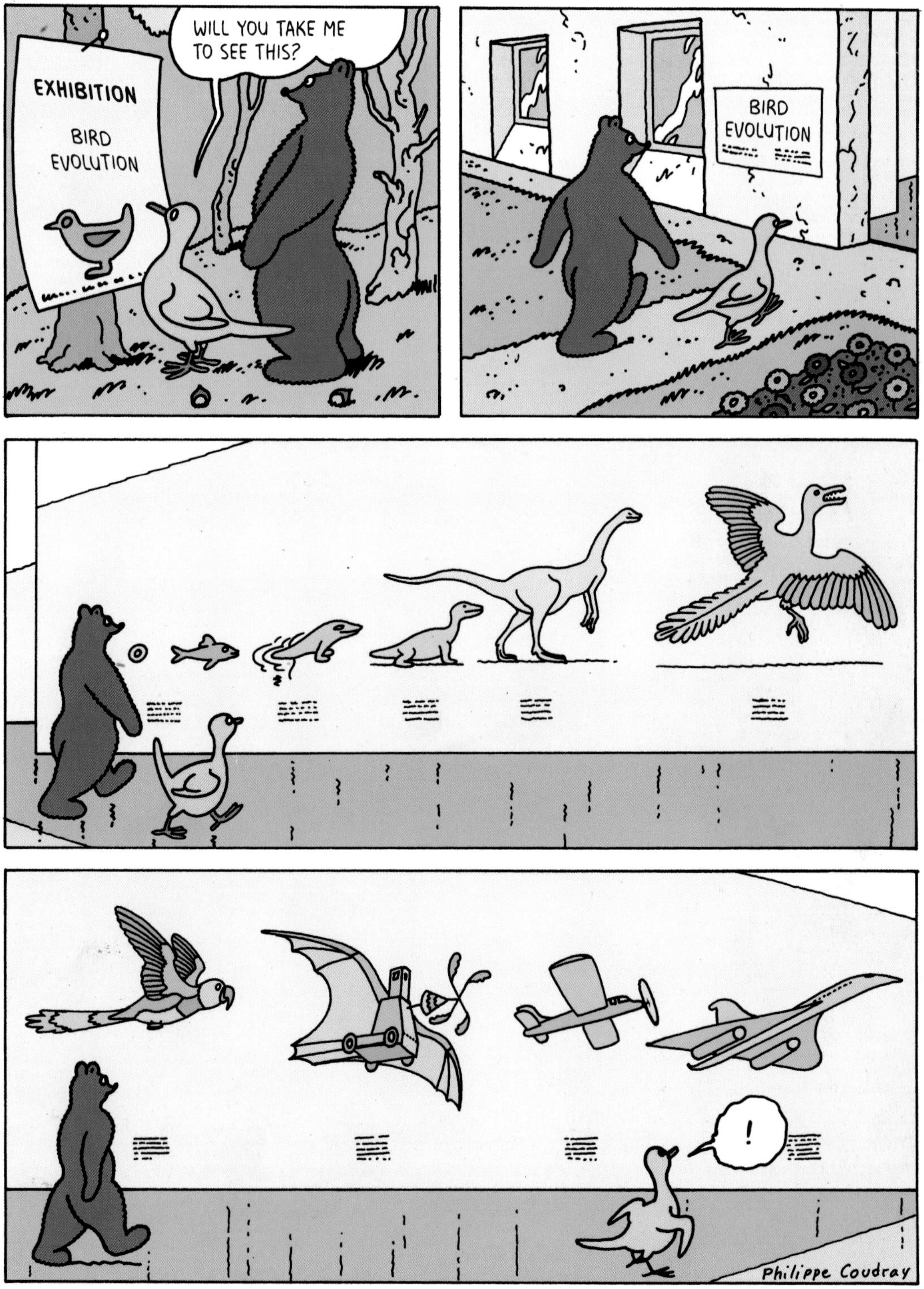
EXHIBITION
BIRD EVOLUTION
WILL YOU TAKE ME TO SEE THIS?
BIRD EVOLUTION
!
Philippe Coudray

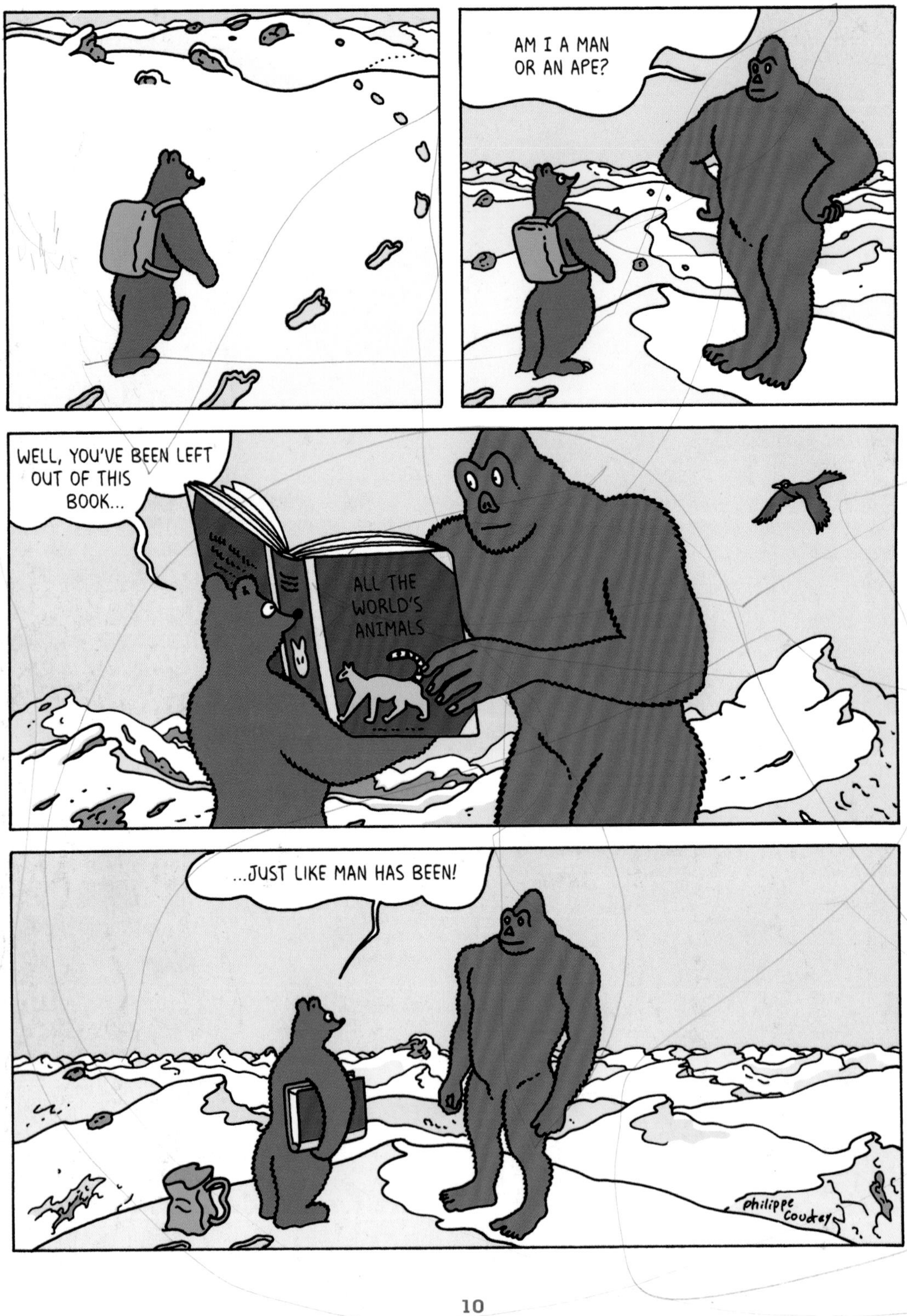
AM I A MAN OR AN APE?
WELL, YOU'VE BEEN LEFT OUT OF THIS BOOK...
ALL THE WORLD'S ANIMALS
...JUST LIKE MAN HAS BEEN!
philippe coudray

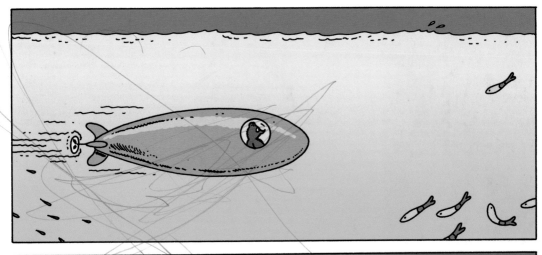

philippe Coudray

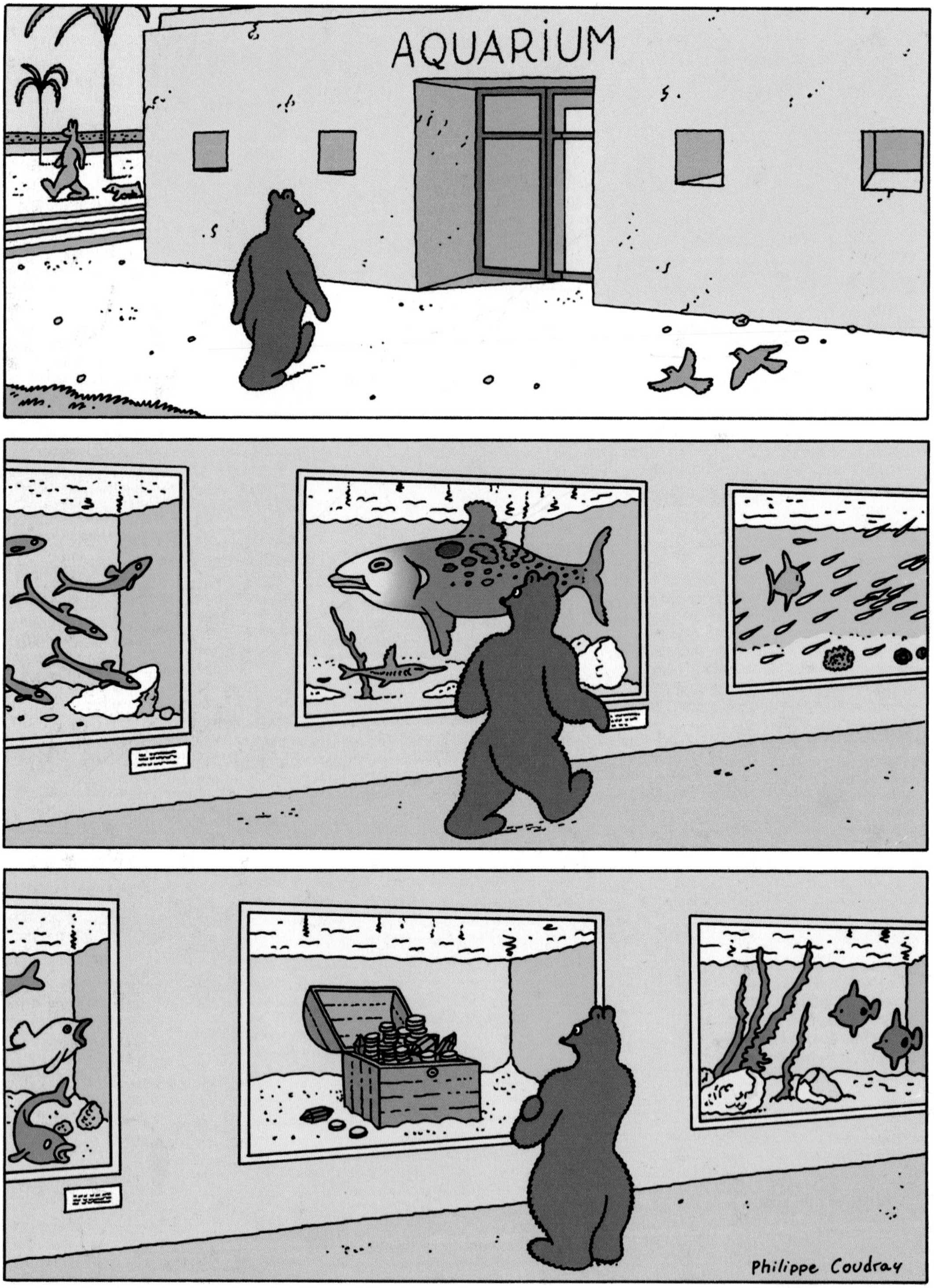
AQUARIUM
Philippe Coudray

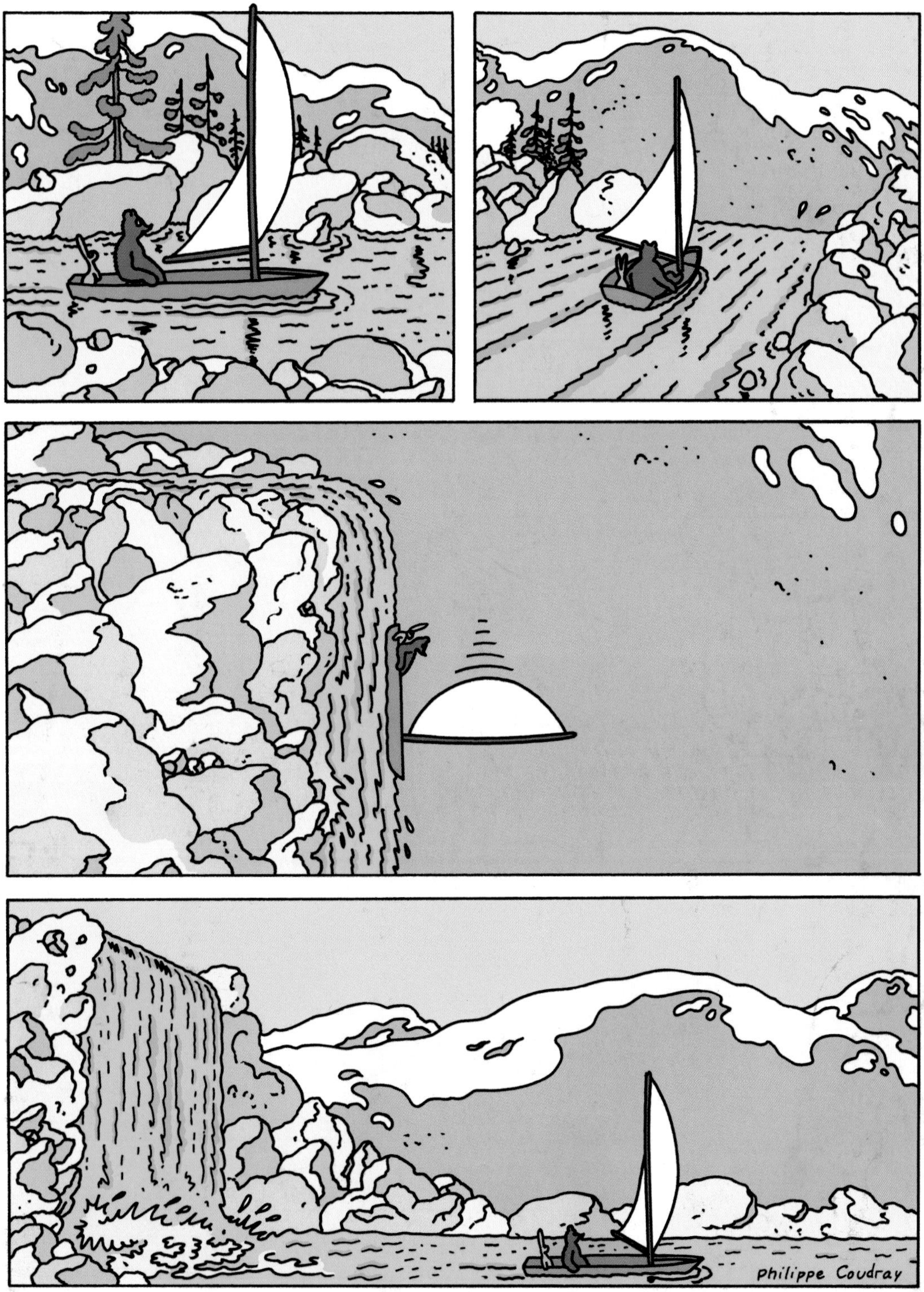
philippe Coudray

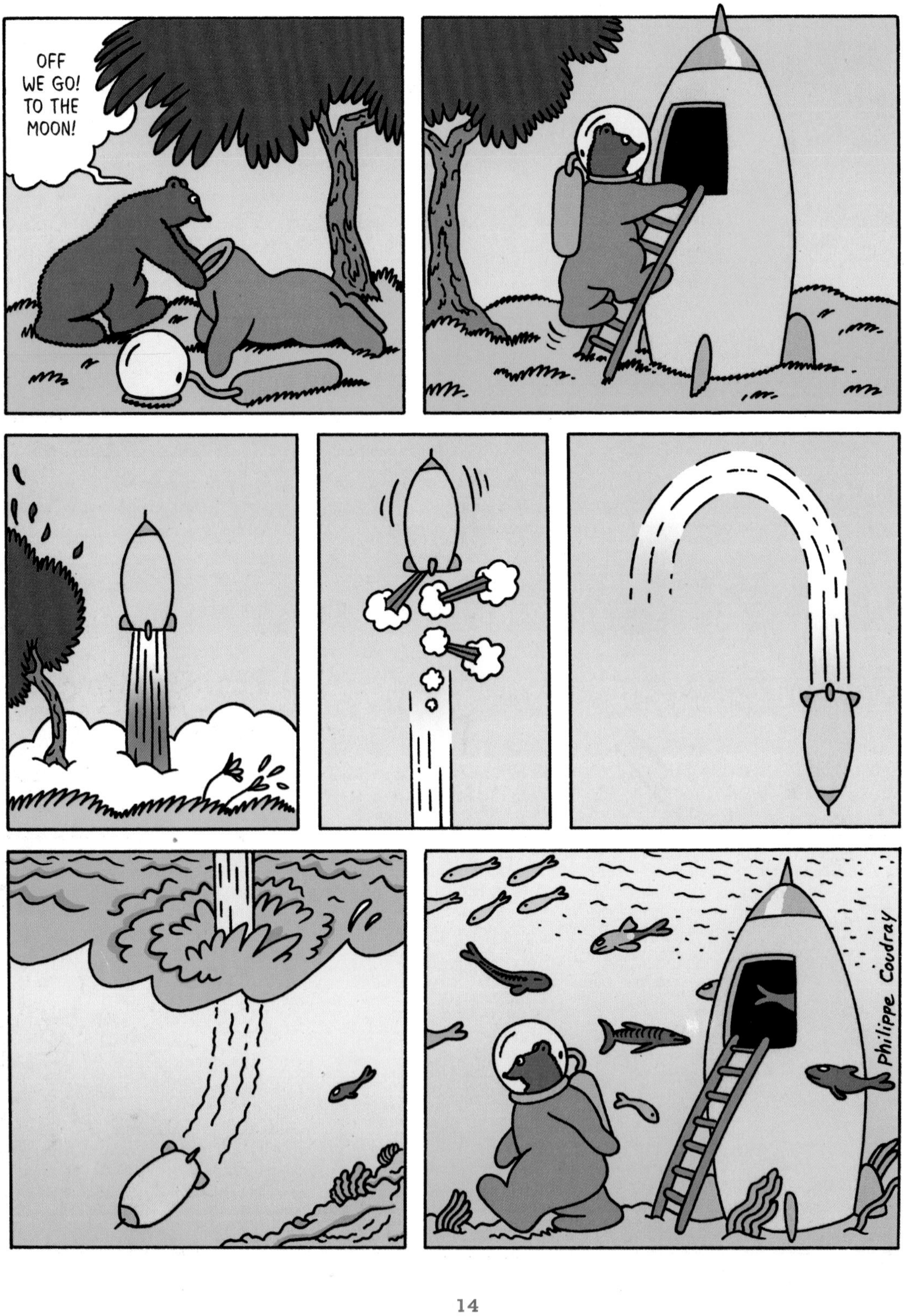
OFF WE GO! TO THE MOON!
Philippe Coudray

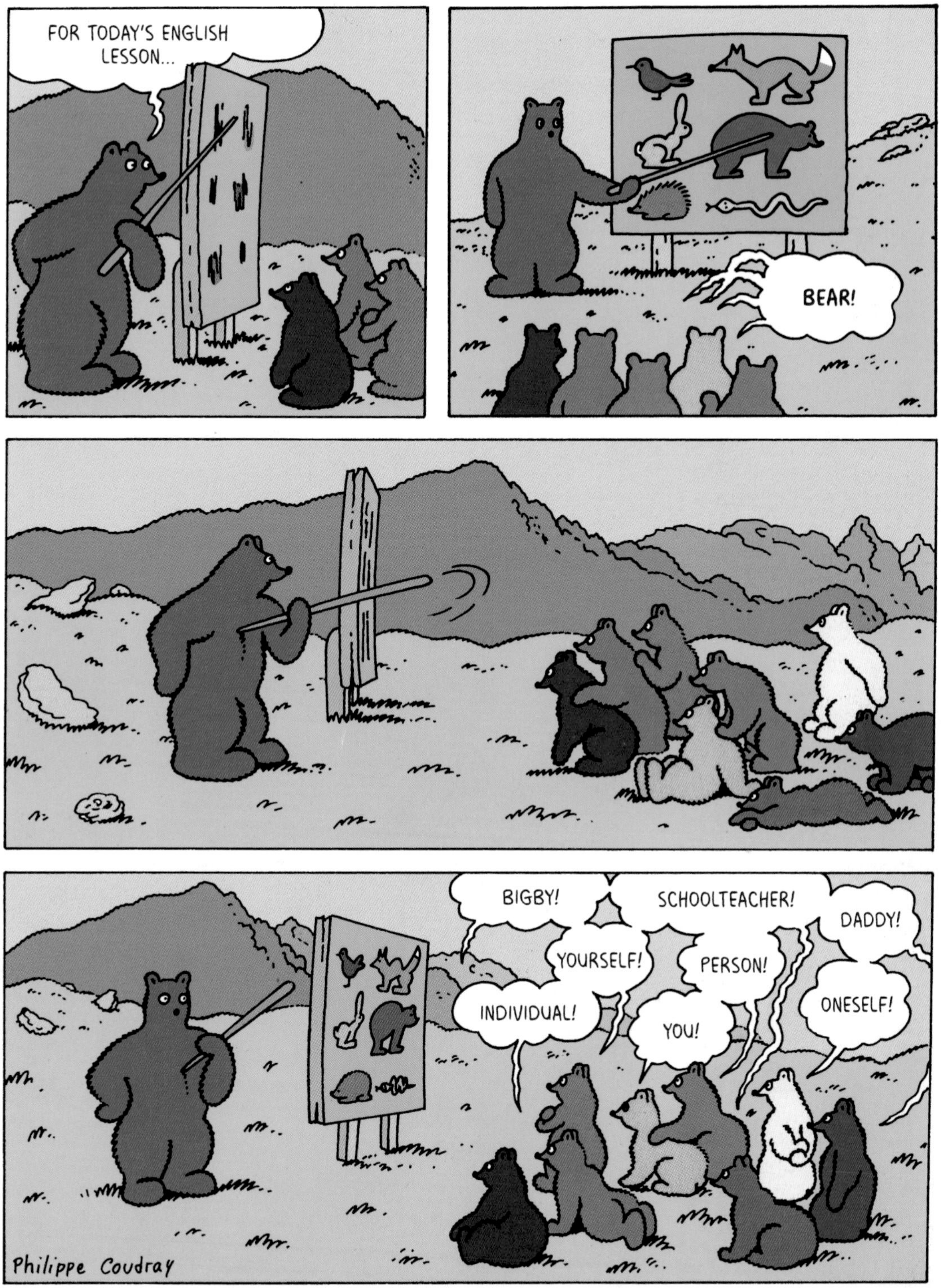
FOR TODAY'S ENGLISH LESSON...
BEAR!
BIGBY!
SCHOOLTEACHER!
DADDY!
YOURSELF!
PERSON!
INDIVIDUAL!
YOU!
ONESELF!
Philippe Coudray

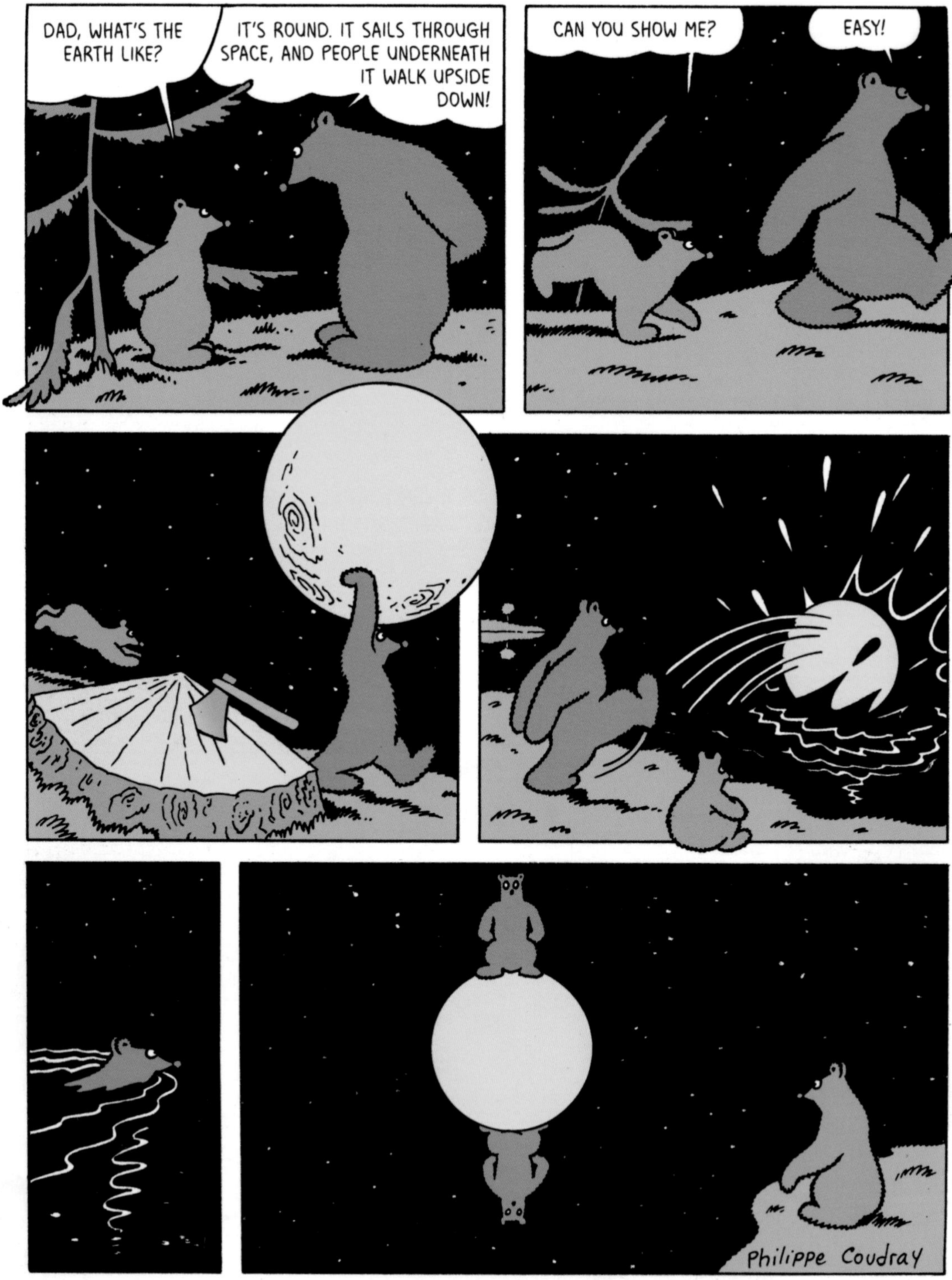
DAD, WHAT'S THE EARTH LIKE?
IT'S ROUND. IT SAILS THROUGH SPACE, AND PEOPLE UNDERNEATH IT WALK UPSIDE DOWN!
CAN YOU SHOW ME?
EASY!
Philippe Coudray

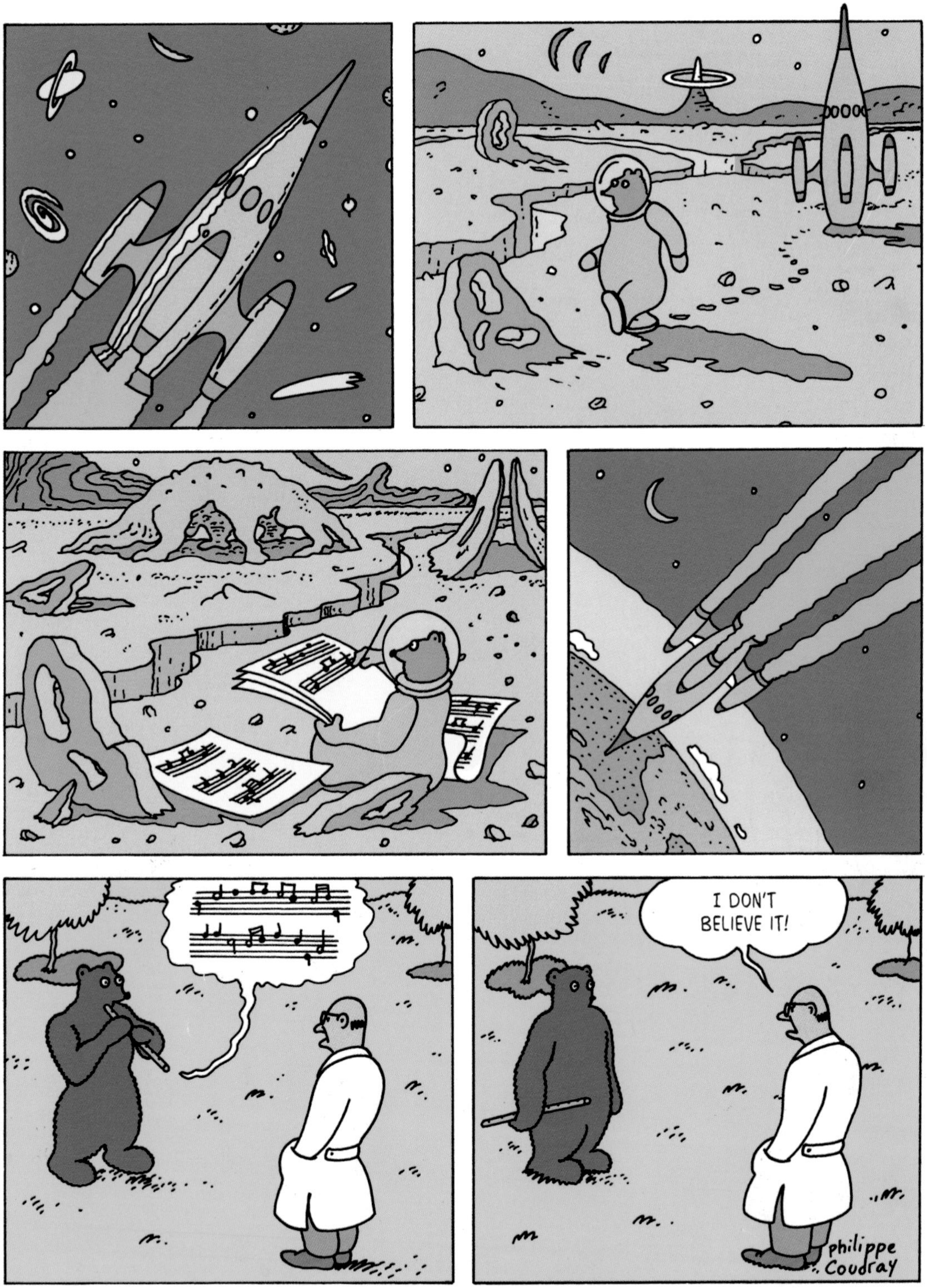
I DON'T BELIEVE IT!
philippe Coudray

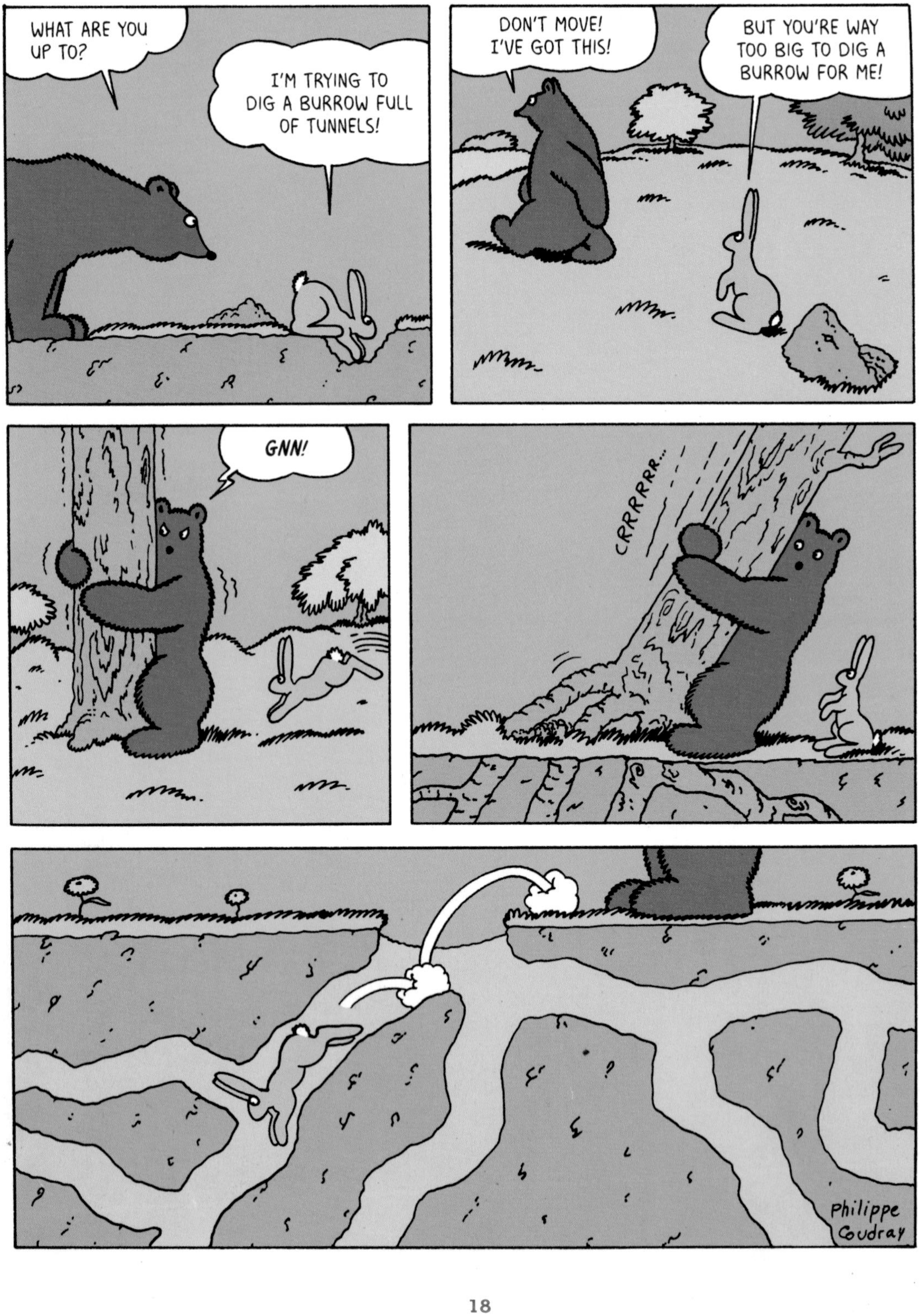
WHAT ARE YOU UP TO?
I'M TRYING TO DIG A BURROW FULL OF TUNNELS!
DON'T MOVE! I'VE GOT THIS!
BUT YOU'RE WAY TOO BIG TO DIG A BURROW FOR ME!
GNN!
CRRRRRR...
Philippe Coudray

MY PLANET IS SO TINY, I'M RUNNING OUT OF SPACE TO PUT MY STUFF!
?
THANKS!
philippe Coudray

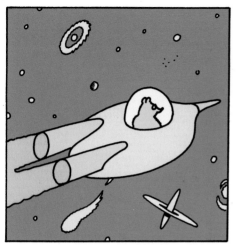

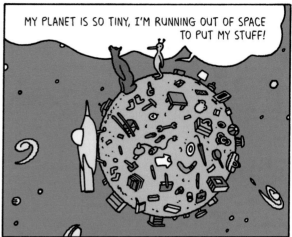

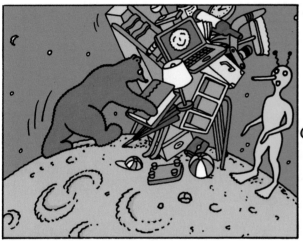

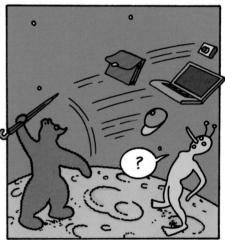

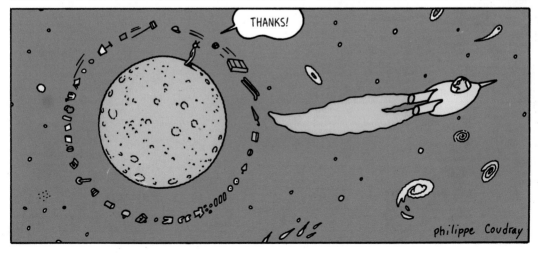

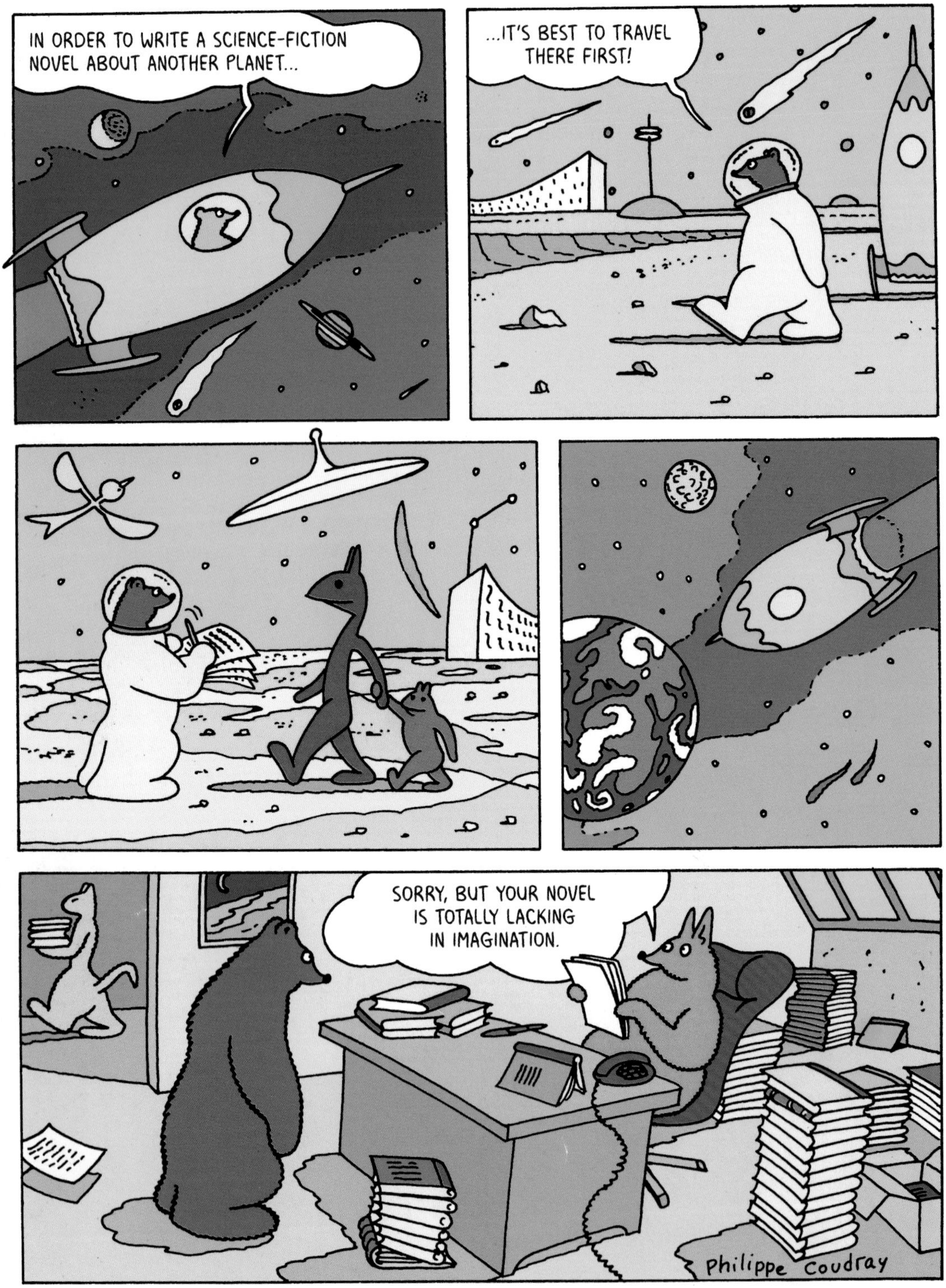
IN ORDER TO WRITE A SCIENCE-FICTION NOVEL ABOUT ANOTHER PLANET...
...IT'S BEST TO TRAVEL THERE FIRST!
SORRY, BUT YOUR NOVEL IS TOTALLY LACKING IN IMAGINATION.
Philippe Coudray

THE INSTRUCTION MANUALS FOR THESE NEW MACHINES ARE GETTING LONGER AND LONGER!
IT'S BECAUSE THEY HAVEN'T EVOLVED ENOUGH YET.
LATER.
I BOUGHT A NEW HI-TECH FOOD PROCESSOR!
INSTRUCTION MANUAL
Philippe Coudray

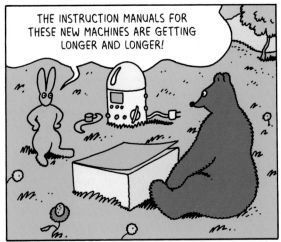

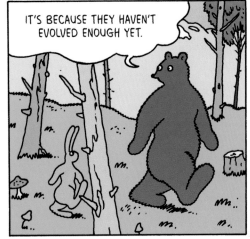

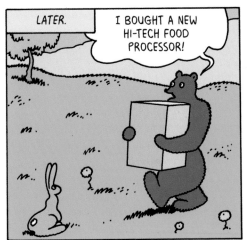

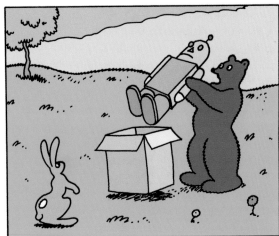

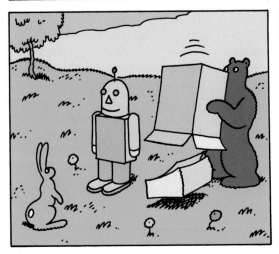

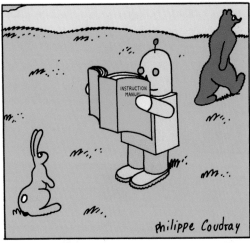

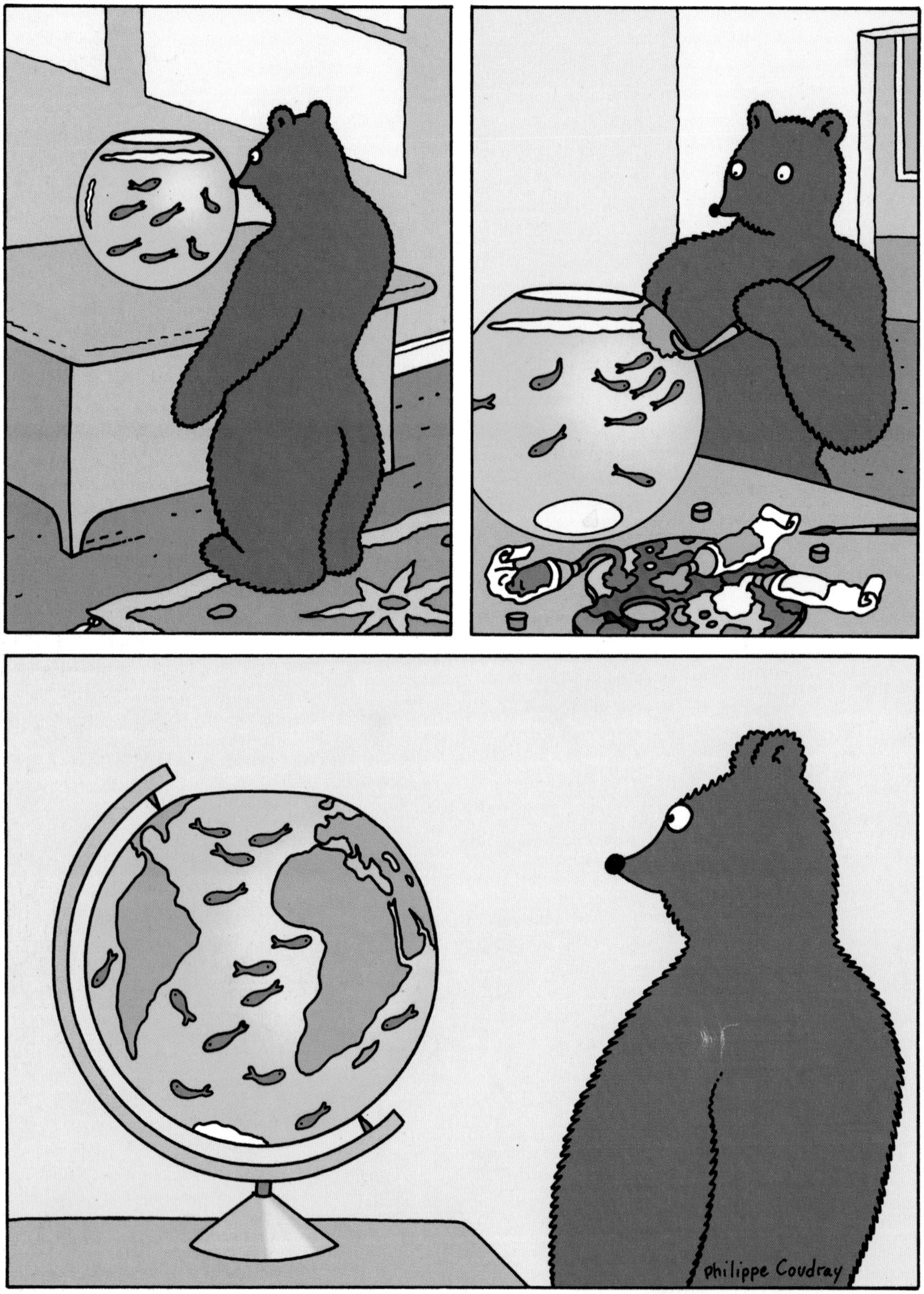
Philippe Coudray

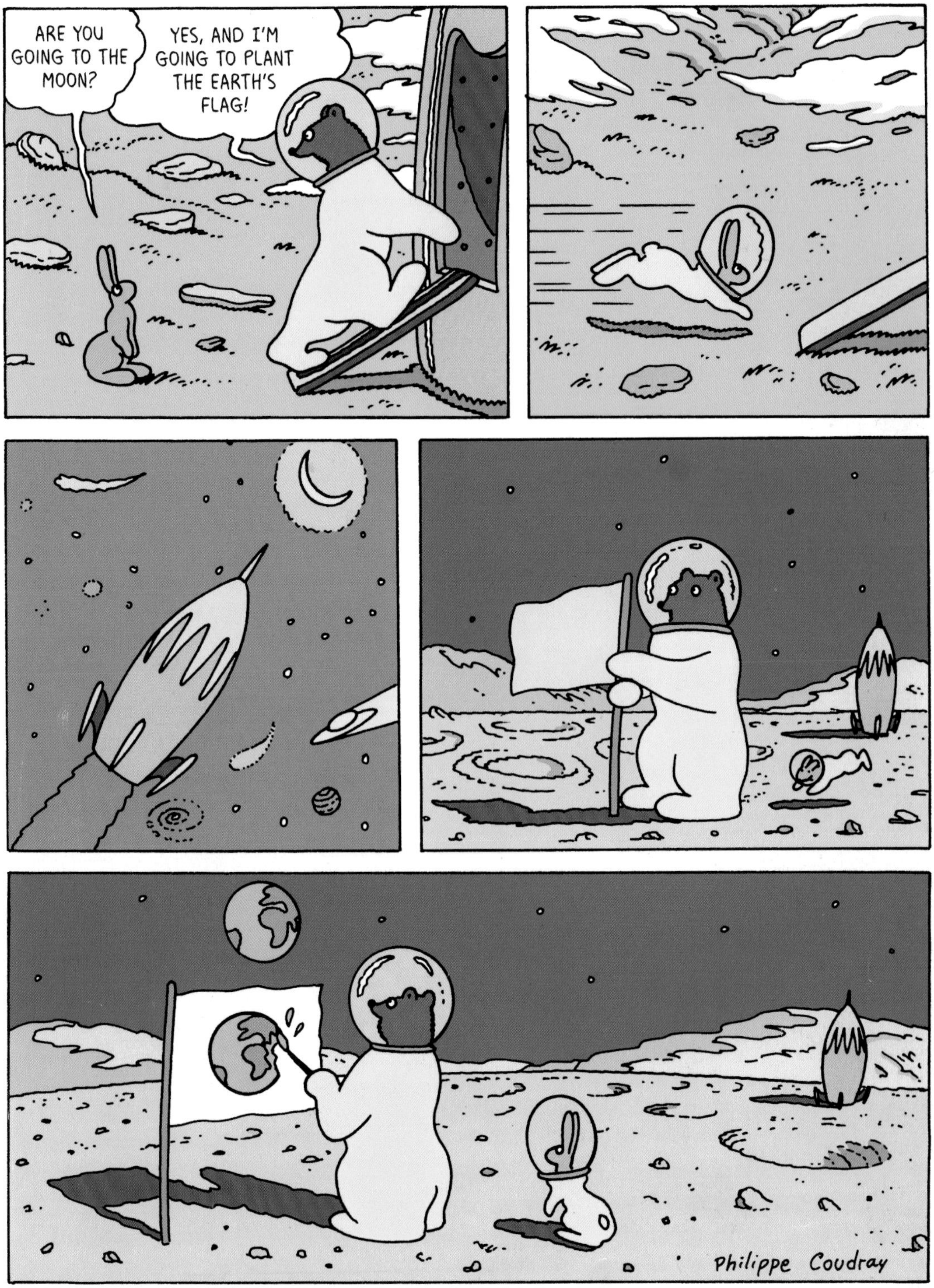
ARE YOU GOING TO THE MOON?
YES, AND I'M GOING TO PLANT THE EARTH'S FLAG!
Philippe Coudray

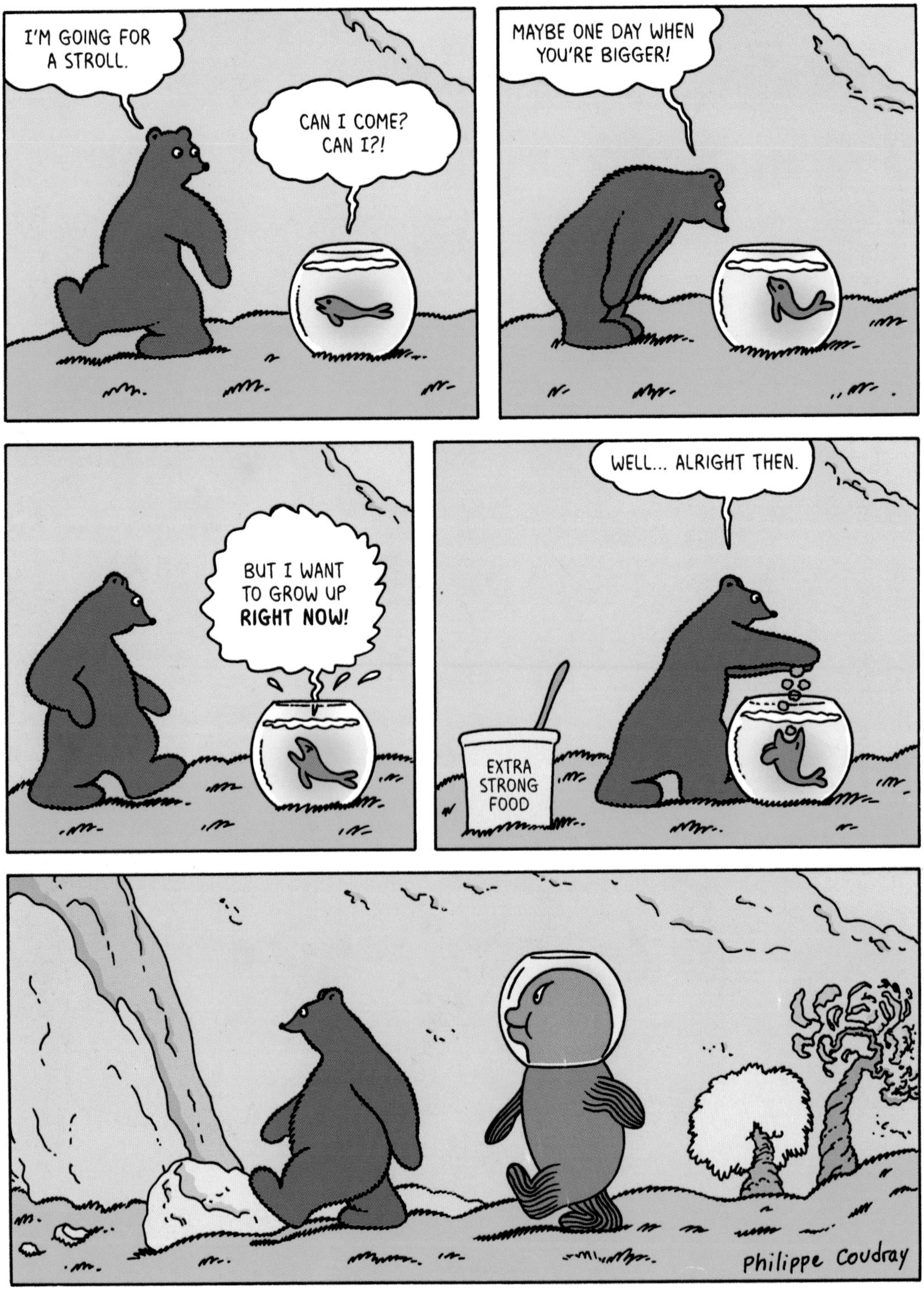
I'M GOING FOR A STROLL.
CAN I COME? CAN I?!
MAYBE ONE DAY WHEN YOU'RE BIGGER!
BUT I WANT TO GROW UP **RIGHT NOW!**
WELL... ALRIGHT THEN.
EXTRA STRONG FOOD
Philippe Coudray

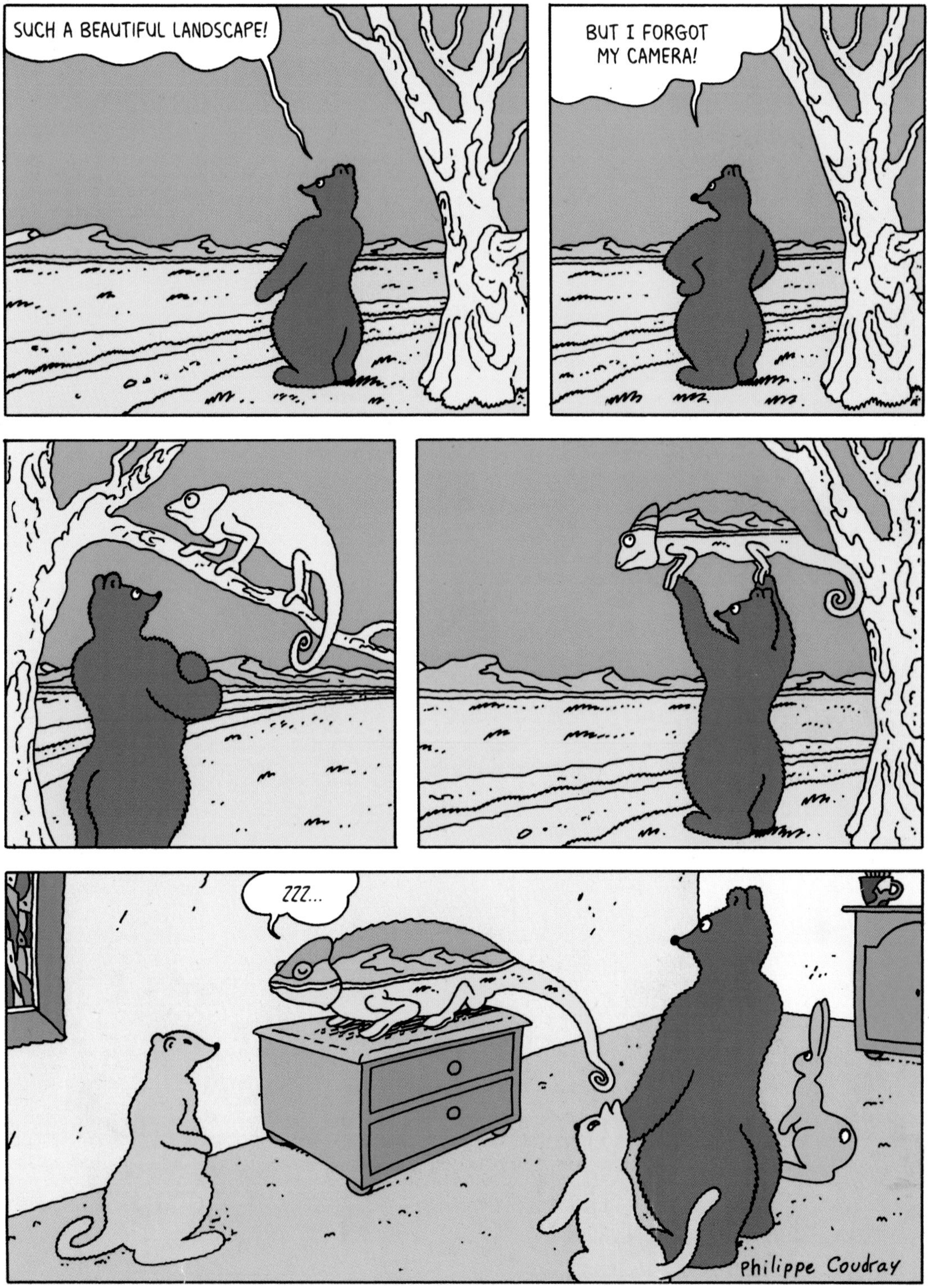

SUCH A BEAUTIFUL LANDSCAPE!
BUT I FORGOT MY CAMERA!
ZZZ...
Philippe Coudray

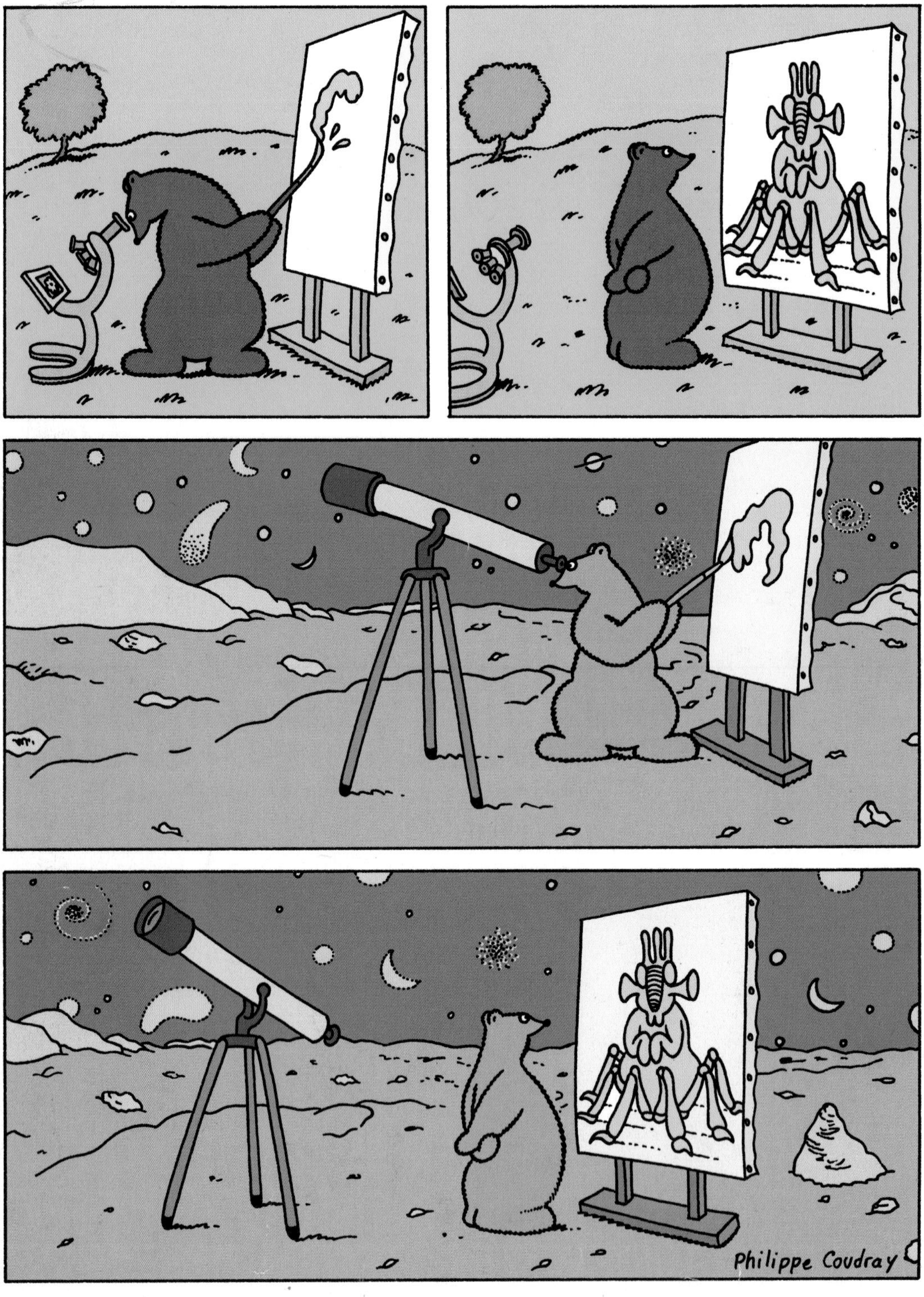
Philippe Coudray

ZZZ...
BIGBY, I'VE GOT A MISSION FOR YOU...
... TO SEE IF THE PLANET MARS IS HOSPITABLE FOR OUR SPECIES!
ZZZ...
IT'S PERFECT!
Philippe Coudray

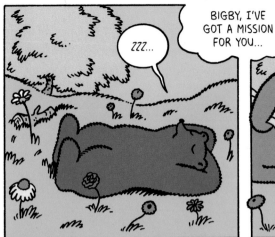

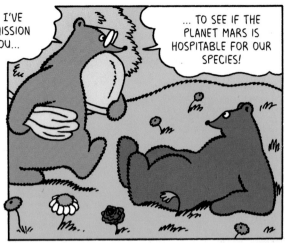

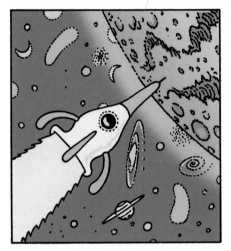

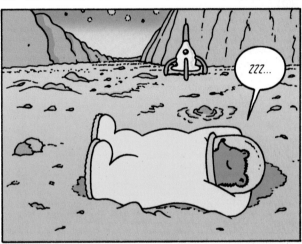

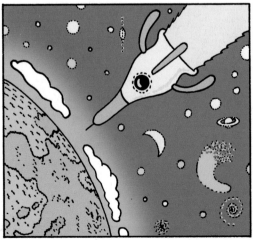

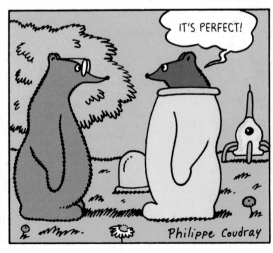

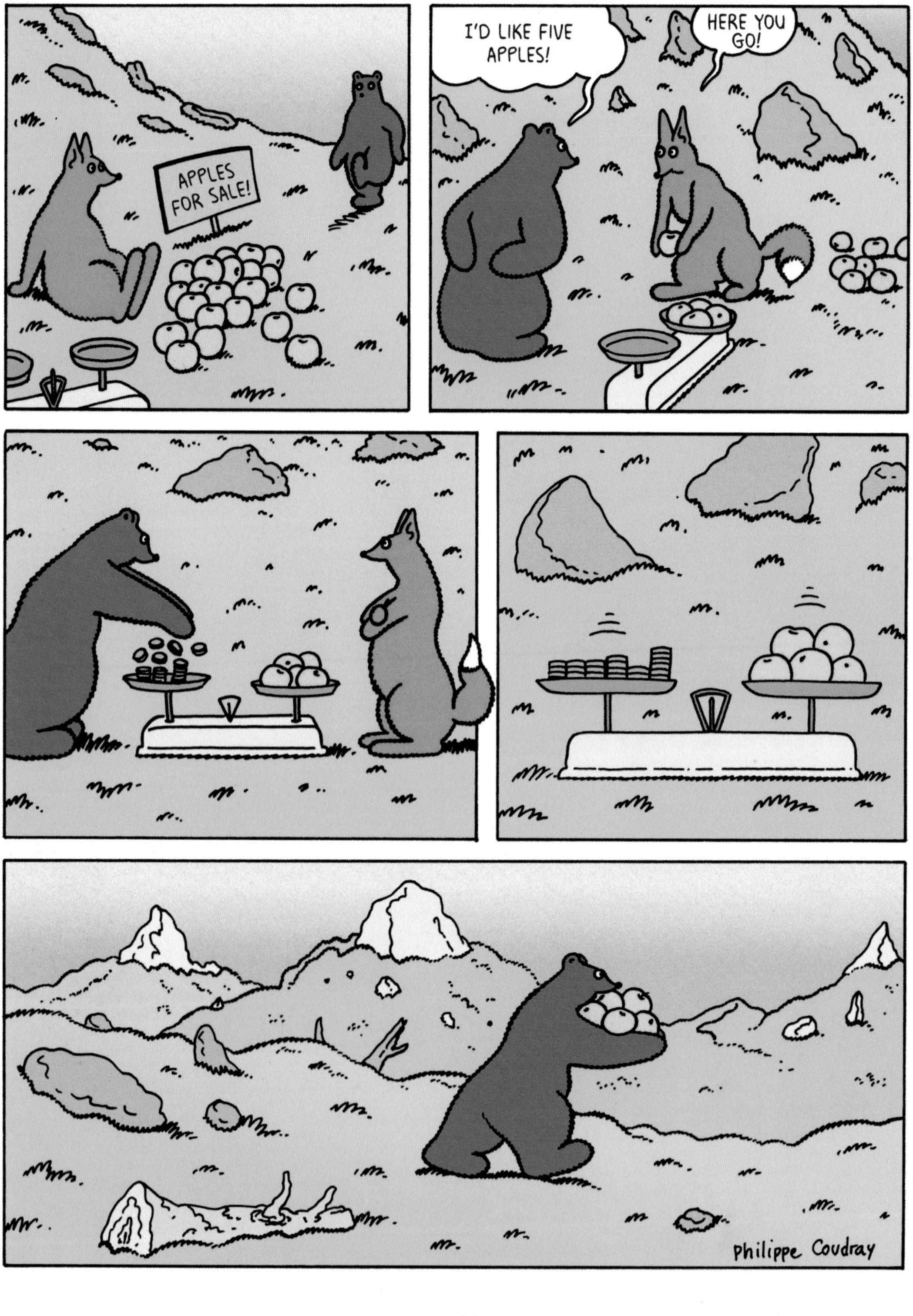
APPLES FOR SALE!
I'D LIKE FIVE APPLES!
HERE YOU GO!
Philippe Coudray

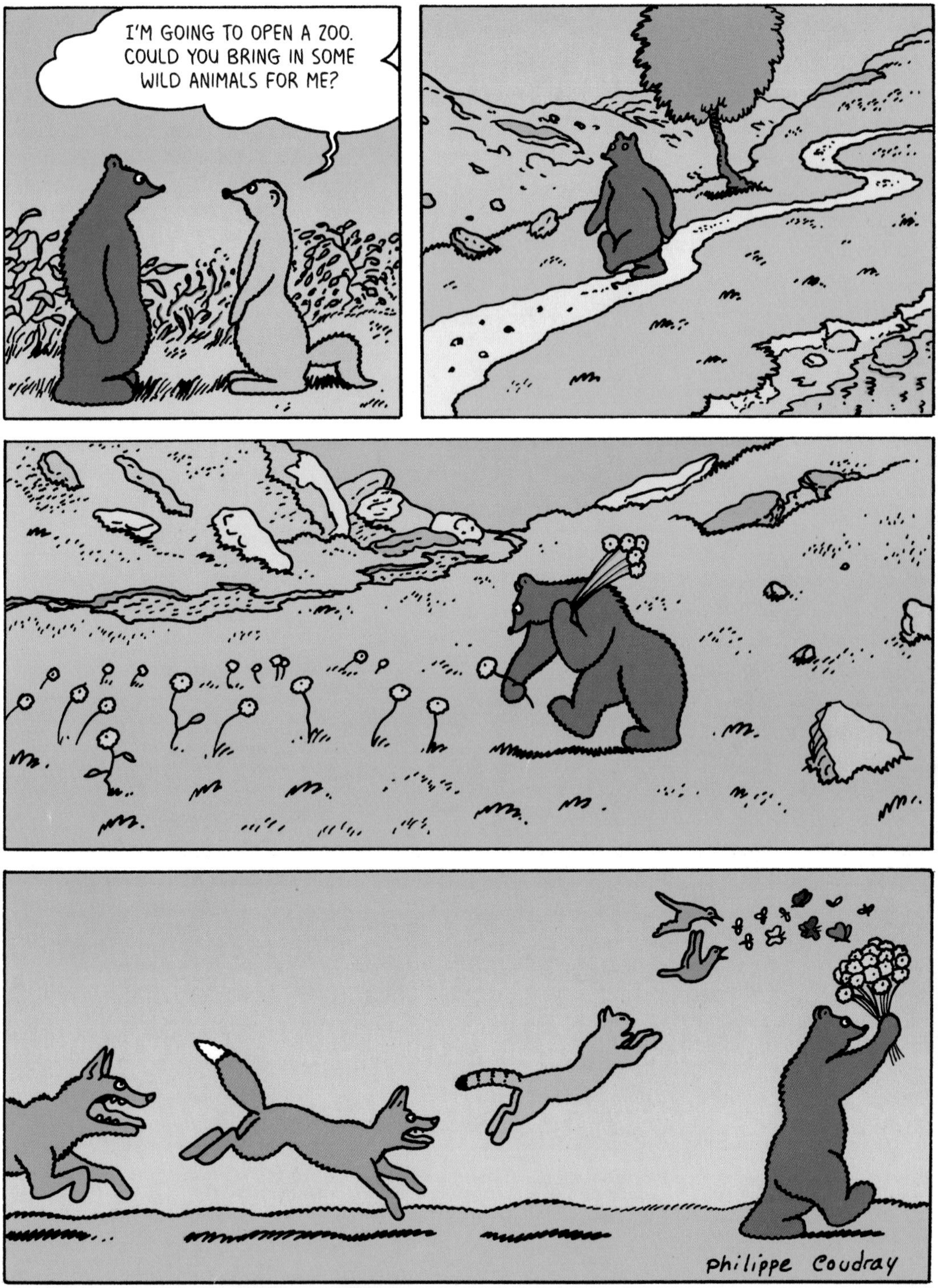
I'M GOING TO OPEN A ZOO. COULD YOU BRING IN SOME WILD ANIMALS FOR ME?
philippe Coudray

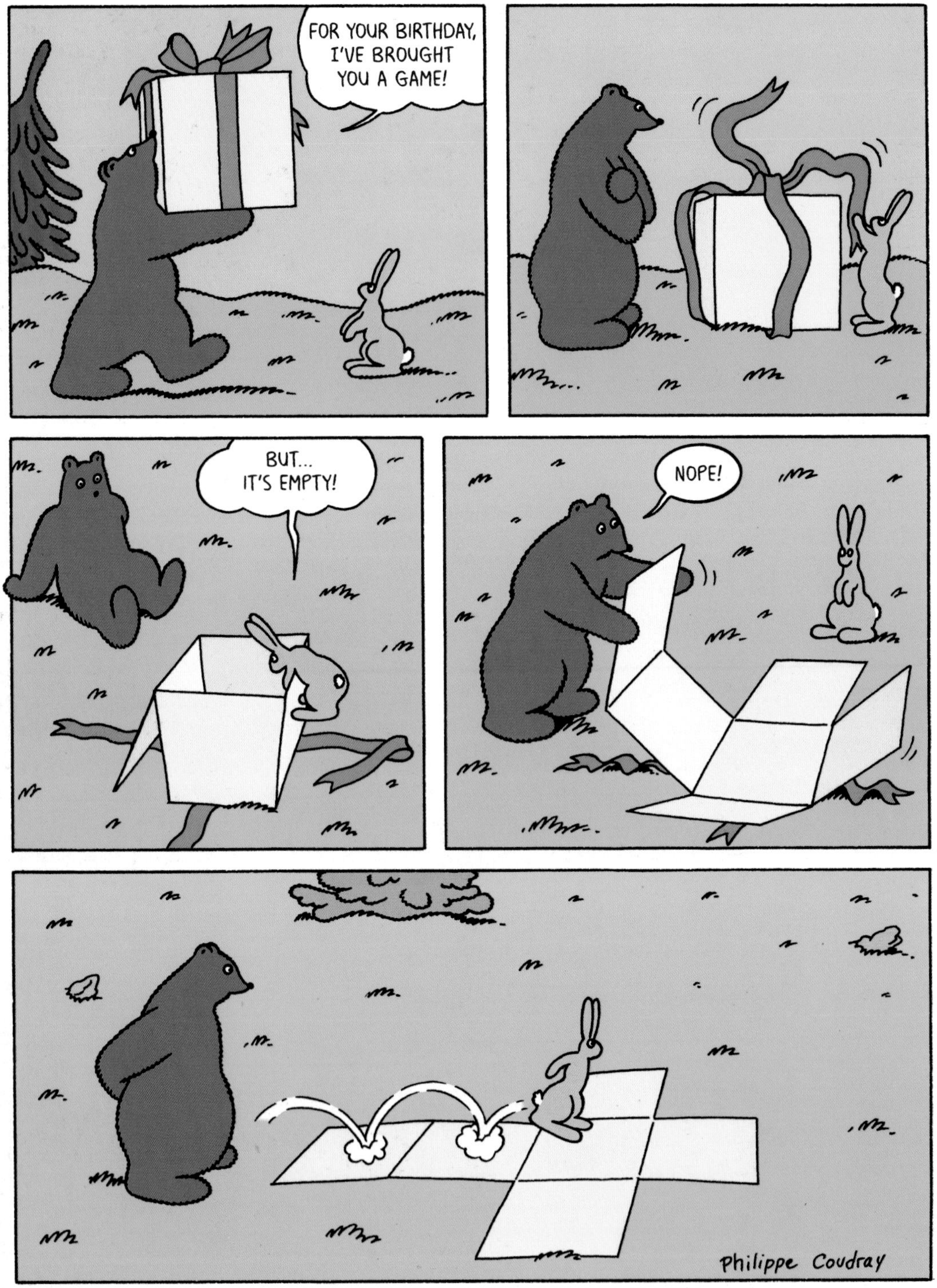
FOR YOUR BIRTHDAY, I'VE BROUGHT YOU A GAME!
BUT... IT'S EMPTY!
NOPE!
Philippe Coudray

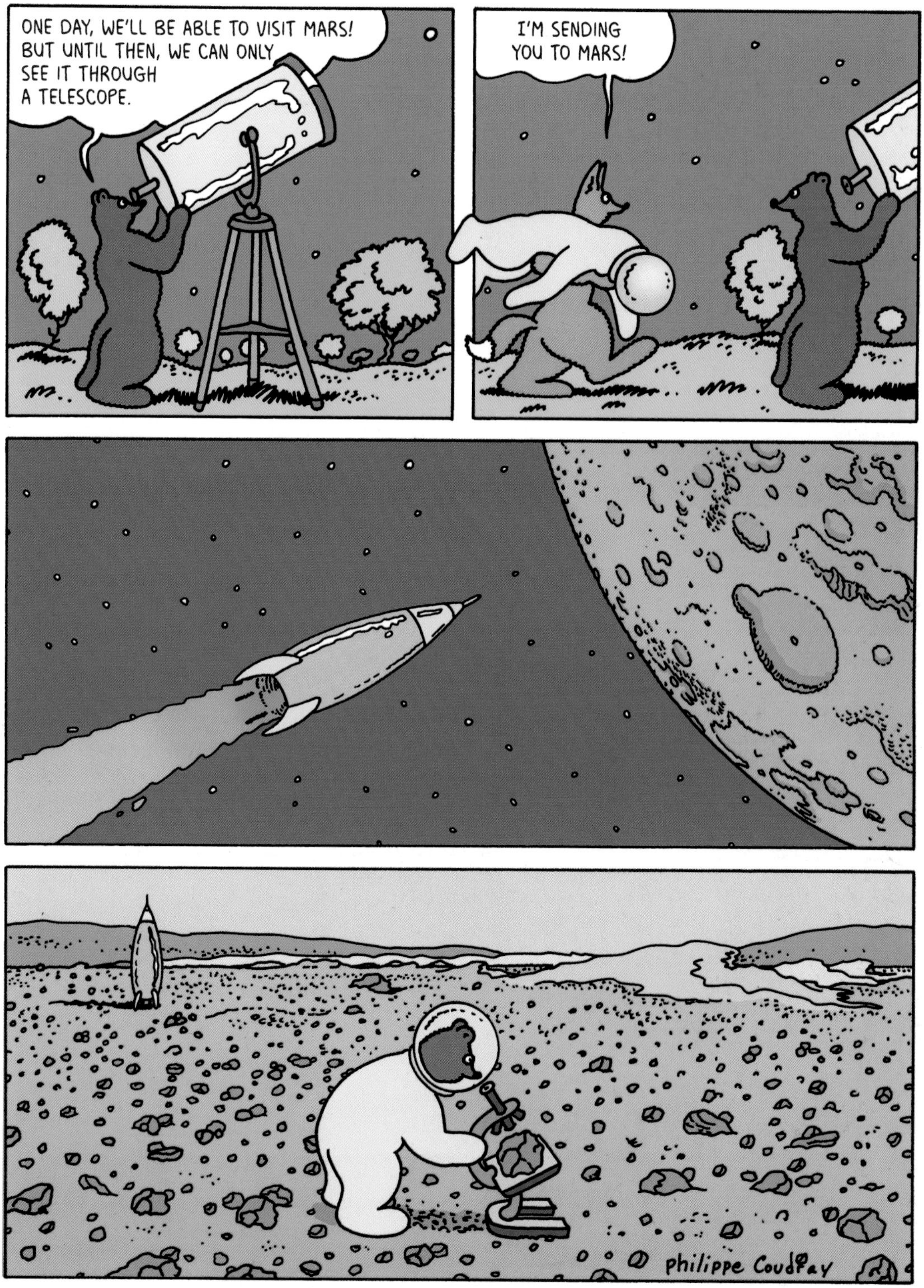
ONE DAY, WE'LL BE ABLE TO VISIT MARS! BUT UNTIL THEN, WE CAN ONLY SEE IT THROUGH A TELESCOPE.
I'M SENDING YOU TO MARS!
philippe Coudray

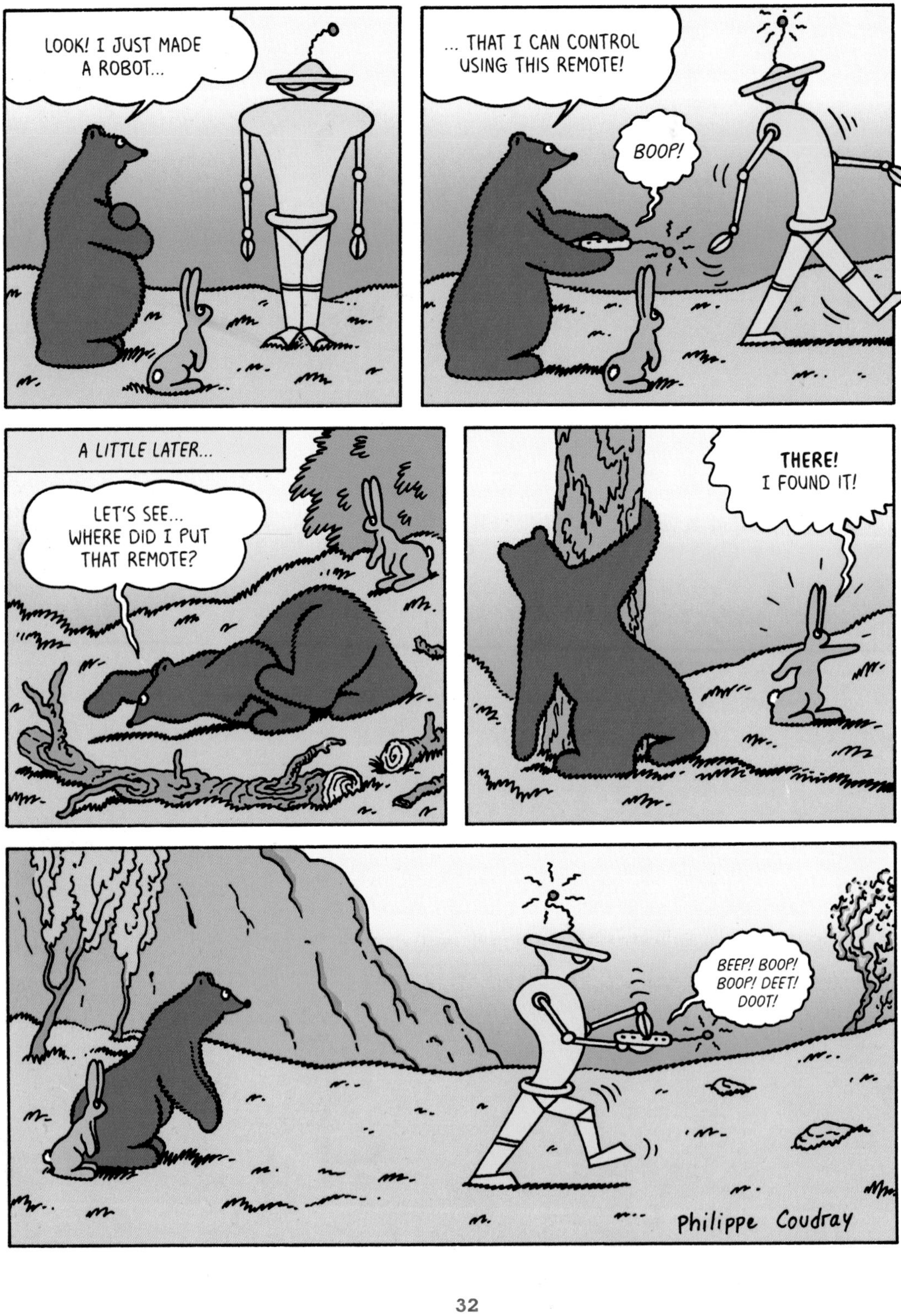
LOOK! I JUST MADE A ROBOT...
... THAT I CAN CONTROL USING THIS REMOTE!
BOOP!
A LITTLE LATER...
LET'S SEE... WHERE DID I PUT THAT REMOTE?
THERE! I FOUND IT!
BEEP! BOOP! BOOP! DEET! DOOT!
Philippe Coudray

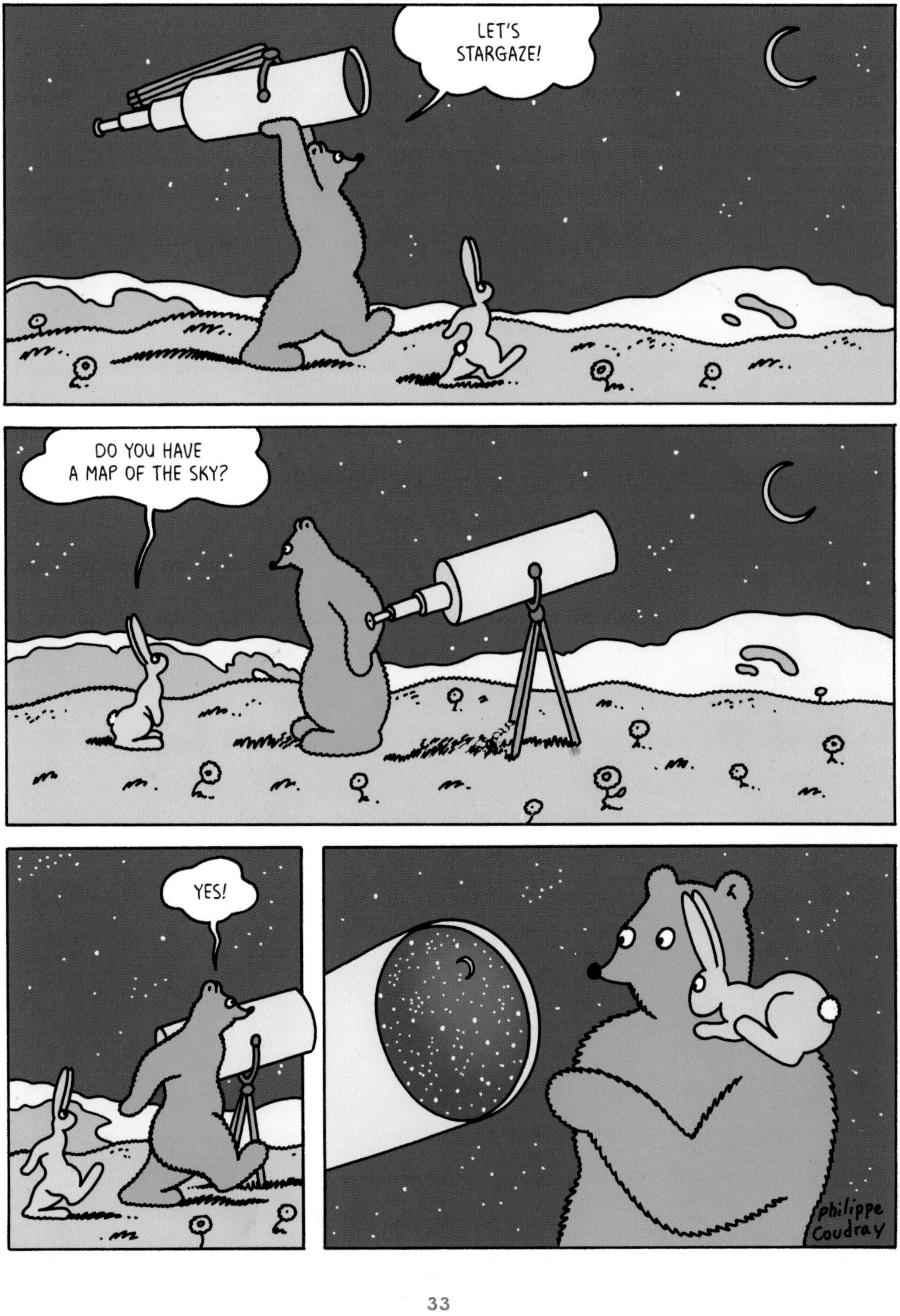
LET'S STARGAZE!
DO YOU HAVE A MAP OF THE SKY?
YES!
philippe Coudray

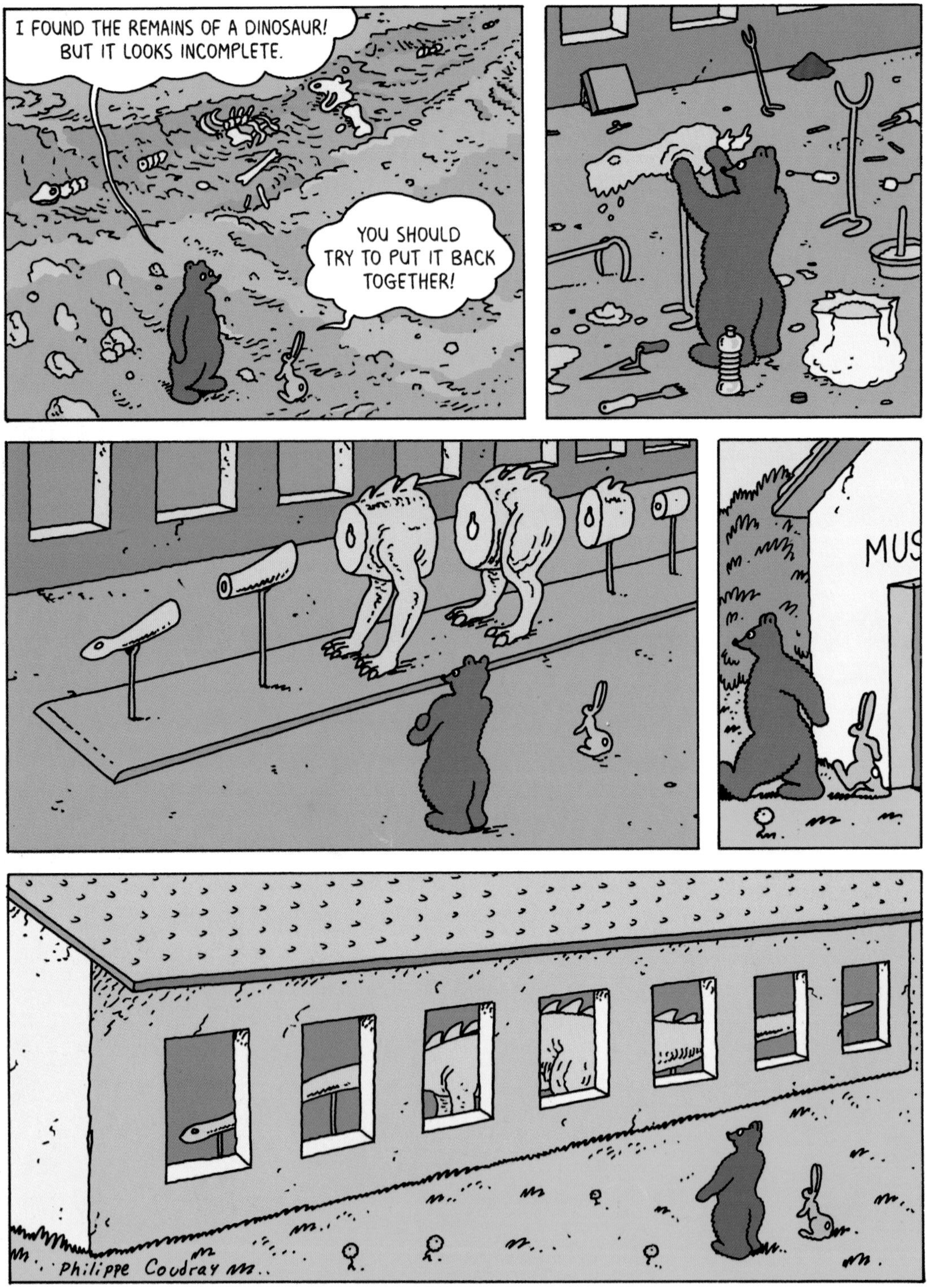
I FOUND THE REMAINS OF A DINOSAUR! BUT IT LOOKS INCOMPLETE.
YOU SHOULD TRY TO PUT IT BACK TOGETHER!
MUS
Philippe Coudray

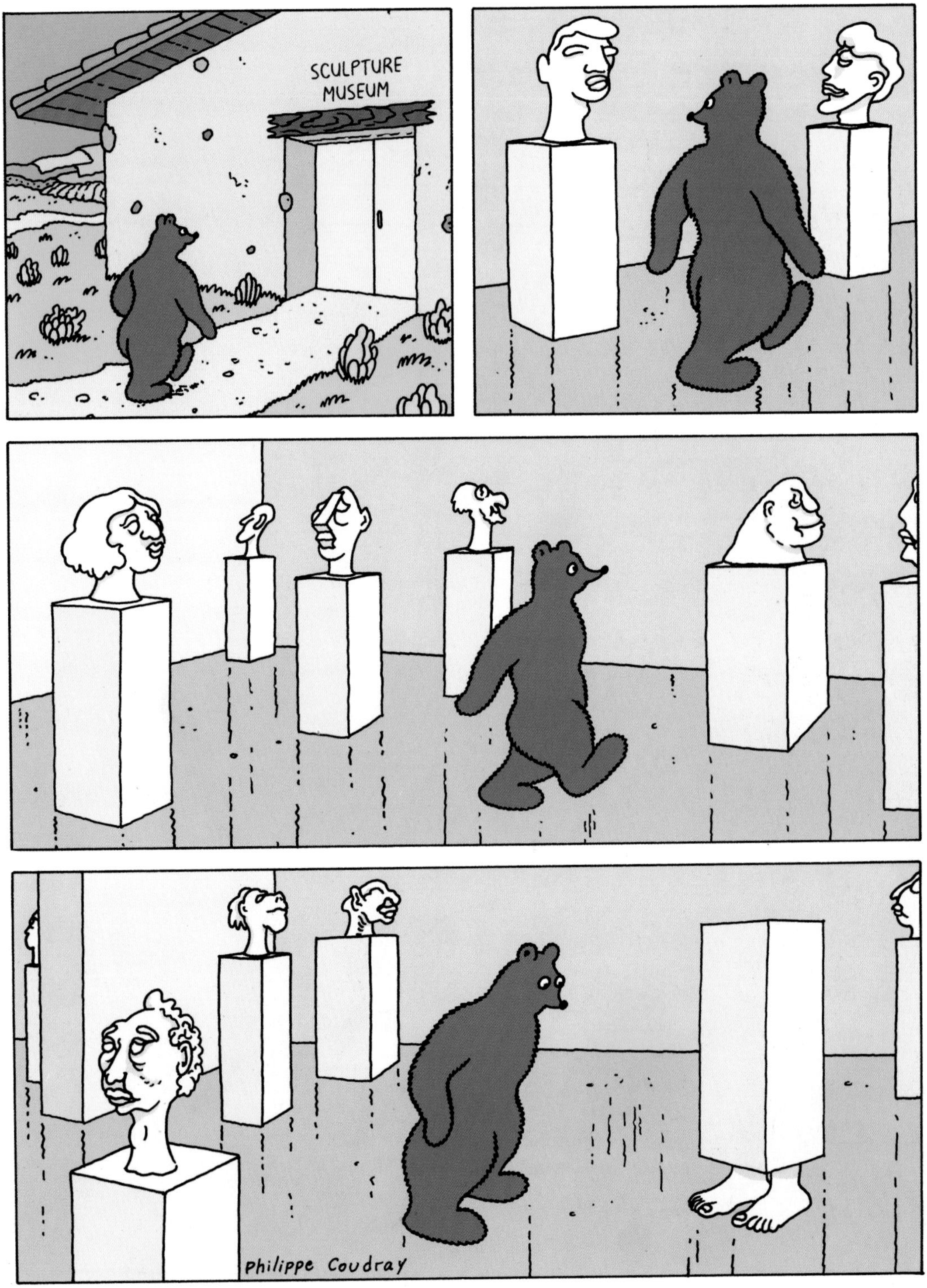
SCULPTURE MUSEUM
Philippe Coudray

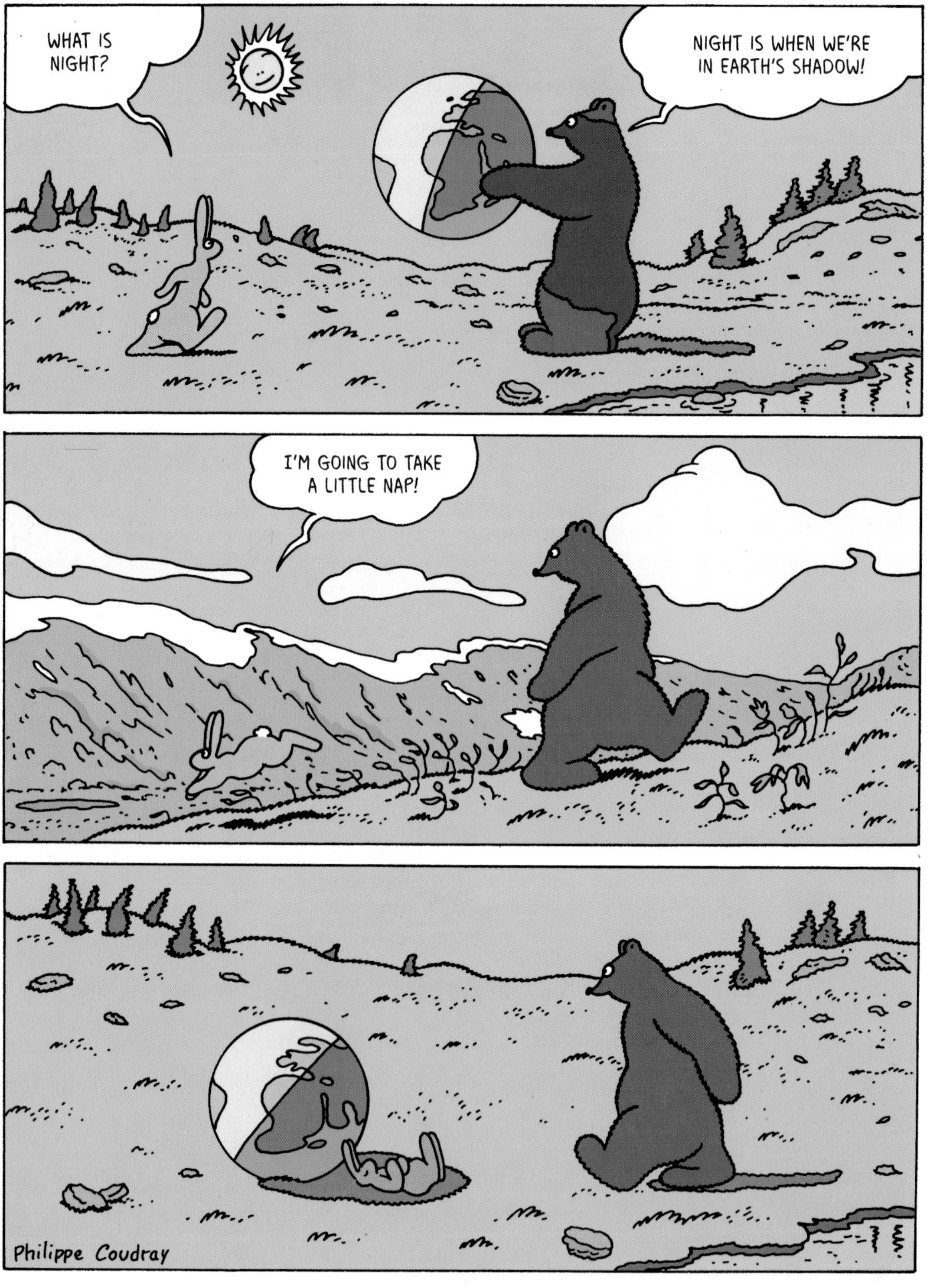
WHAT IS NIGHT?
NIGHT IS WHEN WE'RE IN EARTH'S SHADOW!
I'M GOING TO TAKE A LITTLE NAP!
Philippe Coudray

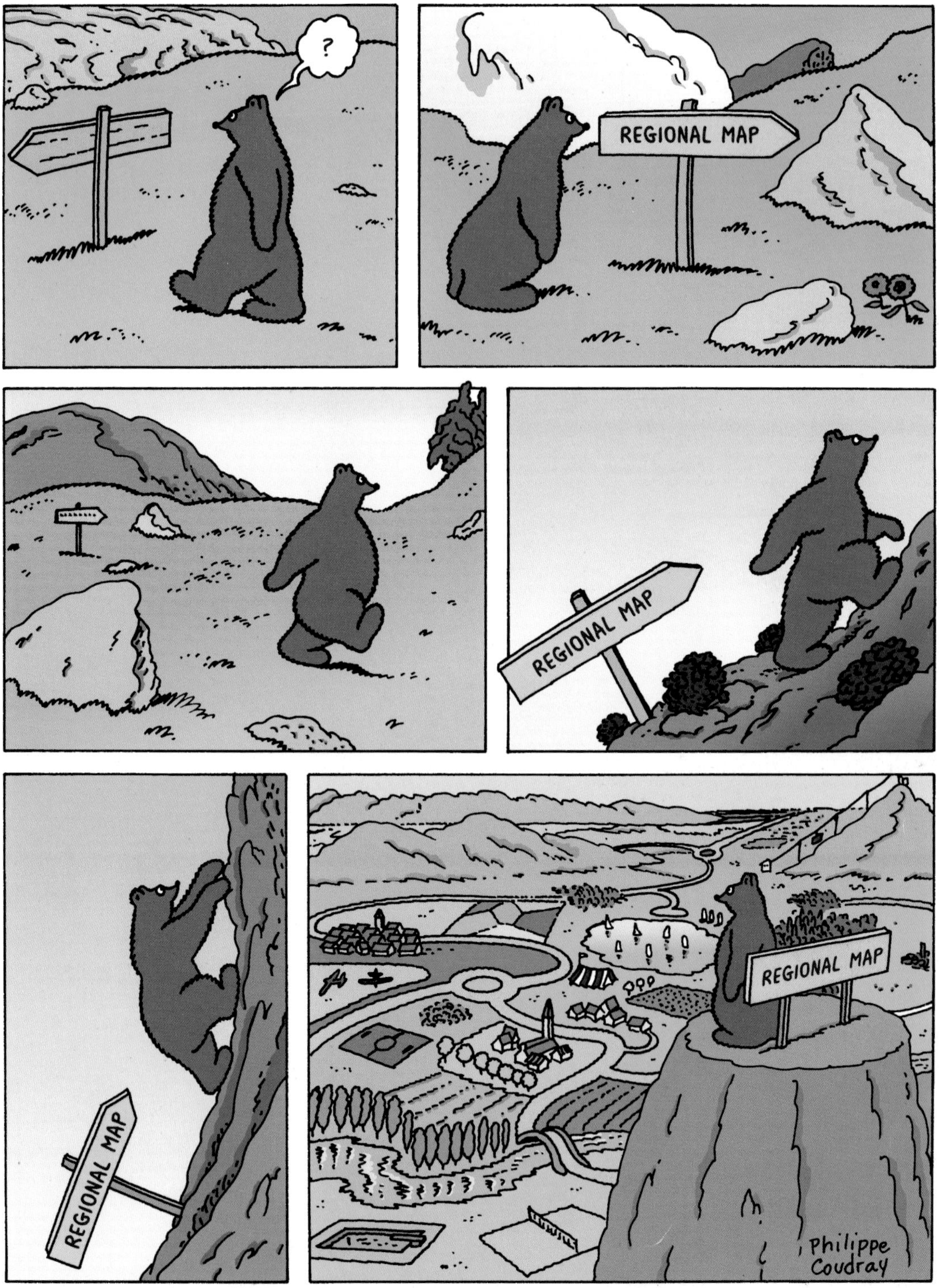
?
REGIONAL MAP
REGIONAL MAP
REGIONAL MAP
REGIONAL MAP
Philippe Coudray

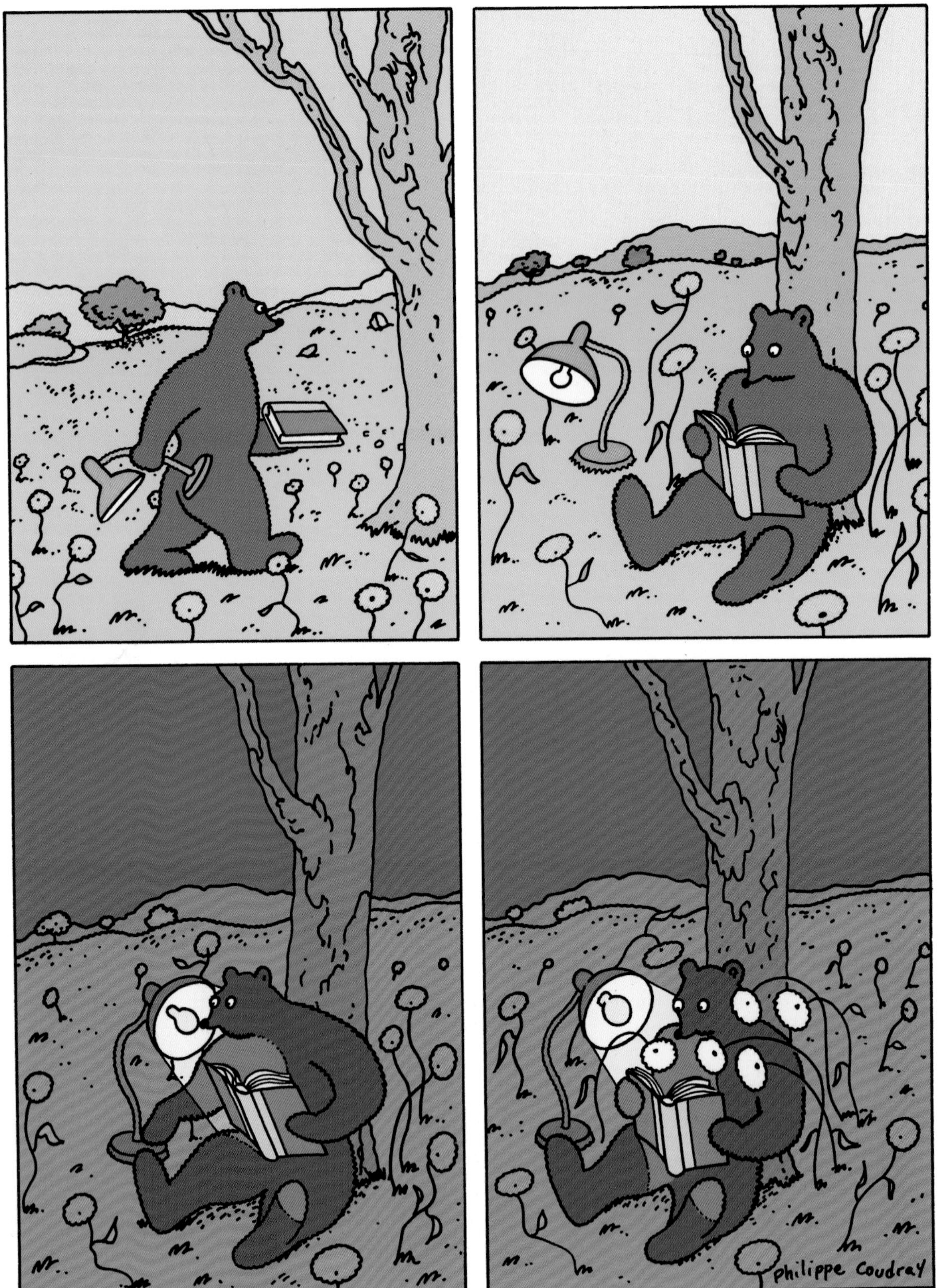
Philippe Coudray

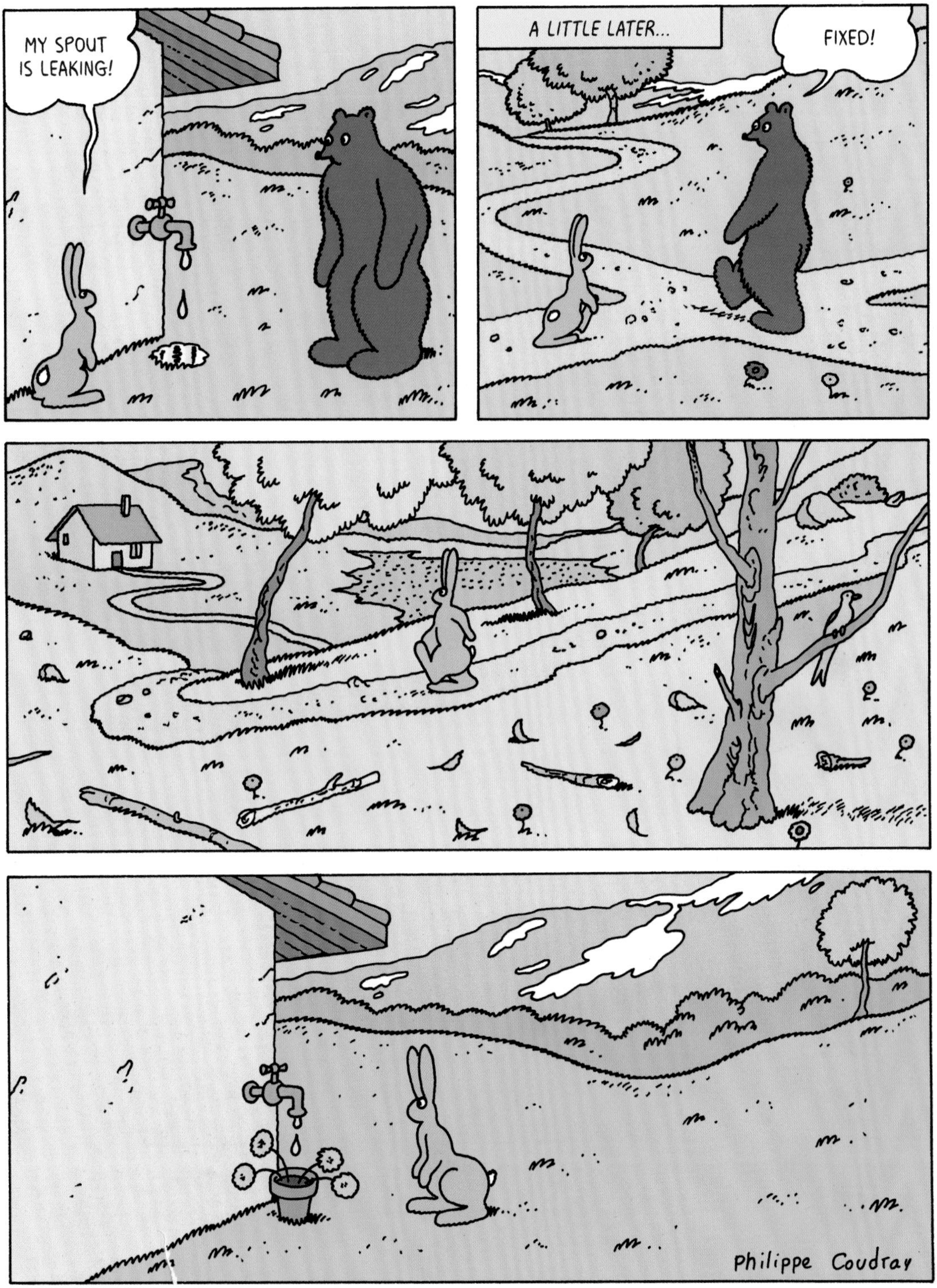
MY SPOUT IS LEAKING!
A LITTLE LATER...
FIXED!
Philippe Coudray

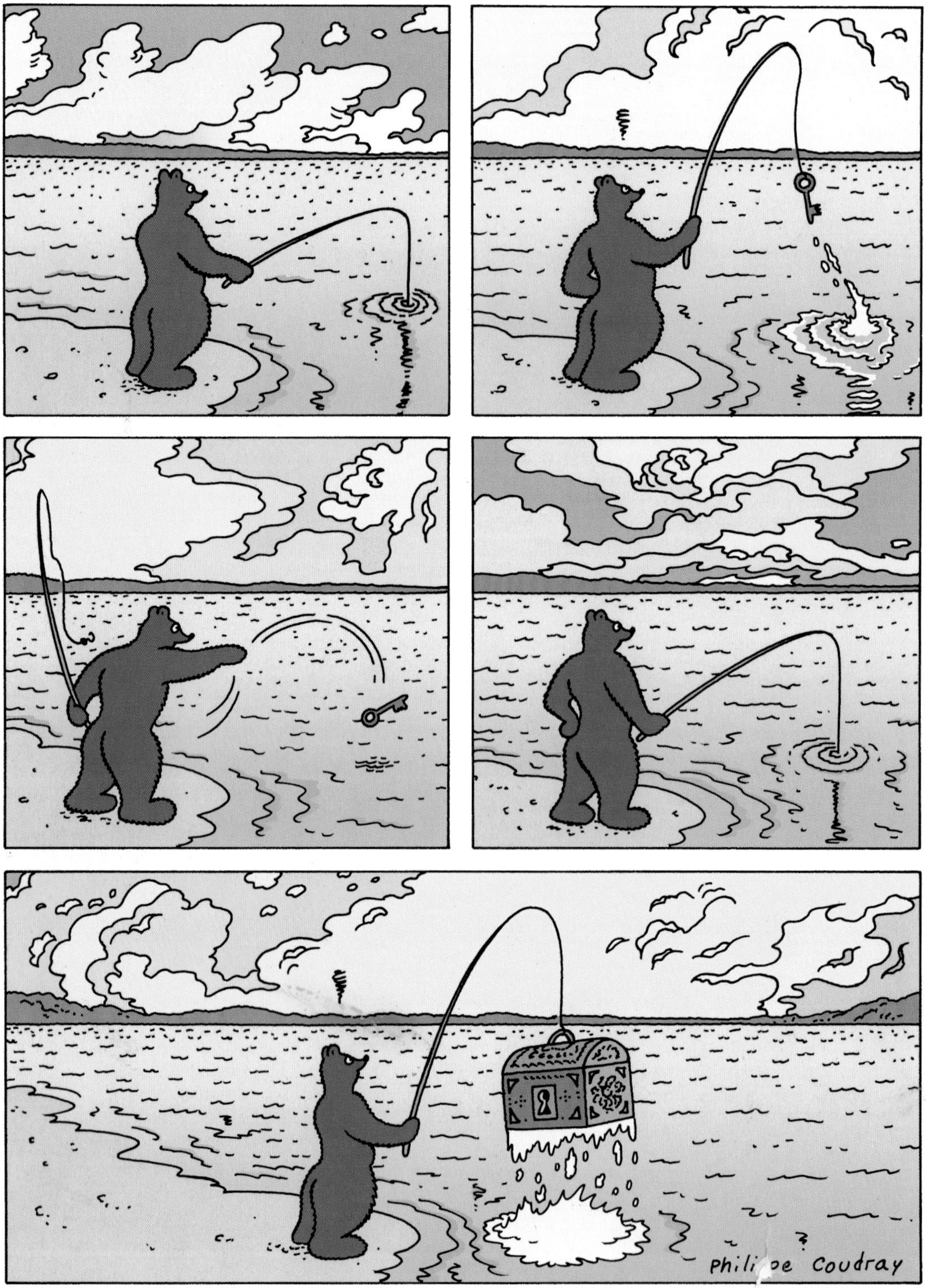
Philippe Coudray

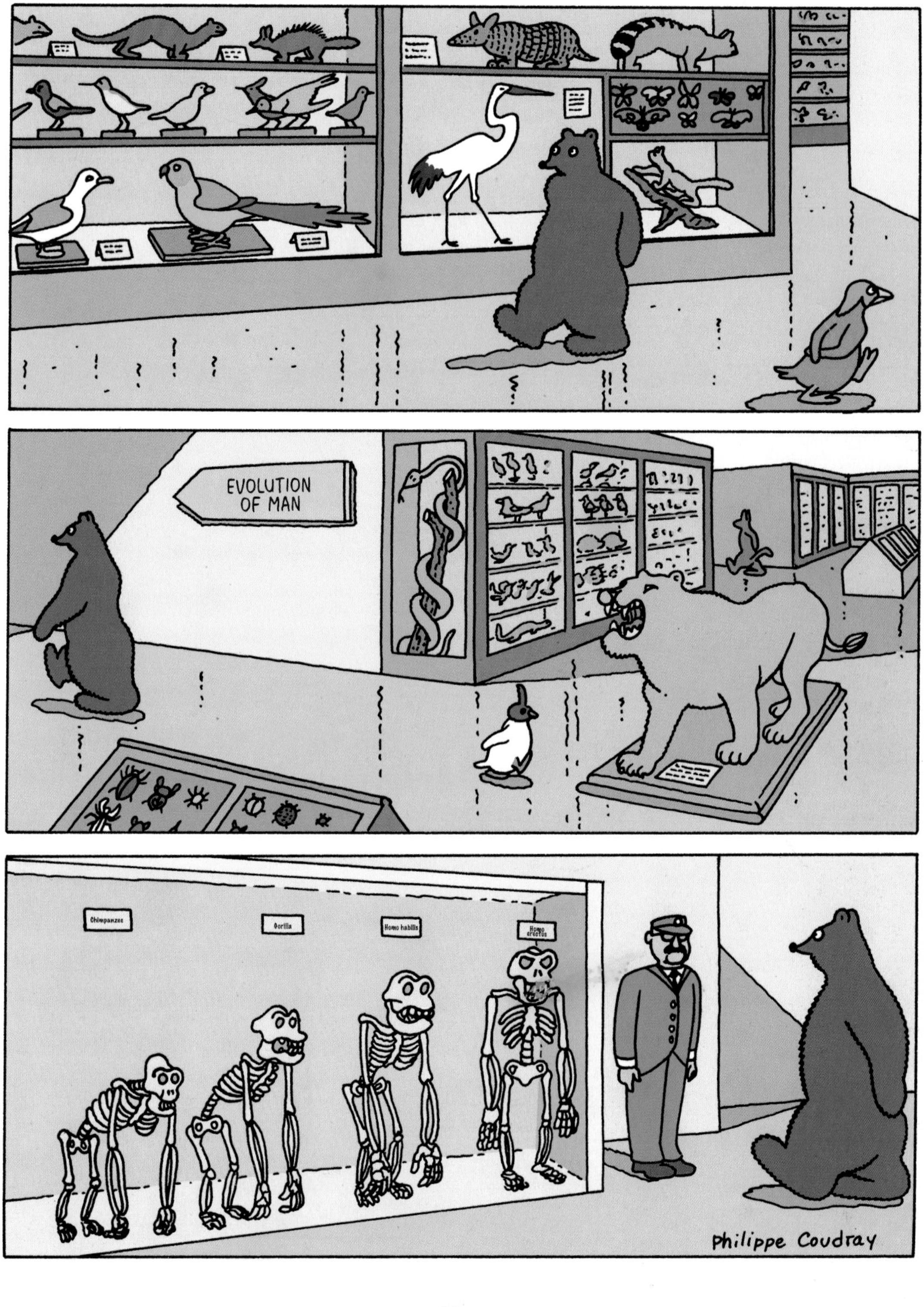
EVOLUTION OF MAN
Chimpanzee
Gorilla
Homo habilis
Homo erectus
Philippe Coudray

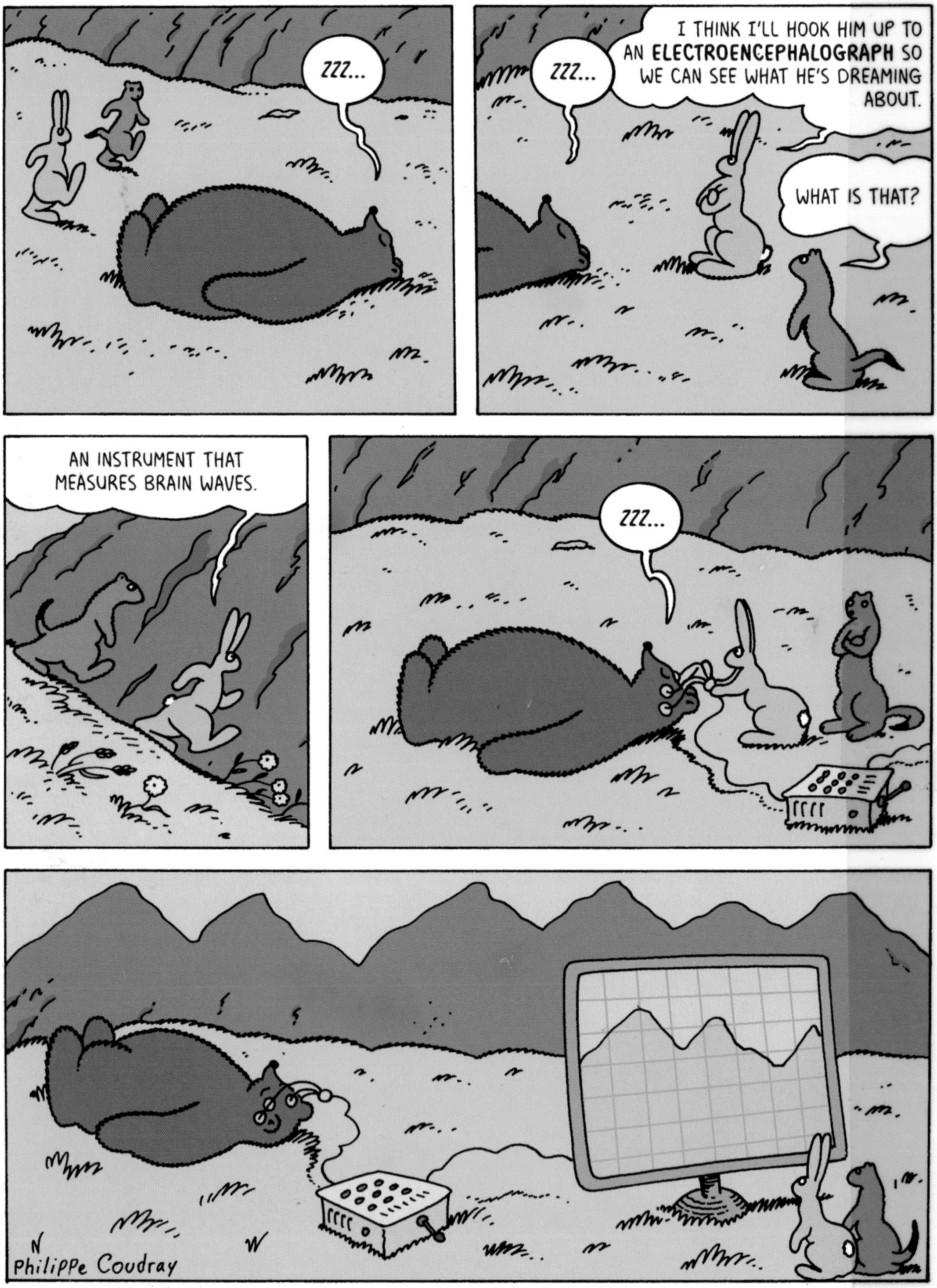
ZZZ...
ZZZ...
I THINK I'LL HOOK HIM UP TO AN **ELECTROENCEPHALOGRAPH** SO WE CAN SEE WHAT HE'S DREAMING ABOUT.
WHAT IS THAT?
AN INSTRUMENT THAT MEASURES BRAIN WAVES.
ZZZ...
Philippe Coudray

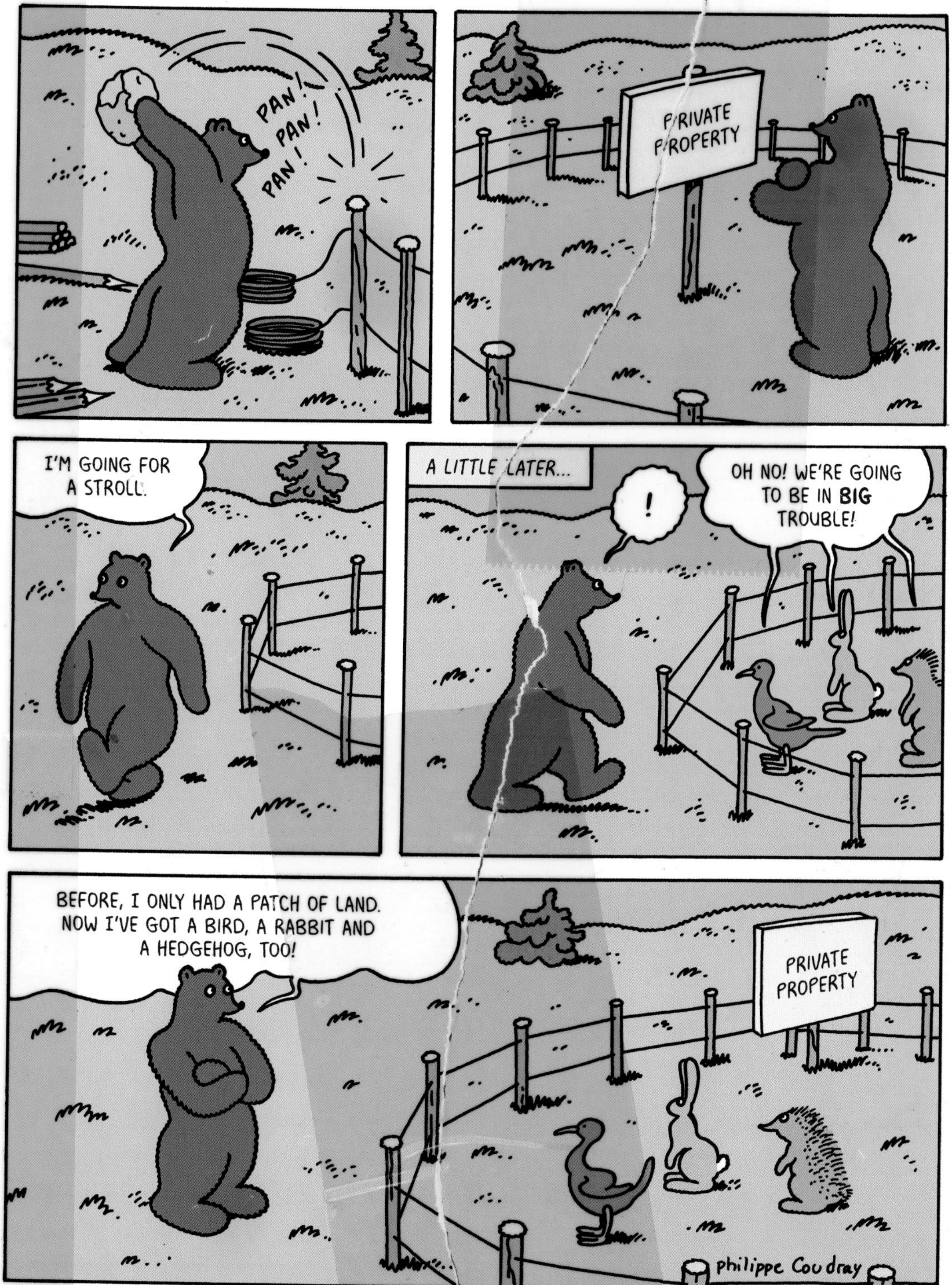
PAN! PAN! PAN!
PRIVATE PROPERTY
I'M GOING FOR A STROLL.
A LITTLE LATER...
!
OH NO! WE'RE GOING TO BE IN **BIG** TROUBLE!
BEFORE, I ONLY HAD A PATCH OF LAND. NOW I'VE GOT A BIRD, A RABBIT AND A HEDGEHOG, TOO!
PRIVATE PROPERTY
philippe Coudray

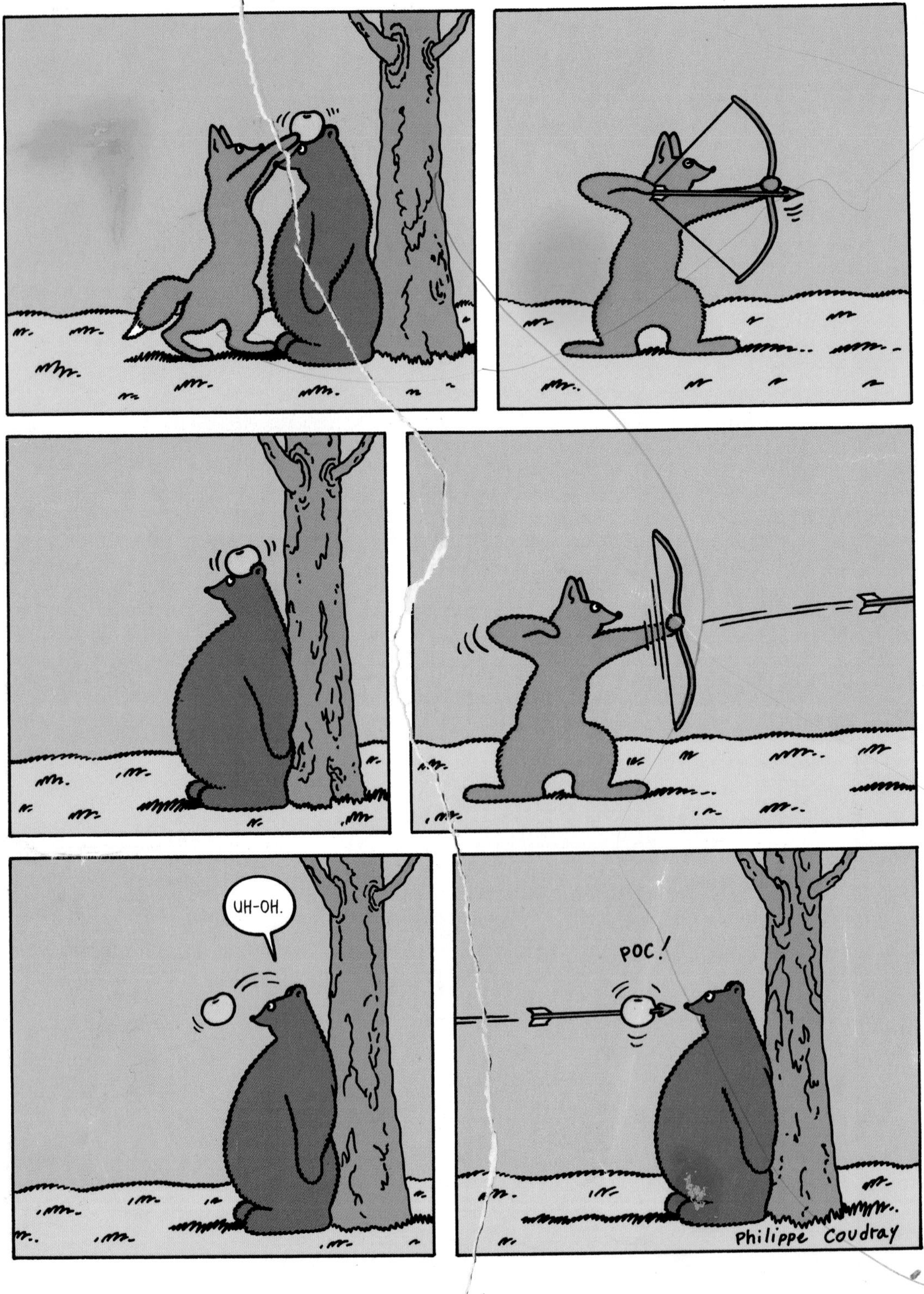
UH-OH.
POC!
Philippe Coudray

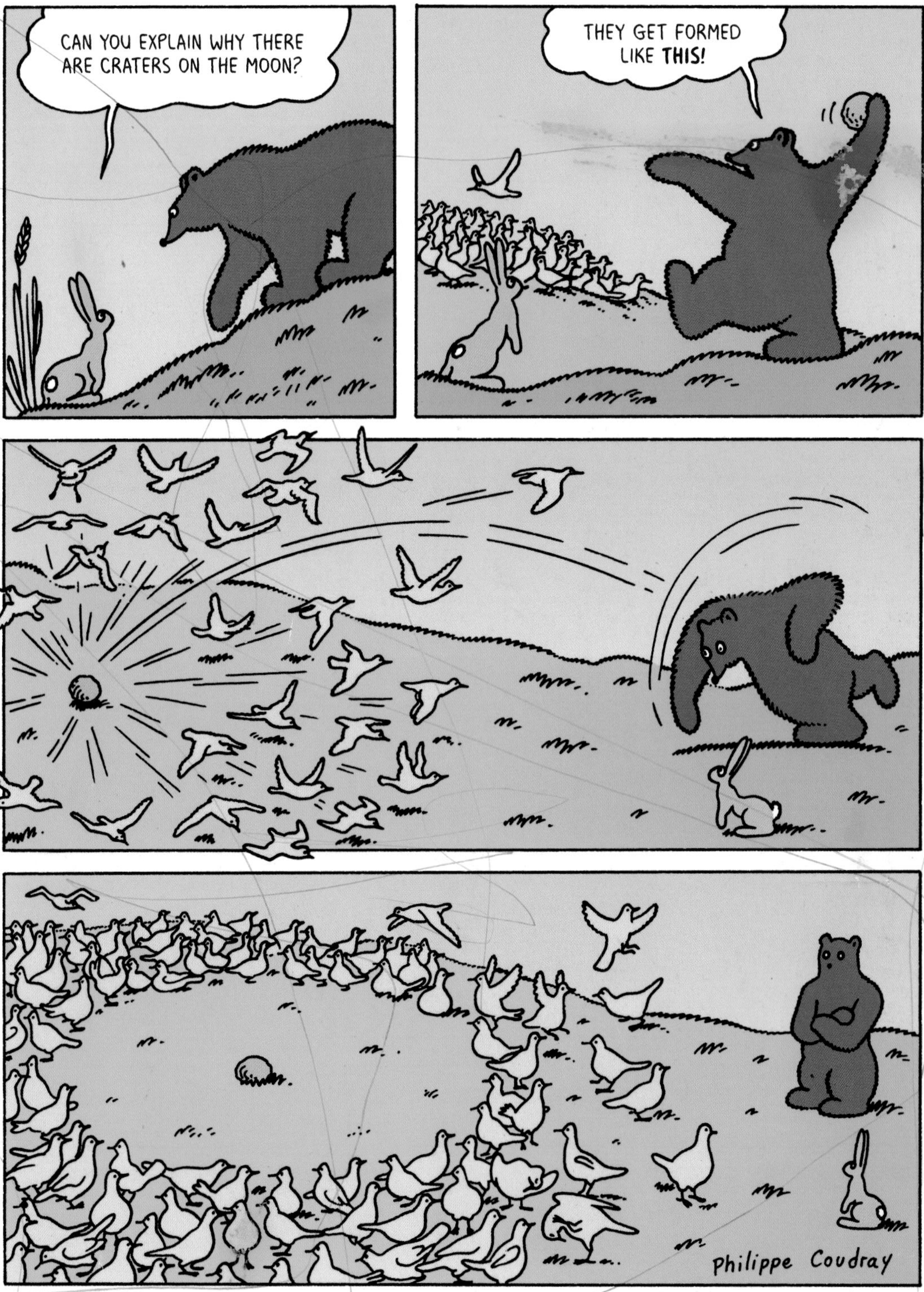
CAN YOU EXPLAIN WHY THERE ARE CRATERS ON THE MOON?
THEY GET FORMED LIKE **THIS!**
Philippe Coudray

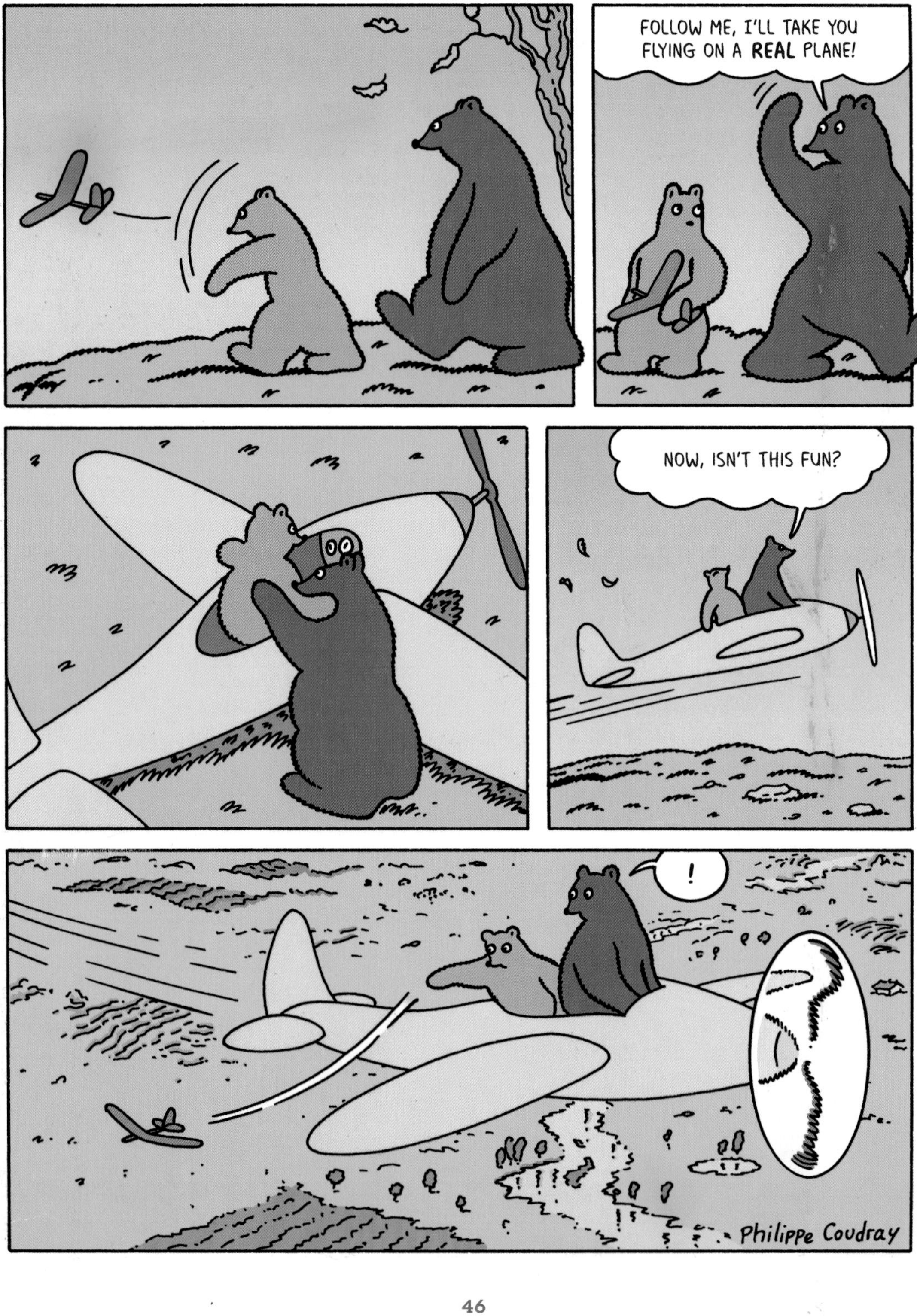
FOLLOW ME, I'LL TAKE YOU FLYING ON A **REAL** PLANE!
NOW, ISN'T THIS FUN?
!
Philippe Coudray

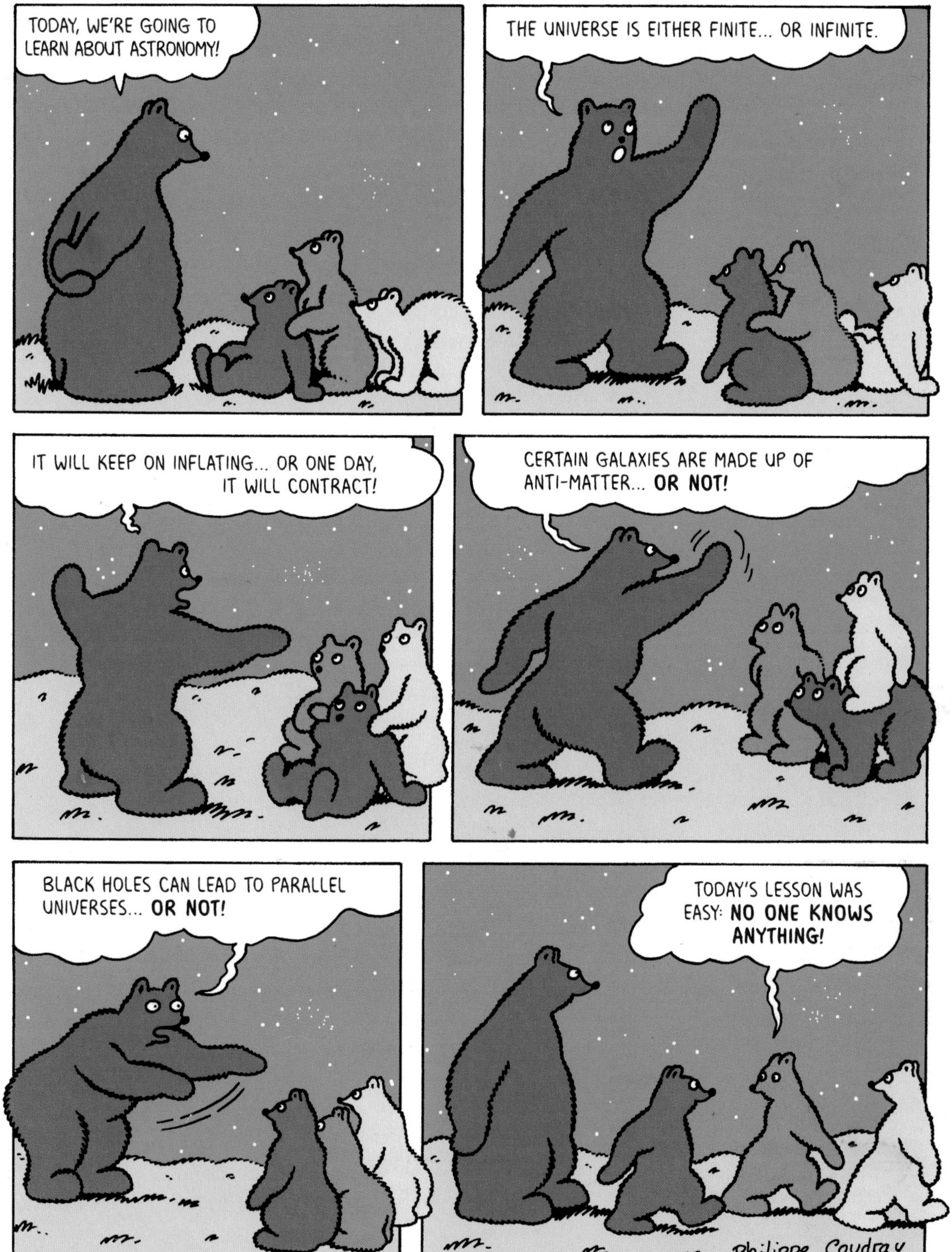
TODAY, WE'RE GOING TO LEARN ABOUT ASTRONOMY!
THE UNIVERSE IS EITHER FINITE... OR INFINITE.
IT WILL KEEP ON INFLATING... OR ONE DAY, IT WILL CONTRACT!
CERTAIN GALAXIES ARE MADE UP OF ANTI-MATTER... **OR NOT!**
BLACK HOLES CAN LEAD TO PARALLEL UNIVERSES... **OR NOT!**
TODAY'S LESSON WAS EASY: **NO ONE KNOWS ANYTHING!**
Philippe Coudray

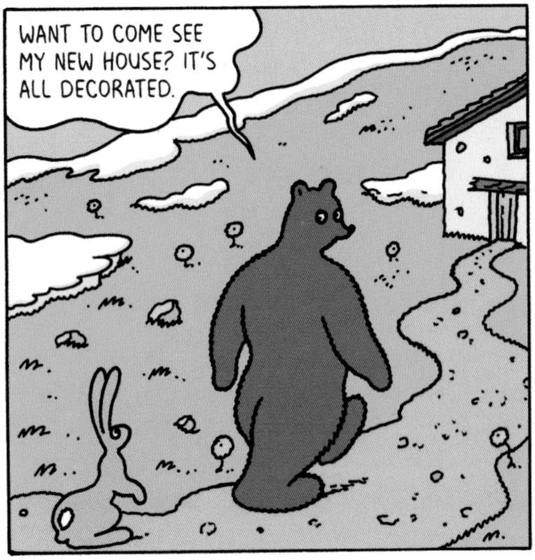
WANT TO COME SEE MY NEW HOUSE? IT'S ALL DECORATED.

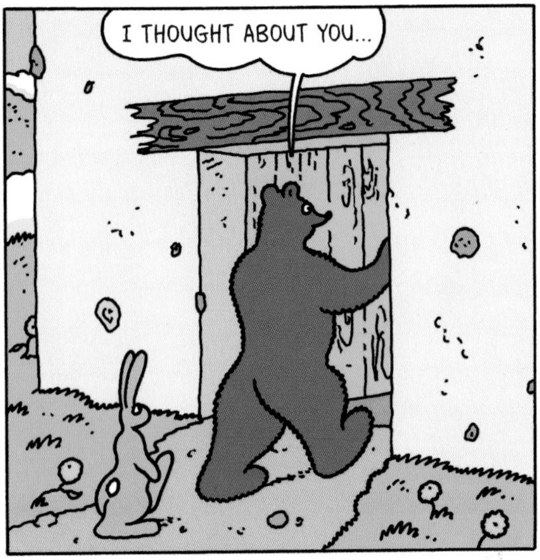
I THOUGHT ABOUT YOU...

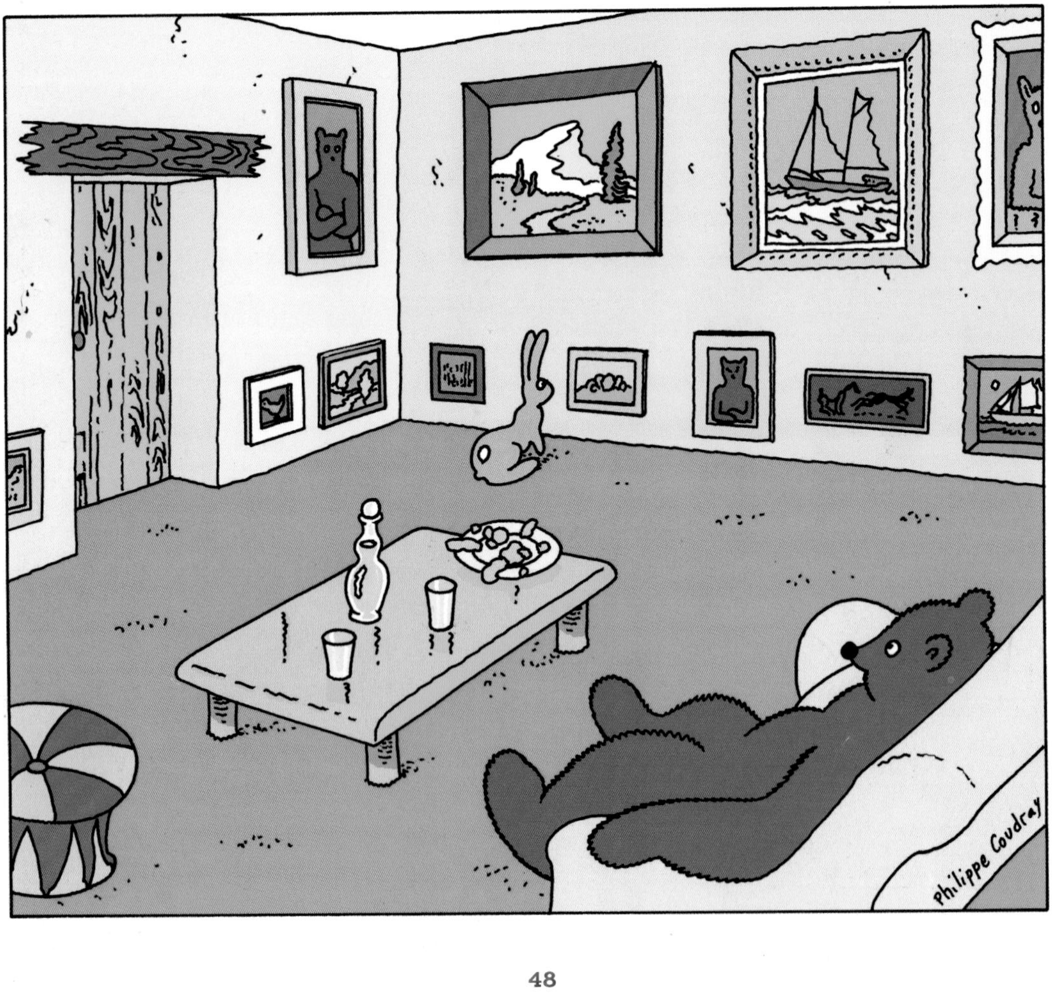
Philippe Coudray

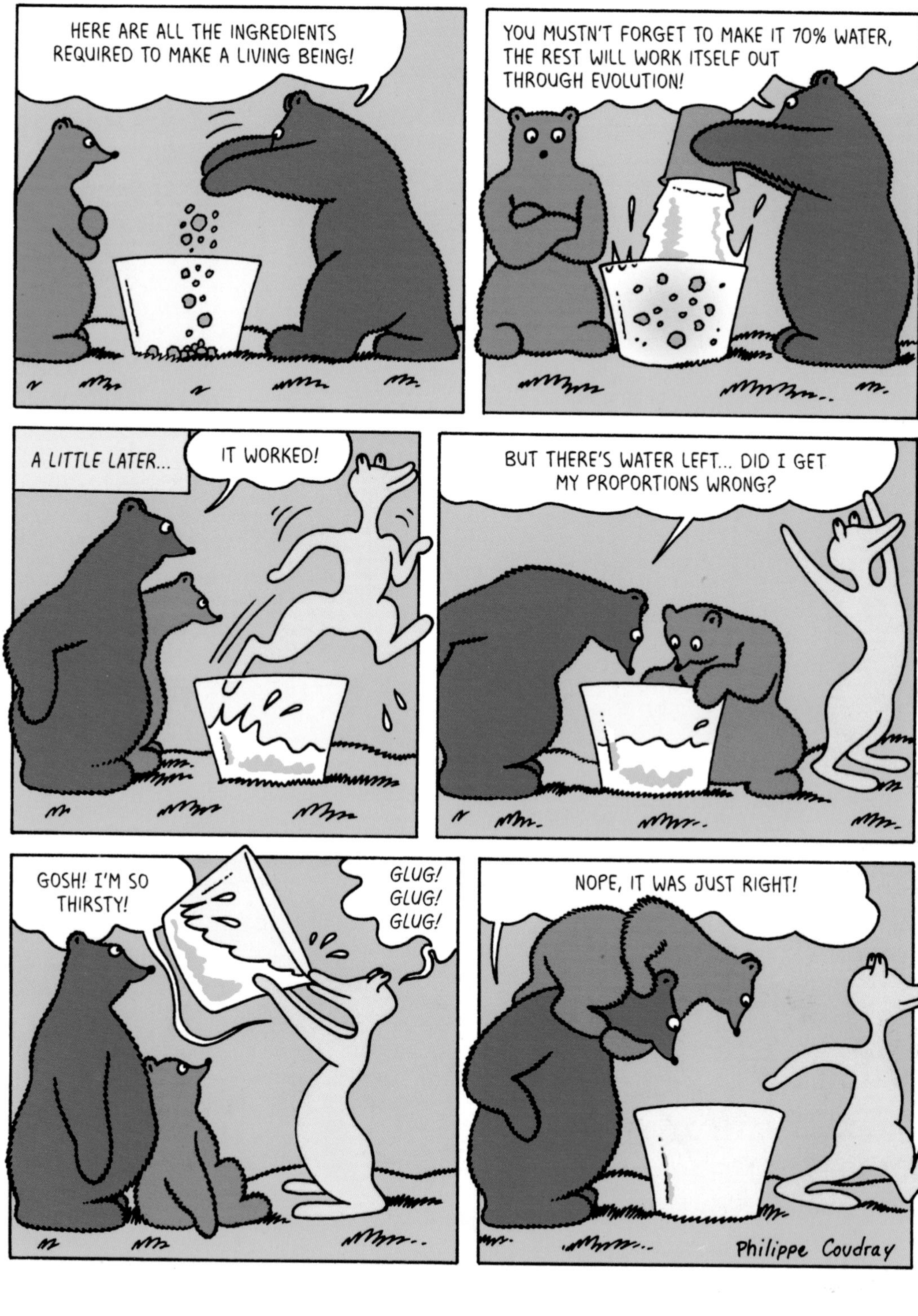
HERE ARE ALL THE INGREDIENTS REQUIRED TO MAKE A LIVING BEING!
YOU MUSTN'T FORGET TO MAKE IT 70% WATER, THE REST WILL WORK ITSELF OUT THROUGH EVOLUTION!
A LITTLE LATER...
IT WORKED!
BUT THERE'S WATER LEFT... DID I GET MY PROPORTIONS WRONG?
GOSH! I'M SO THIRSTY!
GLUG! GLUG! GLUG!
NOPE, IT WAS JUST RIGHT!
Philippe Coudray

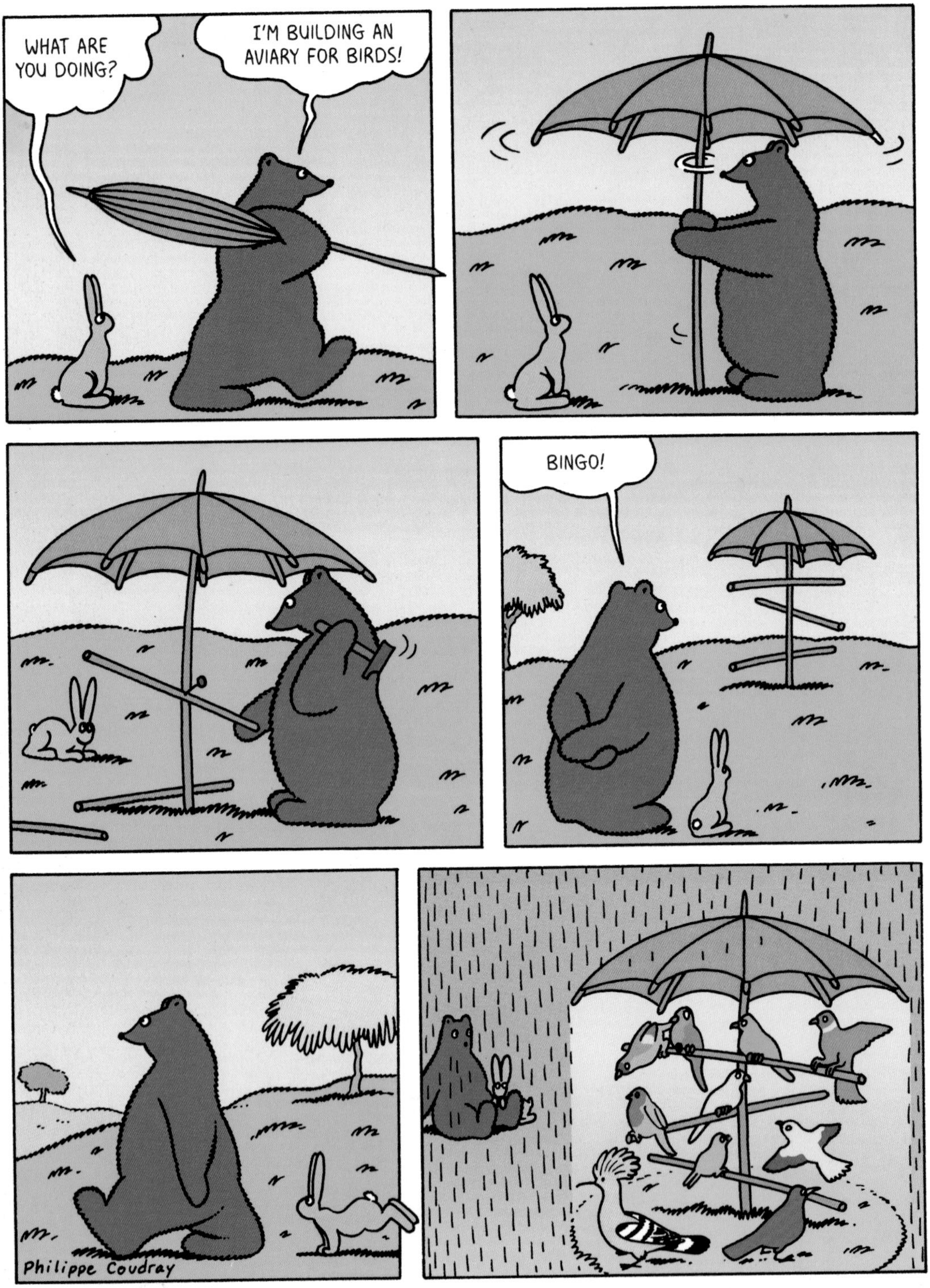
WHAT ARE YOU DOING?
I'M BUILDING AN AVIARY FOR BIRDS!
BINGO!
Philippe Coudray

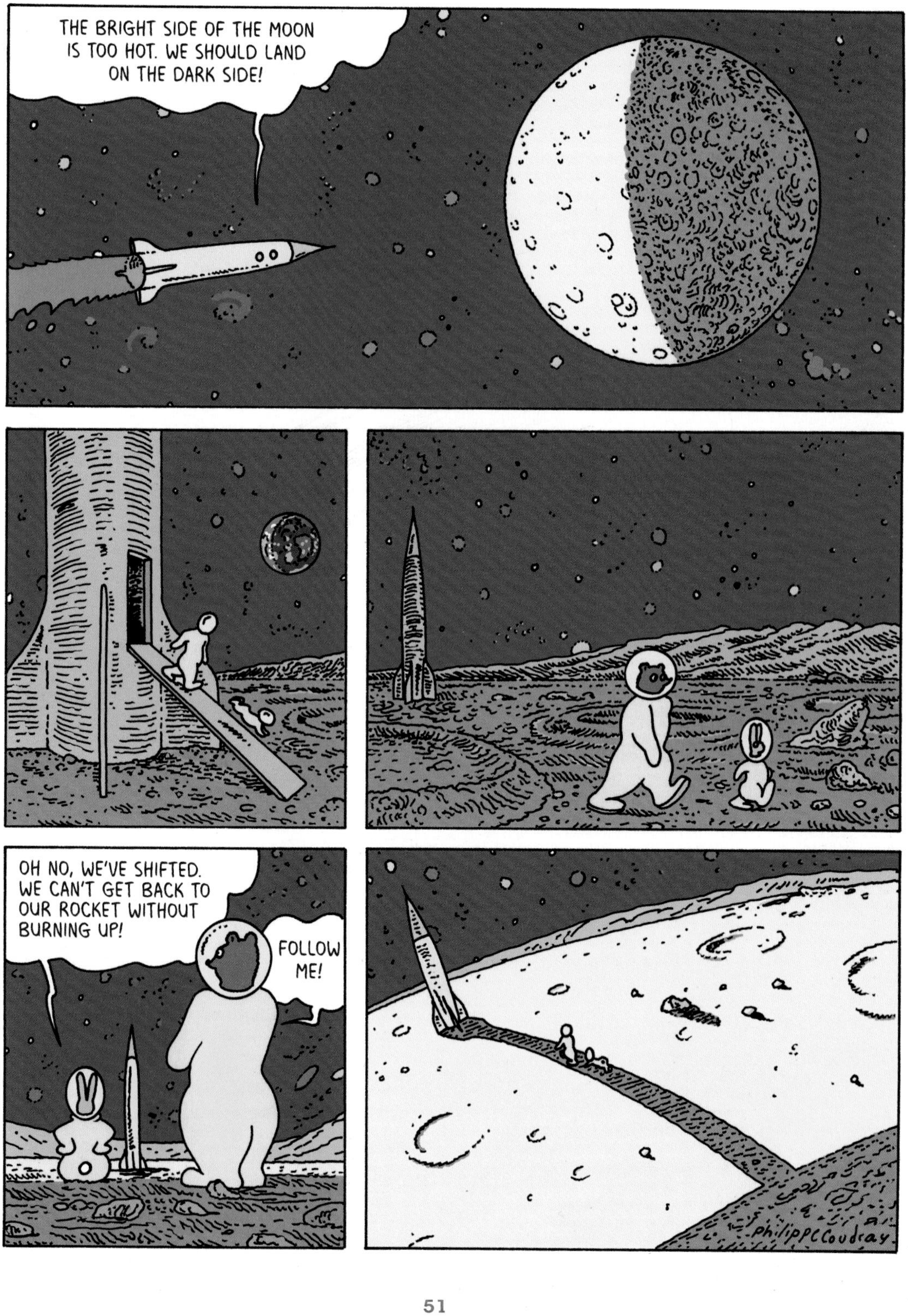
THE BRIGHT SIDE OF THE MOON IS TOO HOT. WE SHOULD LAND ON THE DARK SIDE!
OH NO, WE'VE SHIFTED. WE CAN'T GET BACK TO OUR ROCKET WITHOUT BURNING UP!
FOLLOW ME!
philippeCoudray

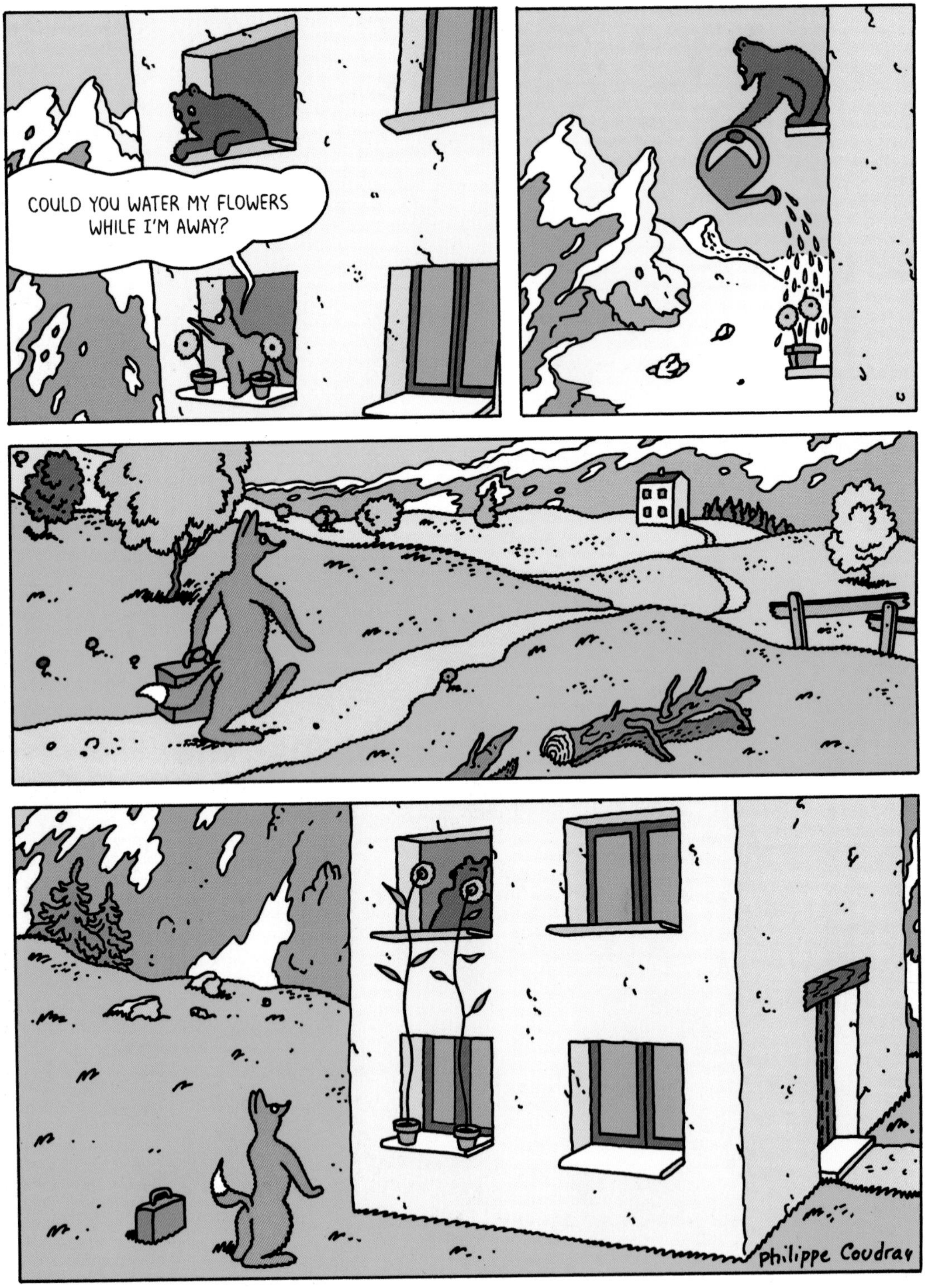
COULD YOU WATER MY FLOWERS WHILE I'M AWAY?
Philippe Coudray

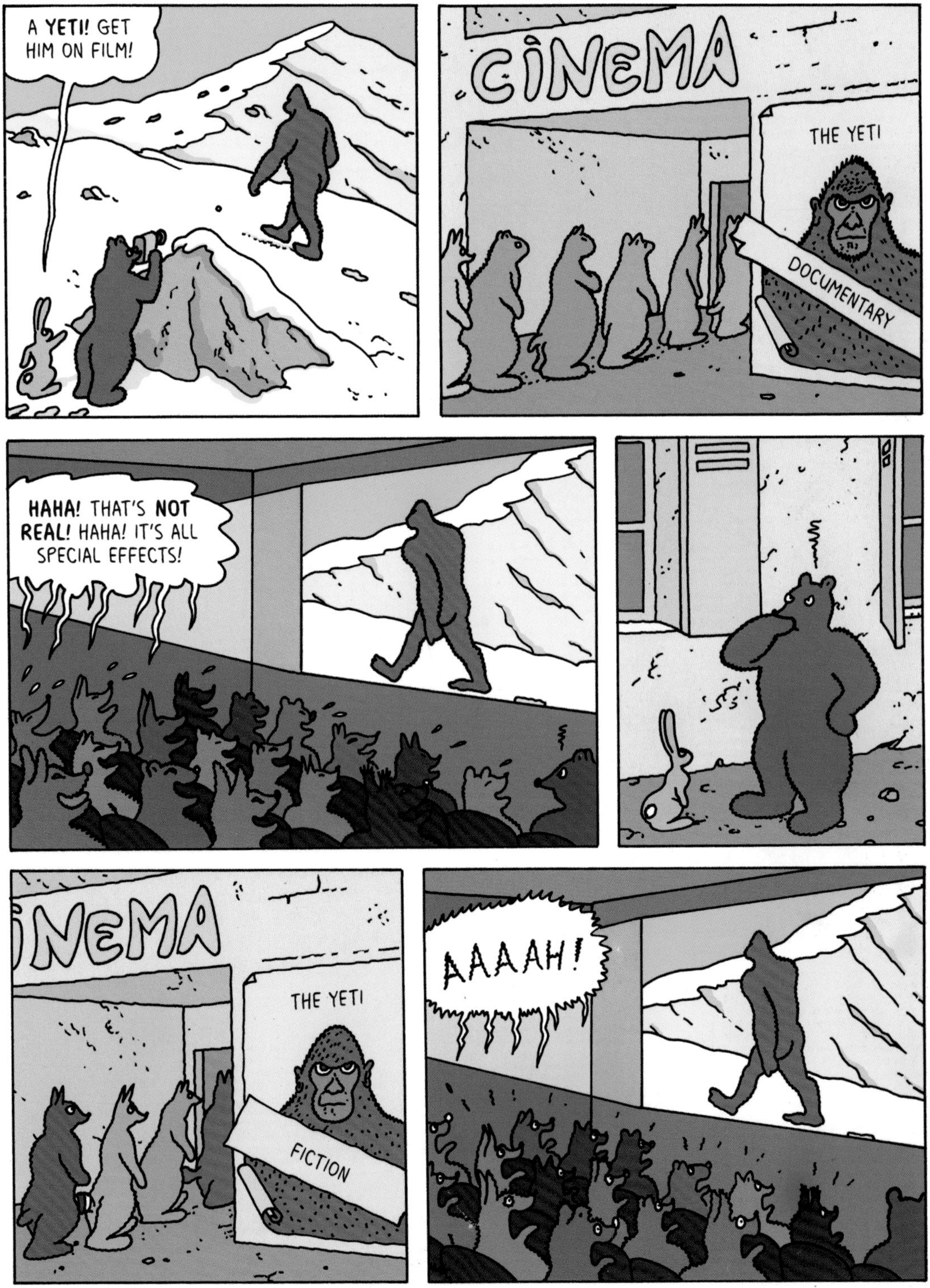

A **YETI!** GET HIM ON FILM!
CINEMA
THE YETI
DOCUMENTARY
HAHA! THAT'S **NOT REAL!** HAHA! IT'S ALL SPECIAL EFFECTS!
CINEMA
THE YETI
FICTION
AAAAH!

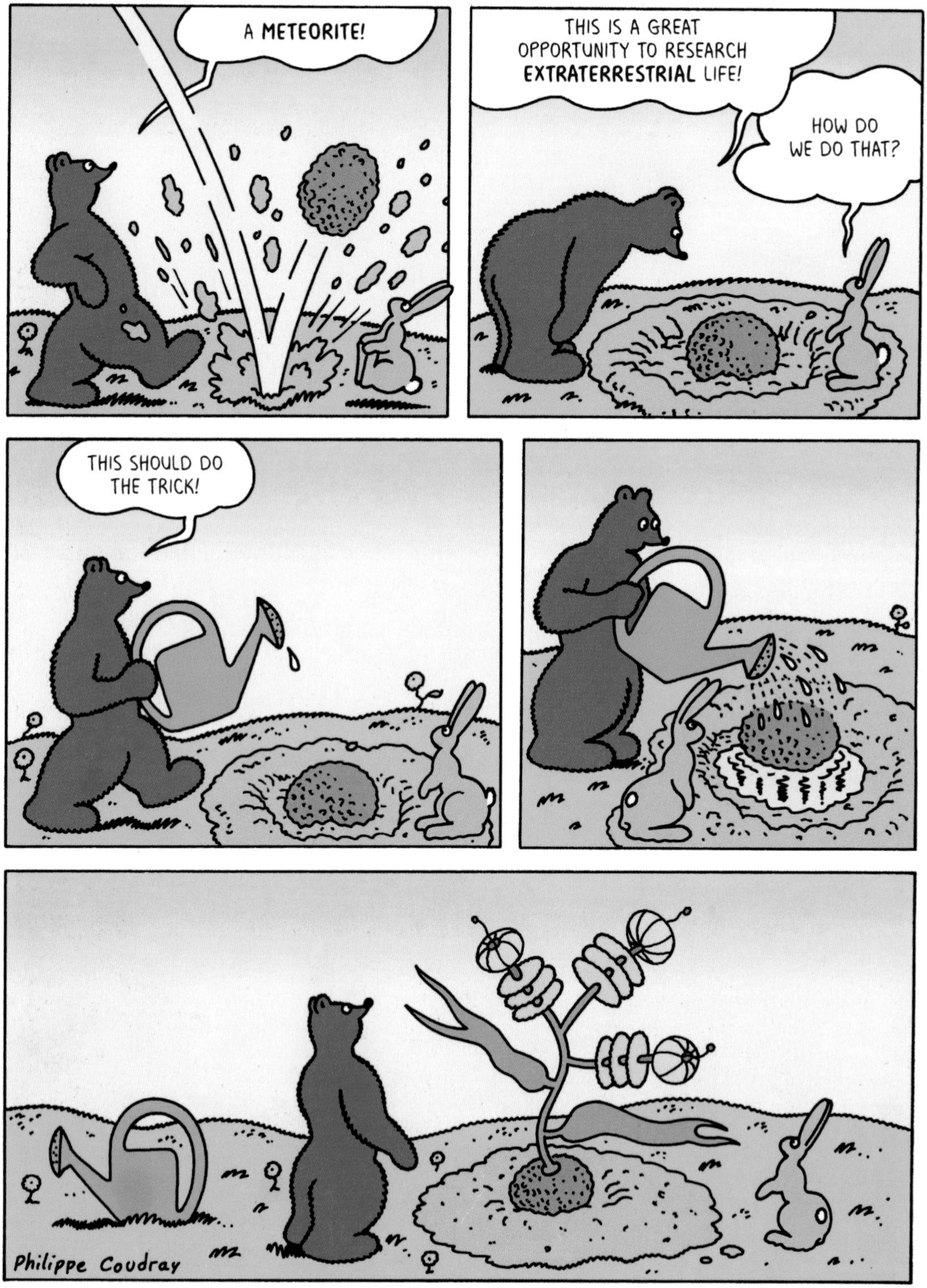
A **METEORITE!**
THIS IS A GREAT OPPORTUNITY TO RESEARCH **EXTRATERRESTRIAL** LIFE!
HOW DO WE DO THAT?
THIS SHOULD DO THE TRICK!
Philippe Coudray

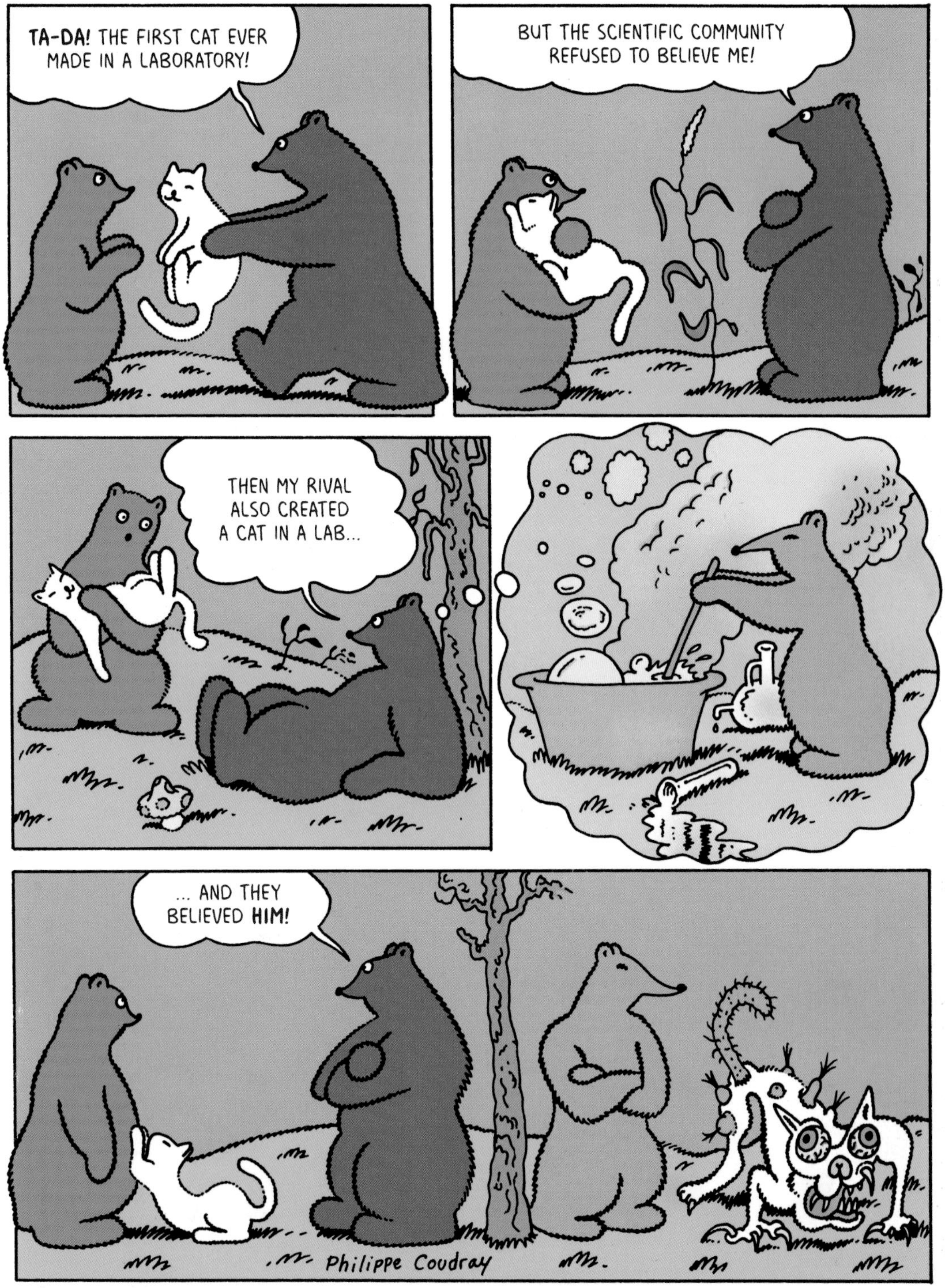
TA-DA! THE FIRST CAT EVER MADE IN A LABORATORY!
BUT THE SCIENTIFIC COMMUNITY REFUSED TO BELIEVE ME!
THEN MY RIVAL ALSO CREATED A CAT IN A LAB...
... AND THEY BELIEVED **HIM!**
Philippe Coudray

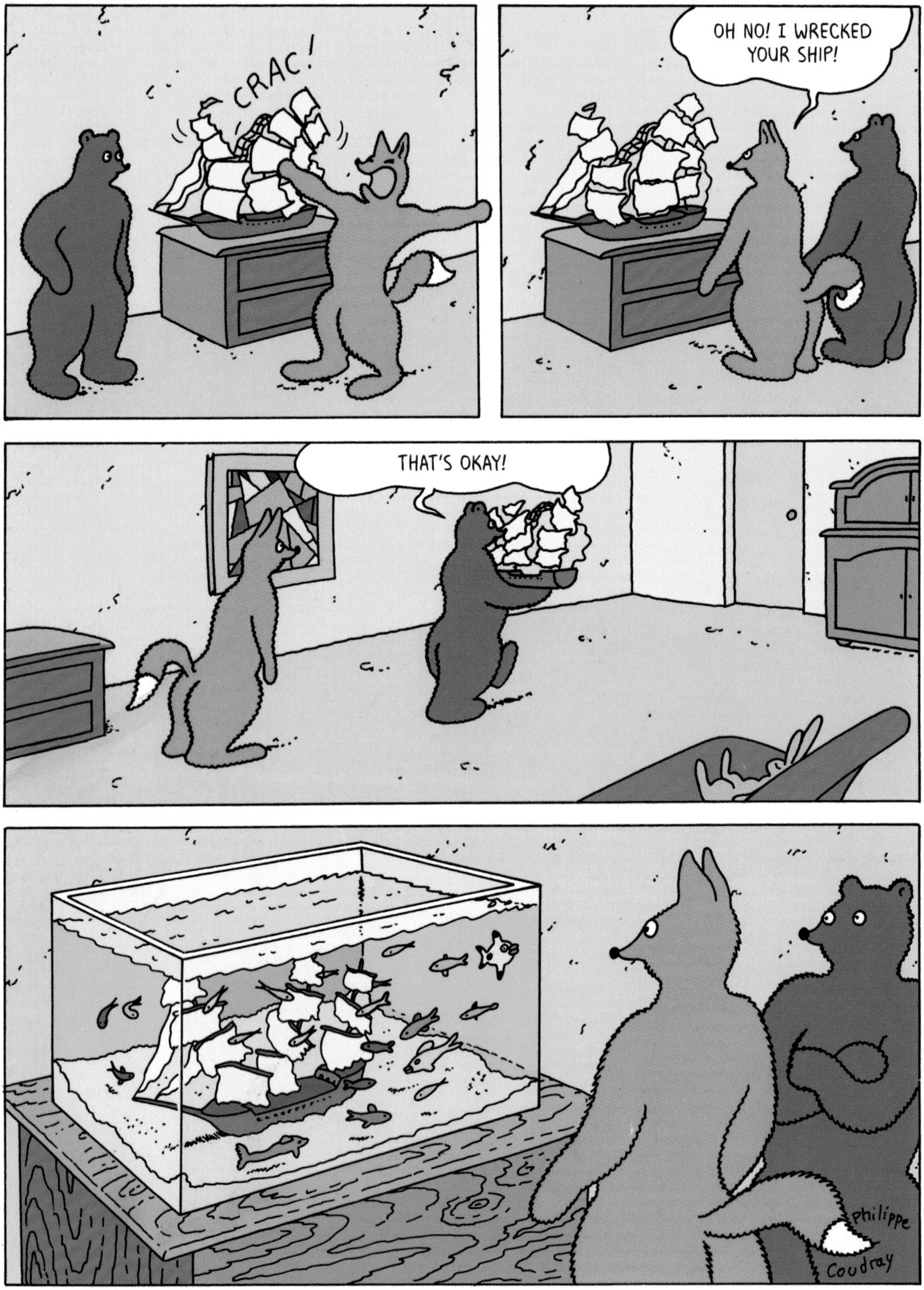
CRAC!
OH NO! I WRECKED YOUR SHIP!
THAT'S OKAY!
philippe Coudray

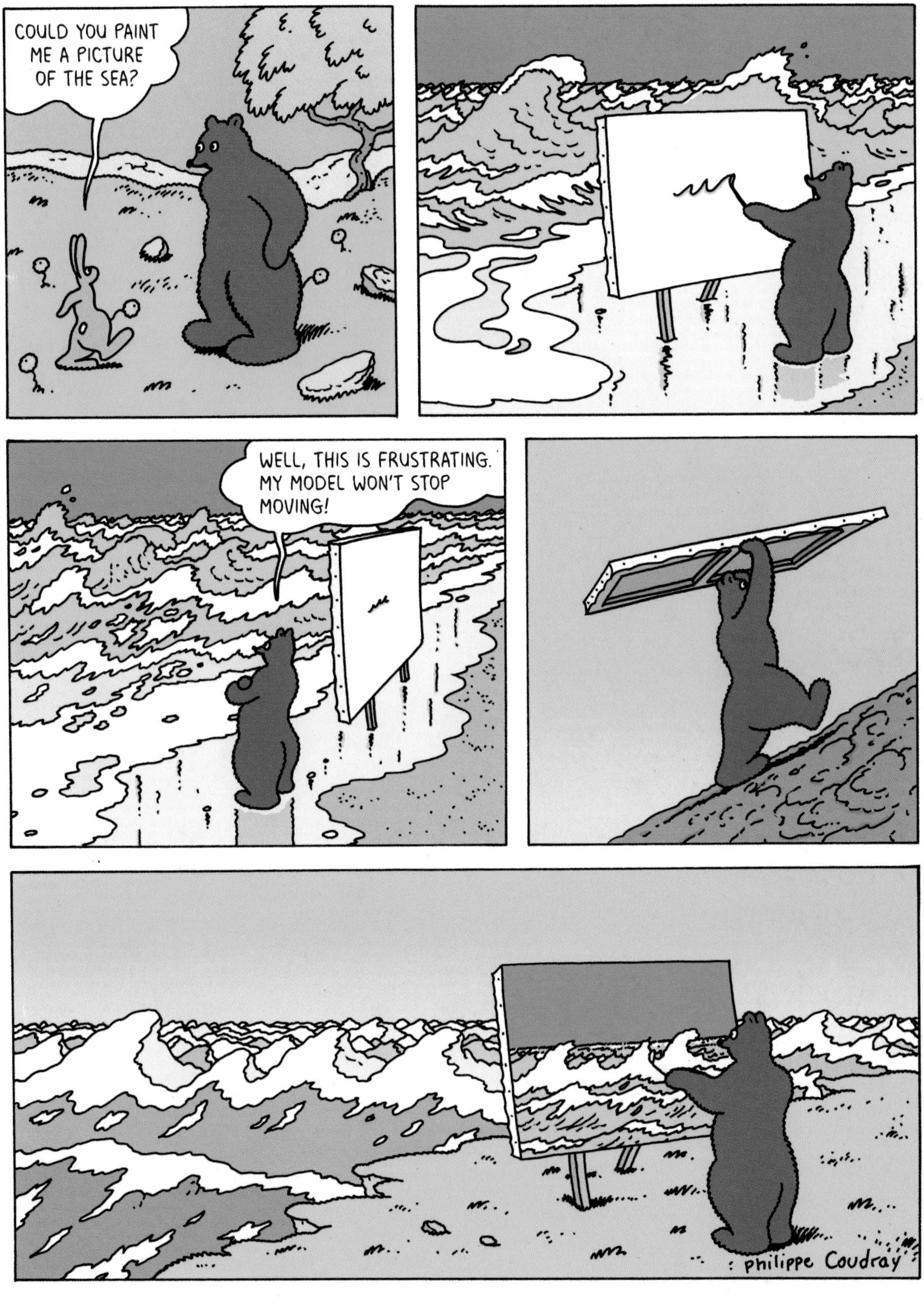
COULD YOU PAINT ME A PICTURE OF THE SEA?
WELL, THIS IS FRUSTRATING. MY MODEL WON'T STOP MOVING!
philippe Coudray

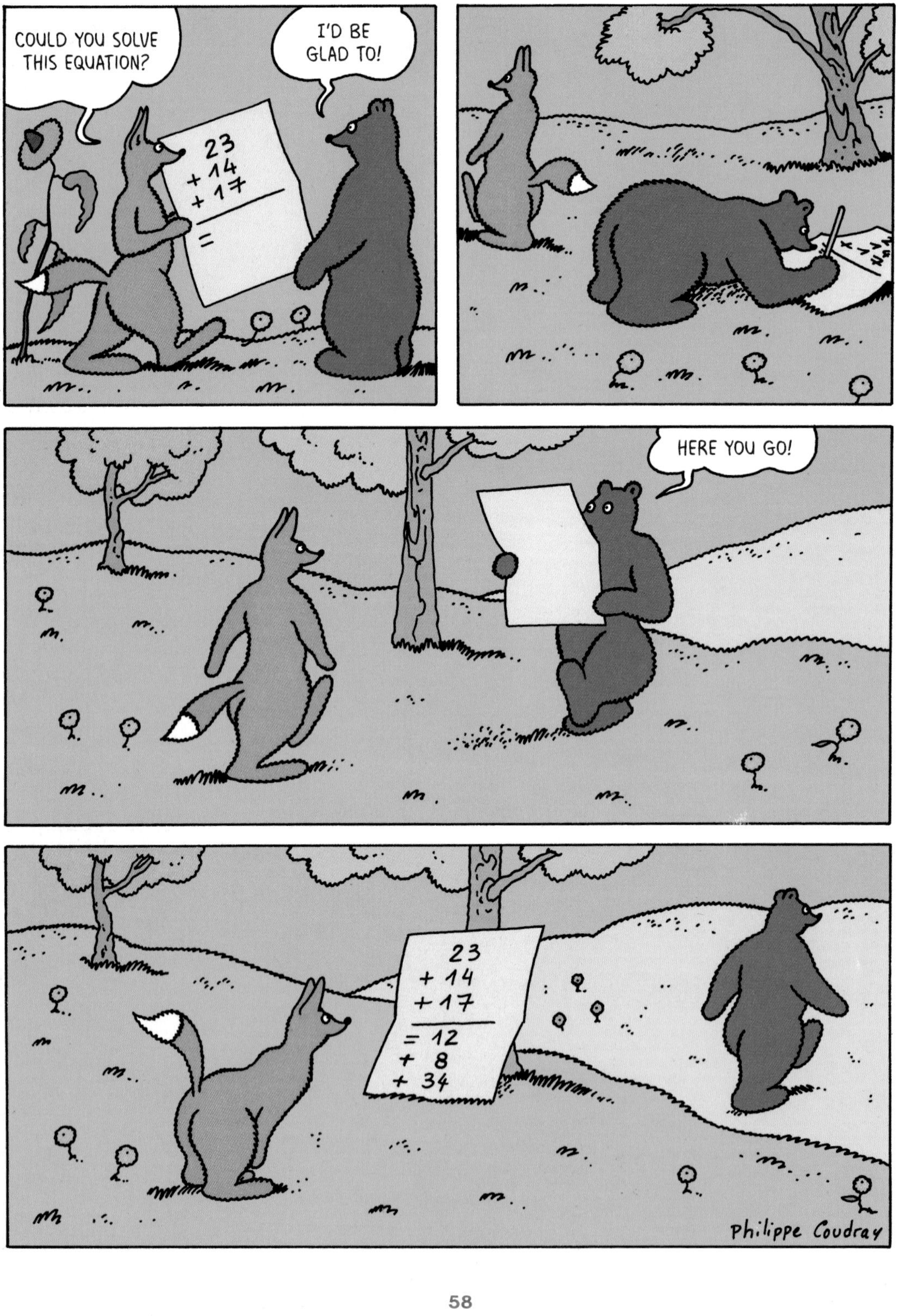
COULD YOU SOLVE THIS EQUATION?
23 + 14 + 17 =
I'D BE GLAD TO!
HERE YOU GO!
23 + 14 + 17 = 12 + 8 + 34
Philippe Coudray

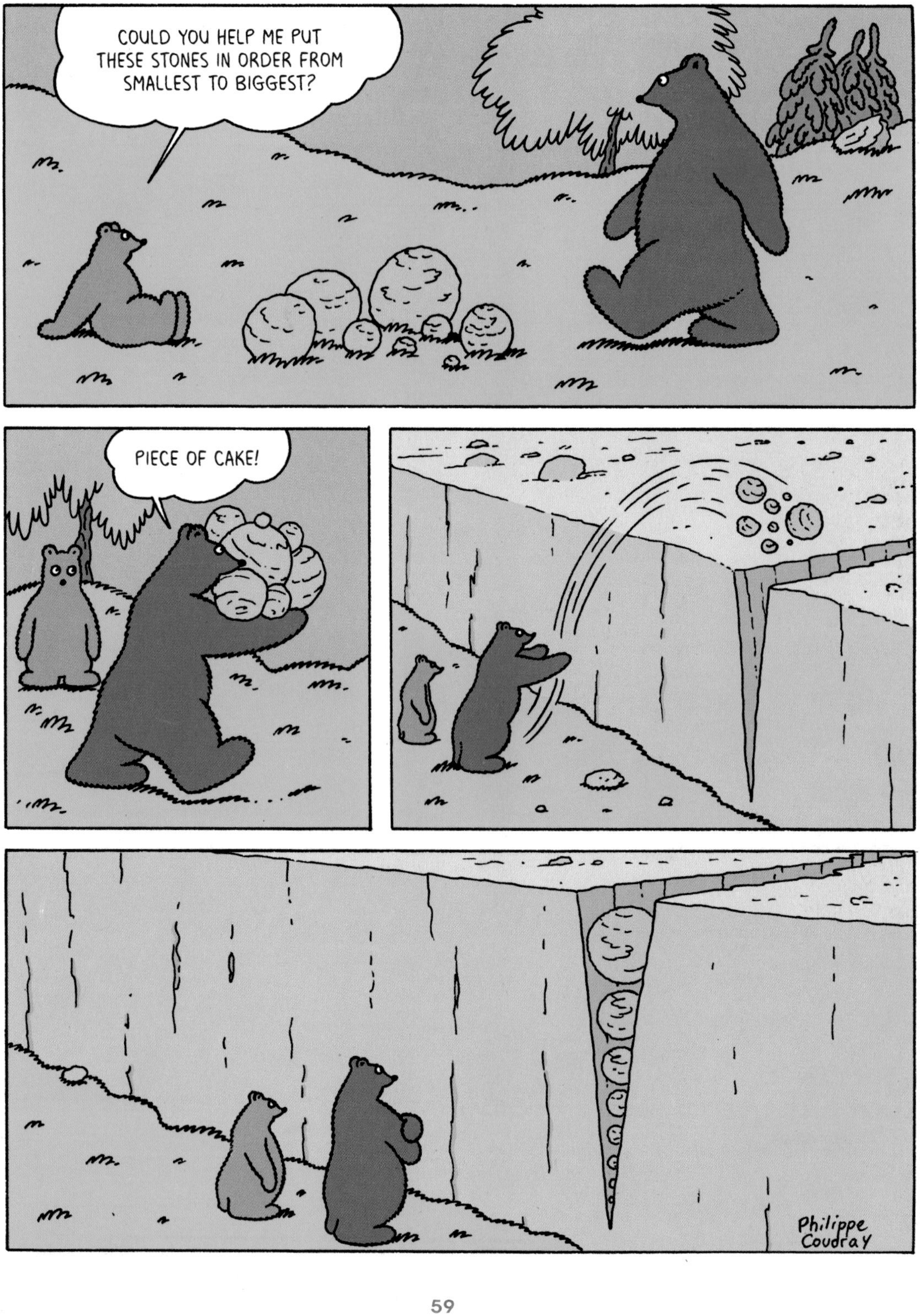
COULD YOU HELP ME PUT THESE STONES IN ORDER FROM SMALLEST TO BIGGEST?
PIECE OF CAKE!
Philippe Coudray

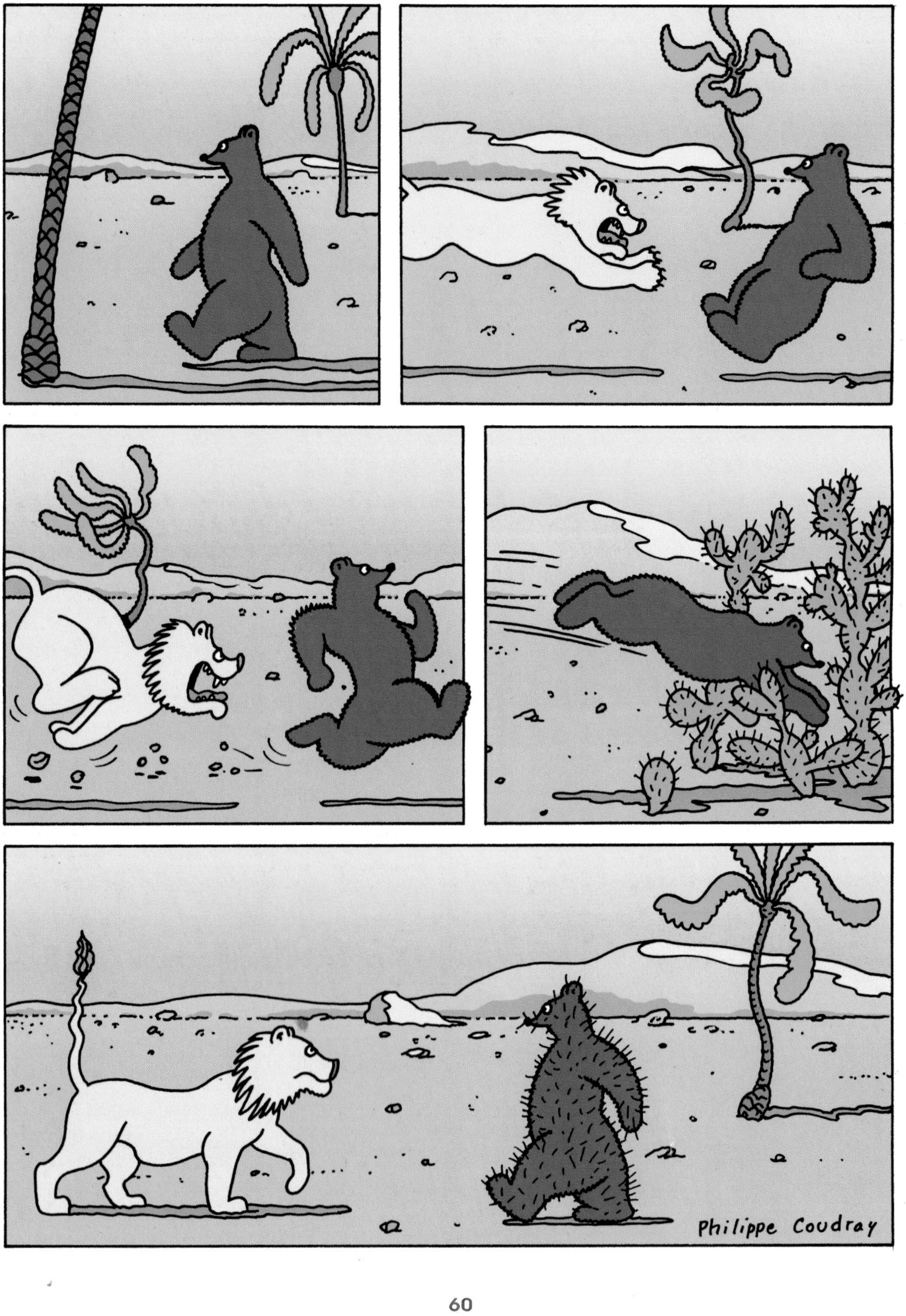
Philippe Coudray

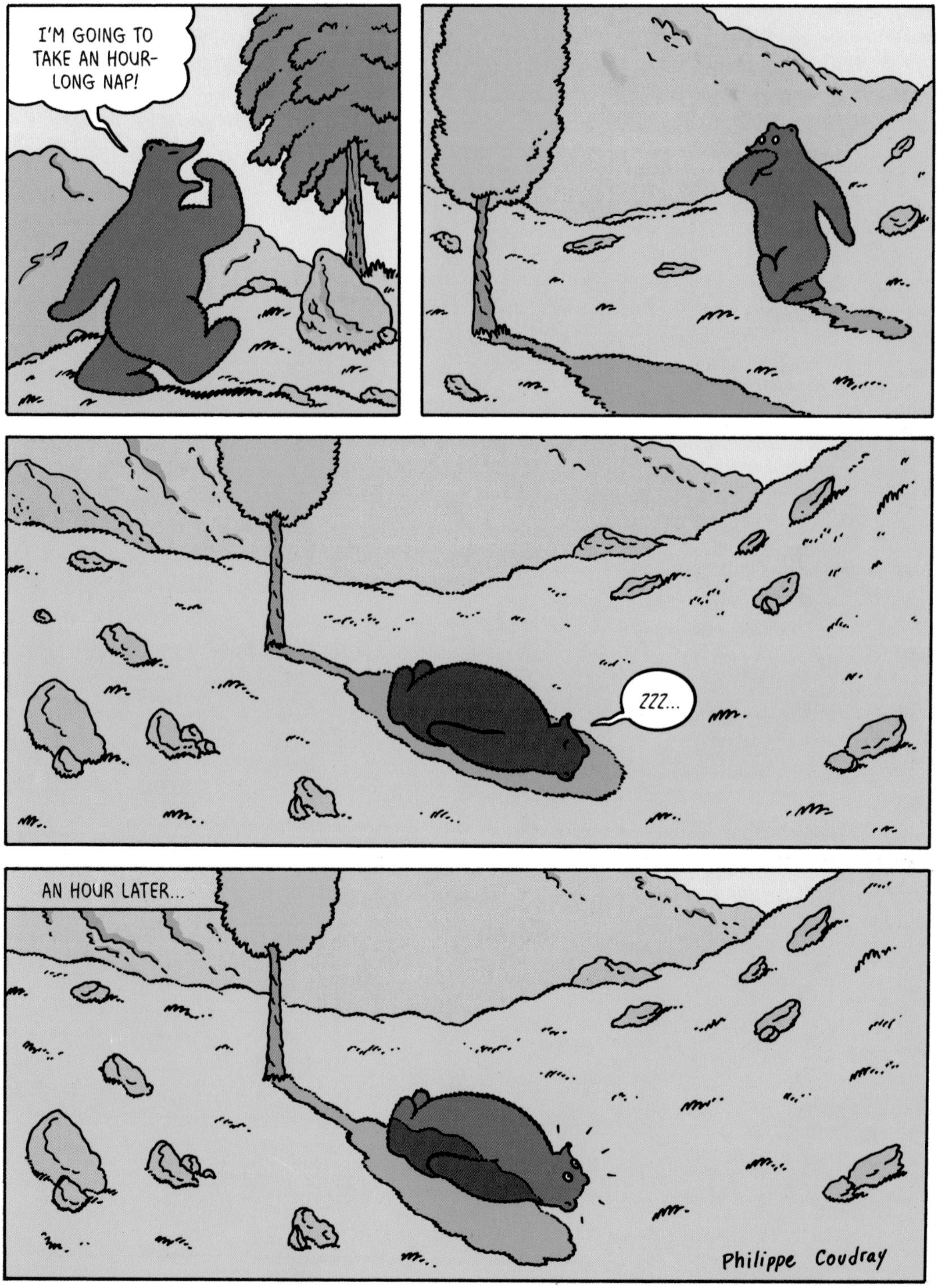
I'M GOING TO TAKE AN HOUR-LONG NAP!
ZZZ...
AN HOUR LATER...
Philippe Coudray

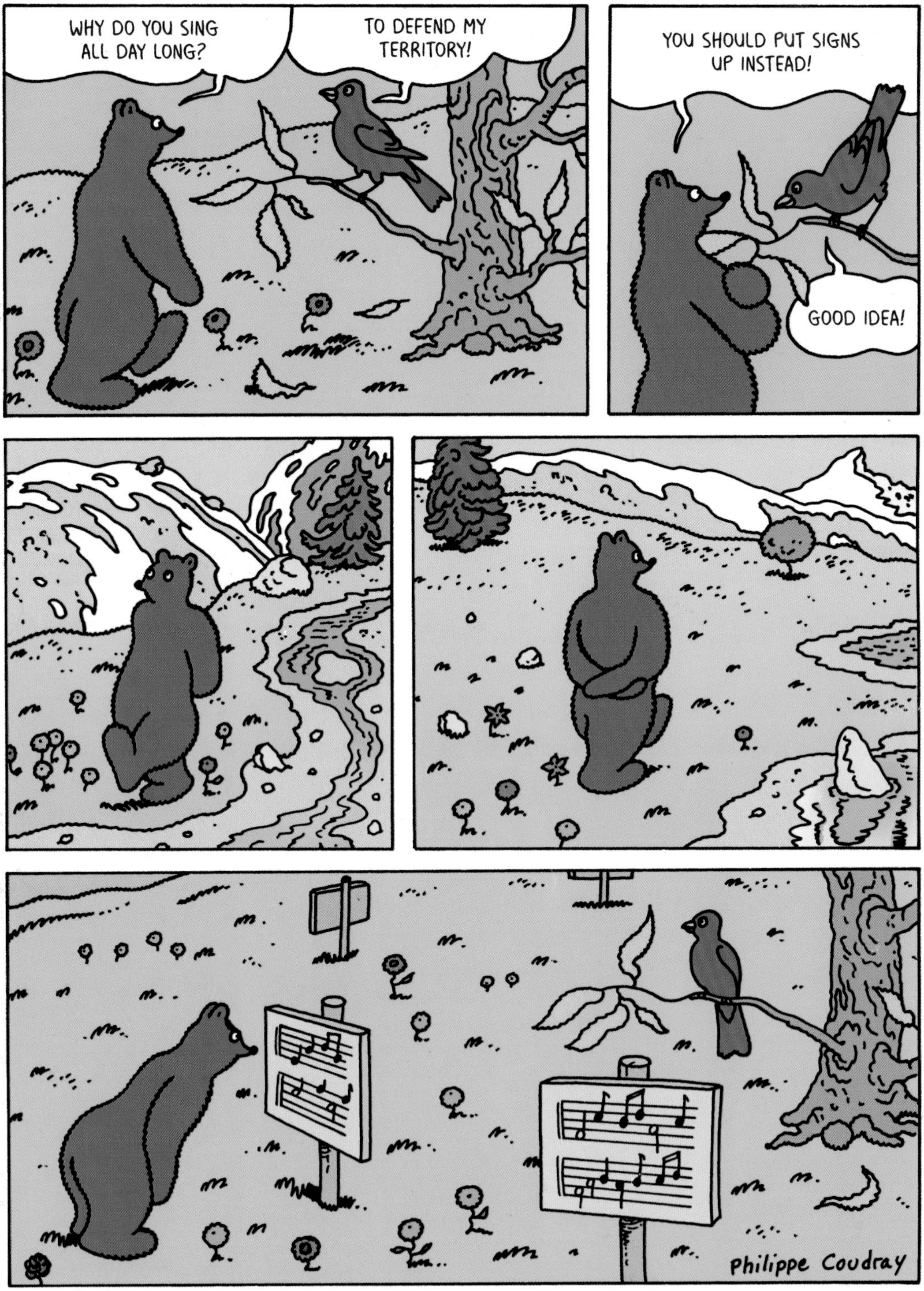
WHY DO YOU SING ALL DAY LONG?
TO DEFEND MY TERRITORY!
YOU SHOULD PUT SIGNS UP INSTEAD!
GOOD IDEA!
Philippe Coudray

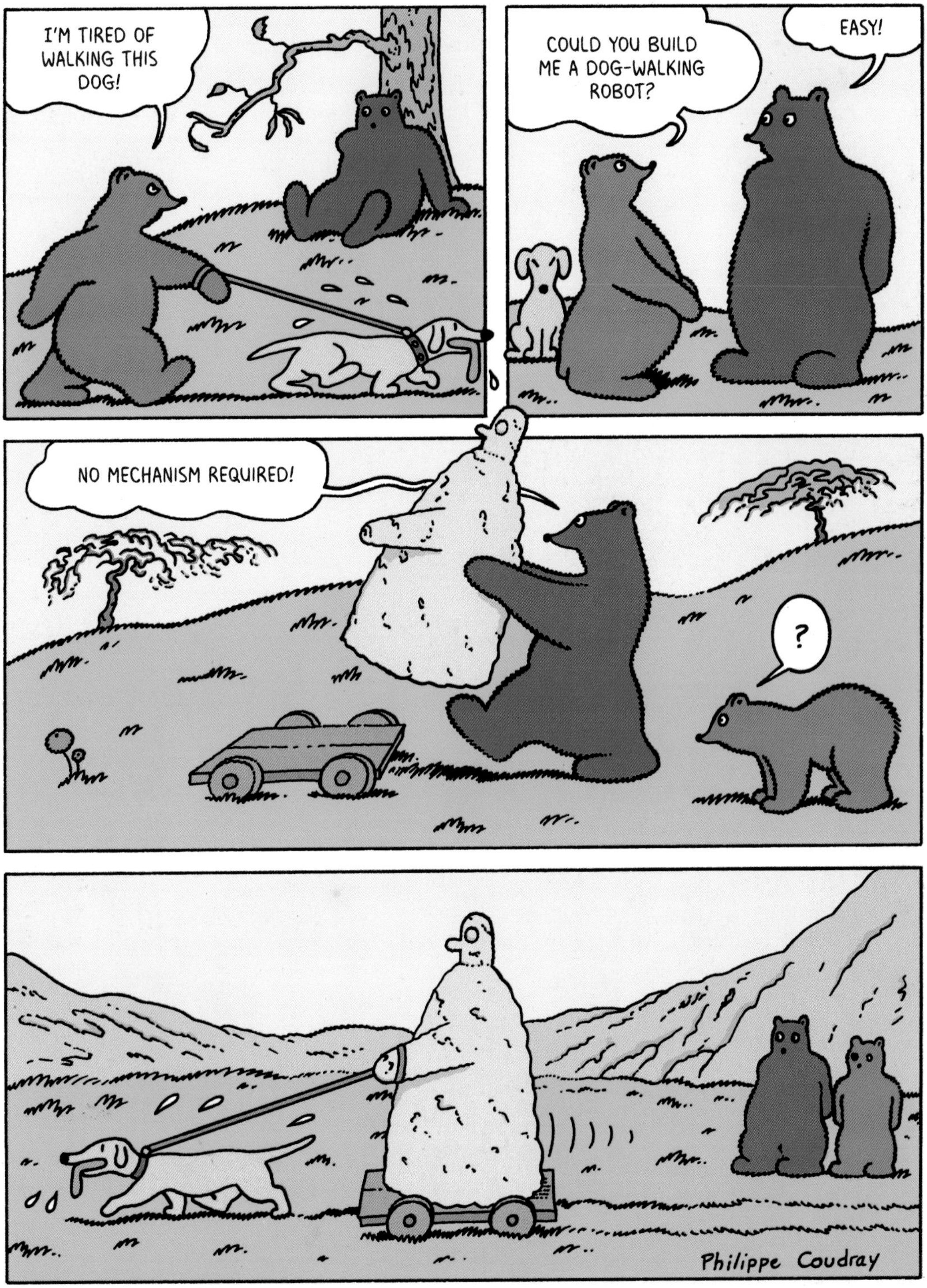
I'M TIRED OF WALKING THIS DOG!
COULD YOU BUILD ME A DOG-WALKING ROBOT?
EASY!
NO MECHANISM REQUIRED!
?
Philippe Coudray

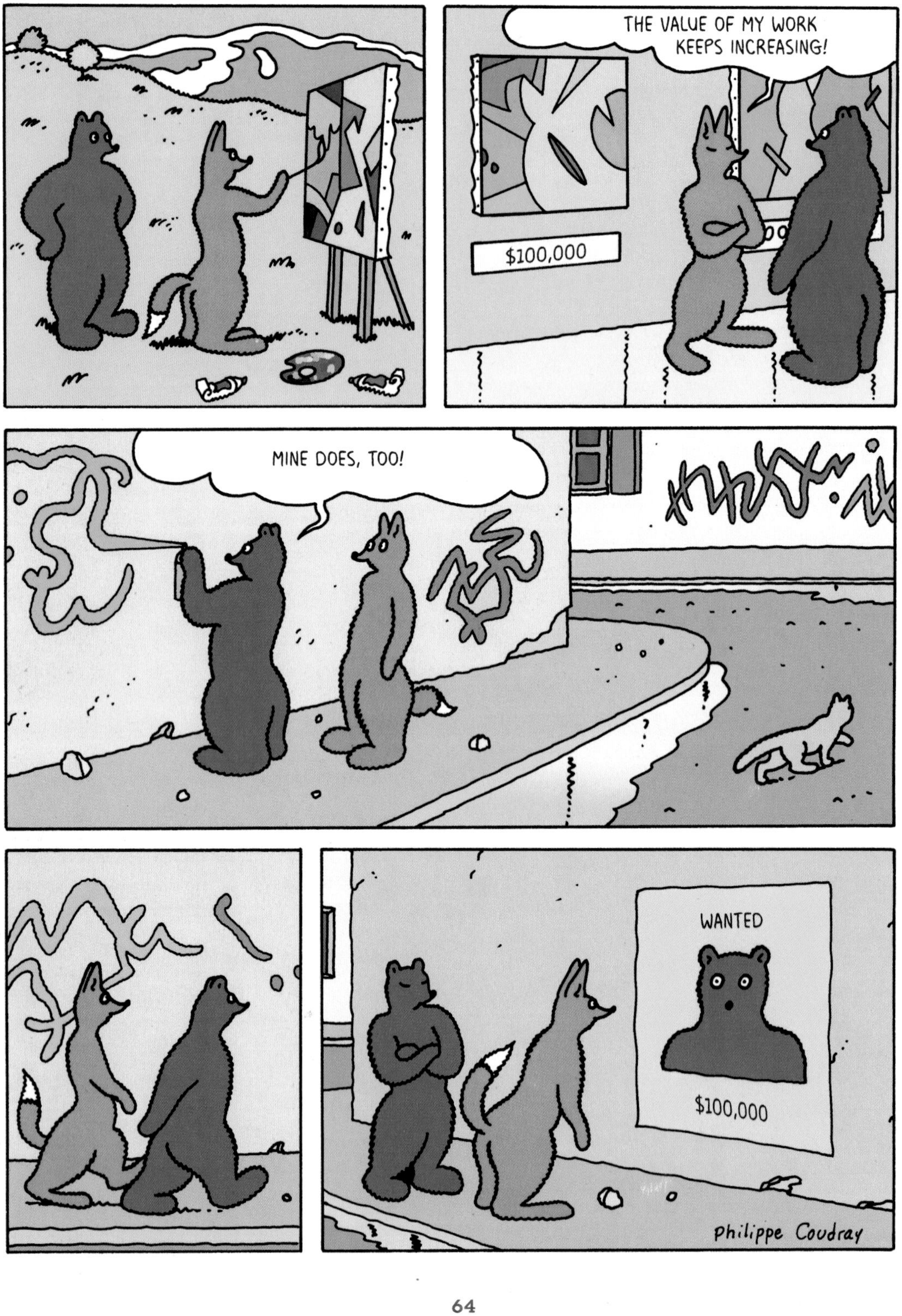

THE VALUE OF MY WORK KEEPS INCREASING!
$100,000
MINE DOES, TOO!
WANTED
$100,000
Philippe Coudray

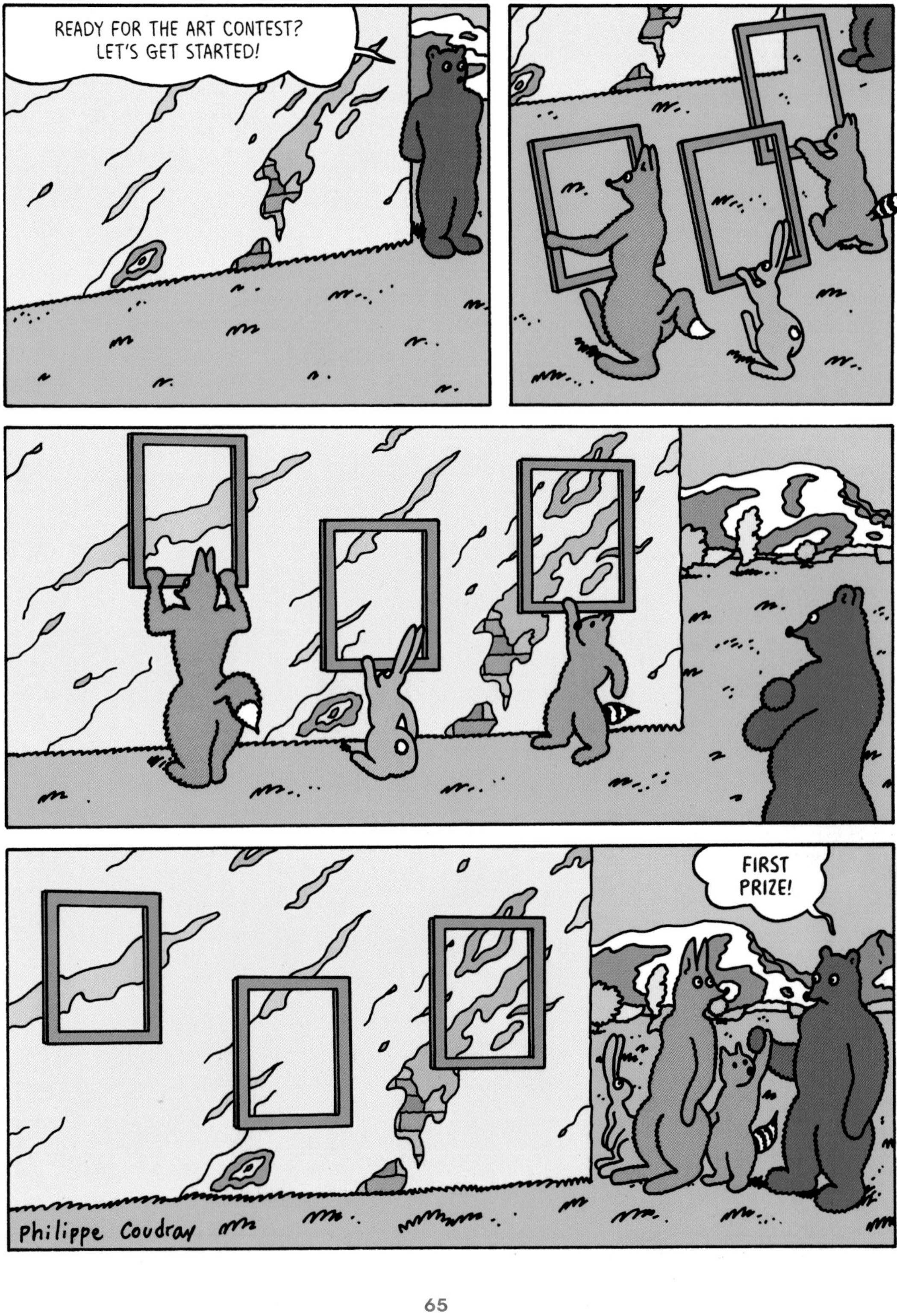
READY FOR THE ART CONTEST? LET'S GET STARTED!
FIRST PRIZE!
Philippe Coudray

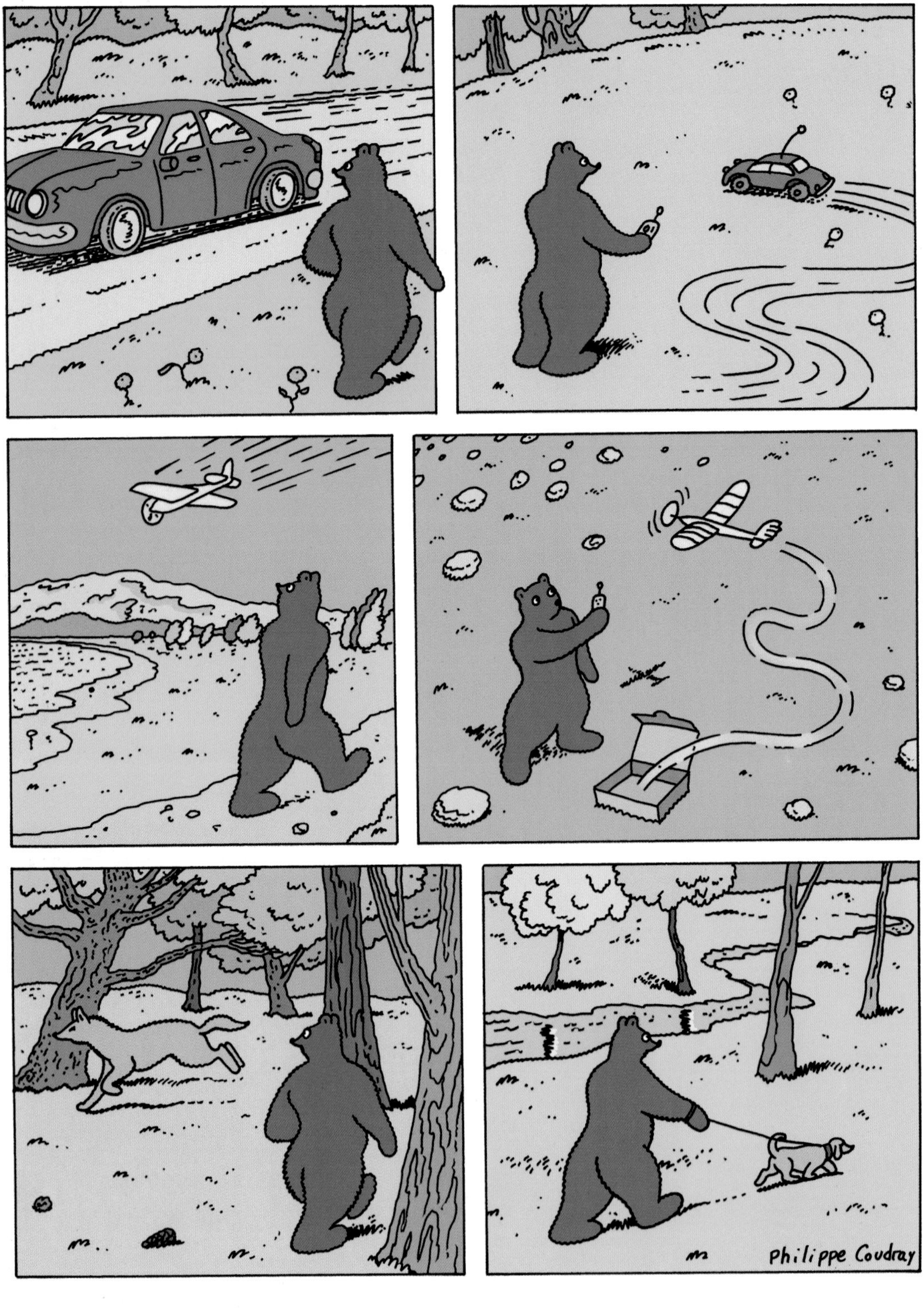
Philippe Coudray

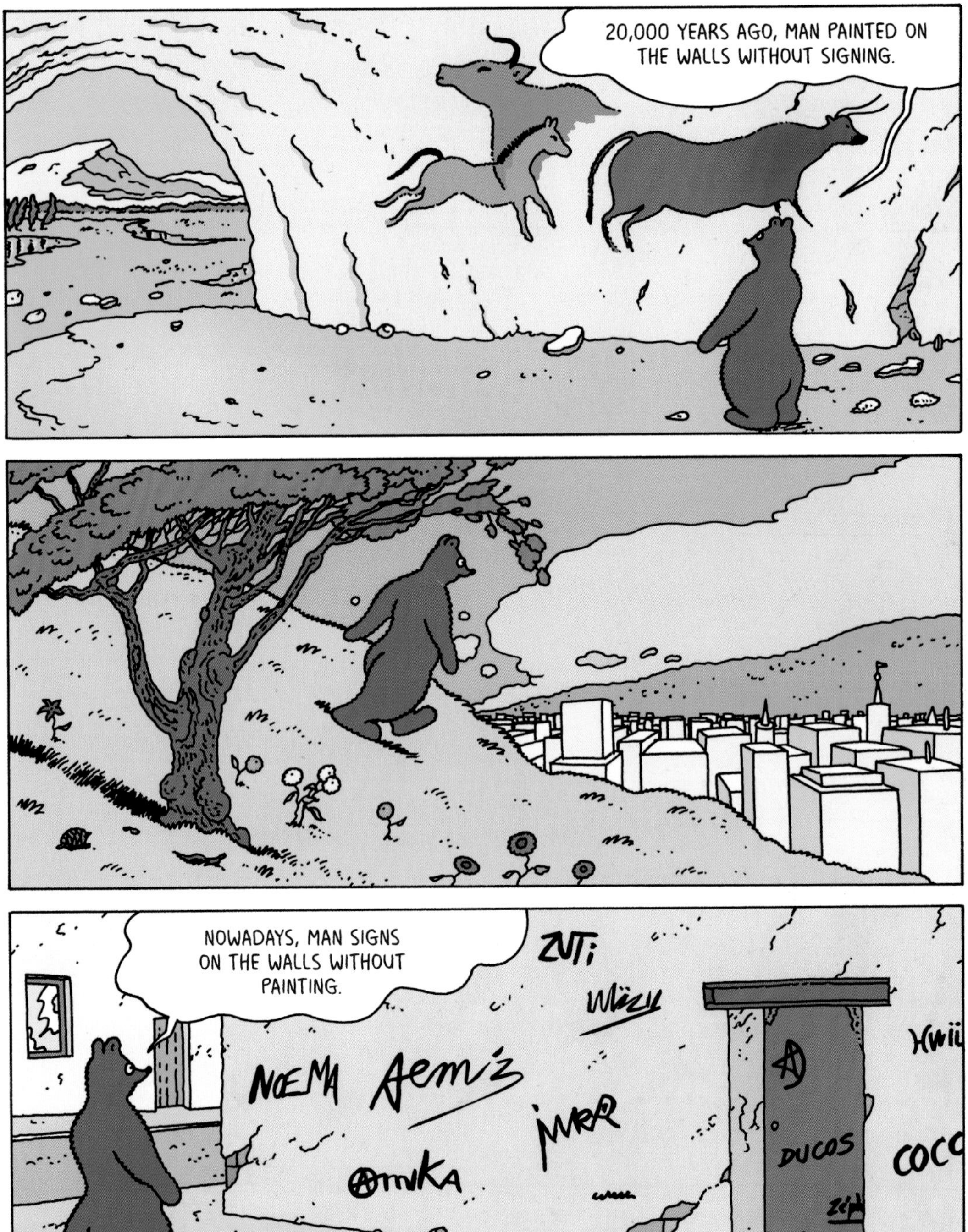
20,000 YEARS AGO, MAN PAINTED ON THE WALLS WITHOUT SIGNING.
NOWADAYS, MAN SIGNS ON THE WALLS WITHOUT PAINTING.
Philippe Coudray

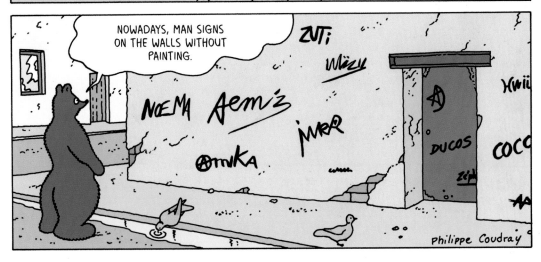

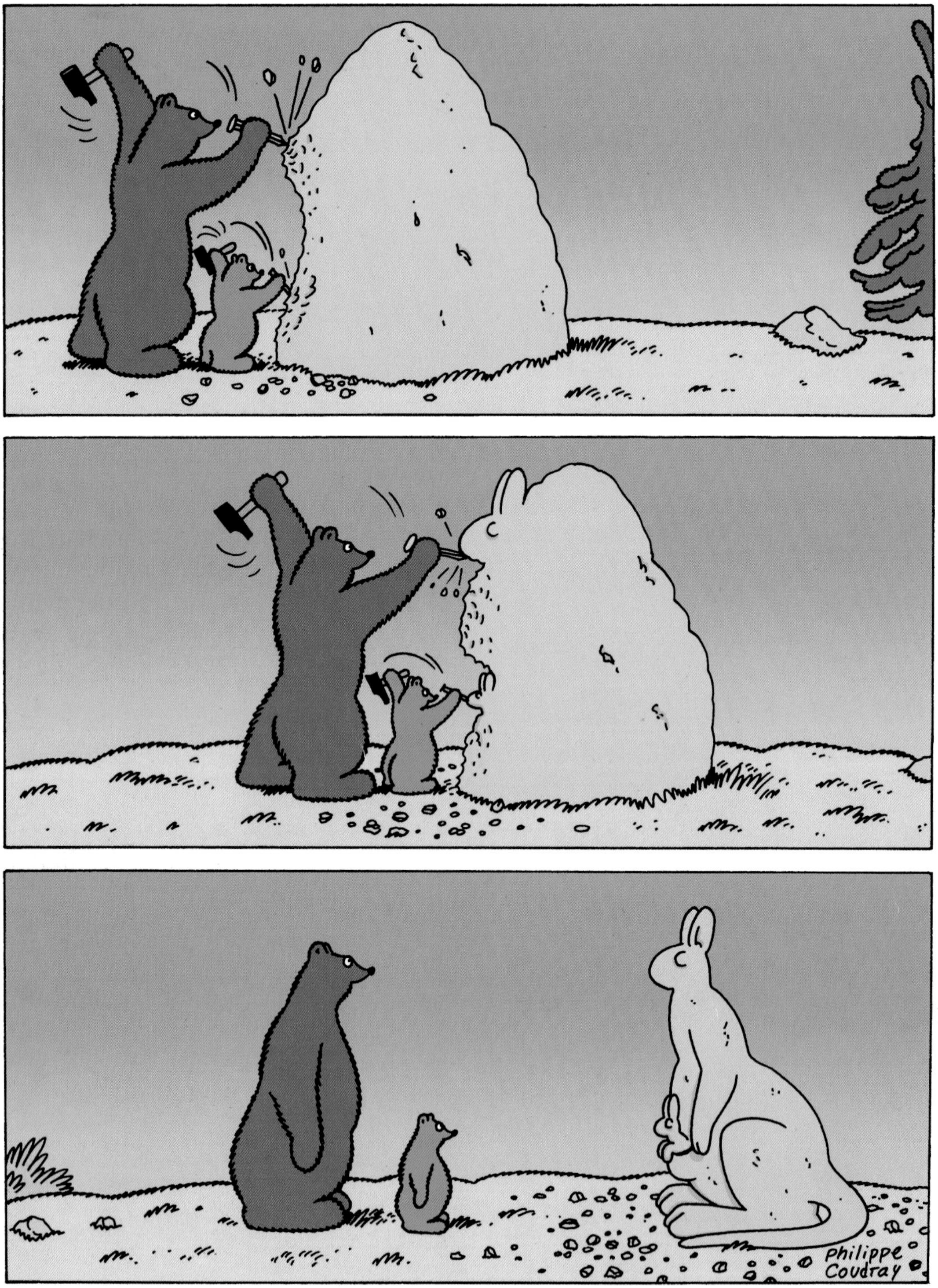
Philippe
Coudray

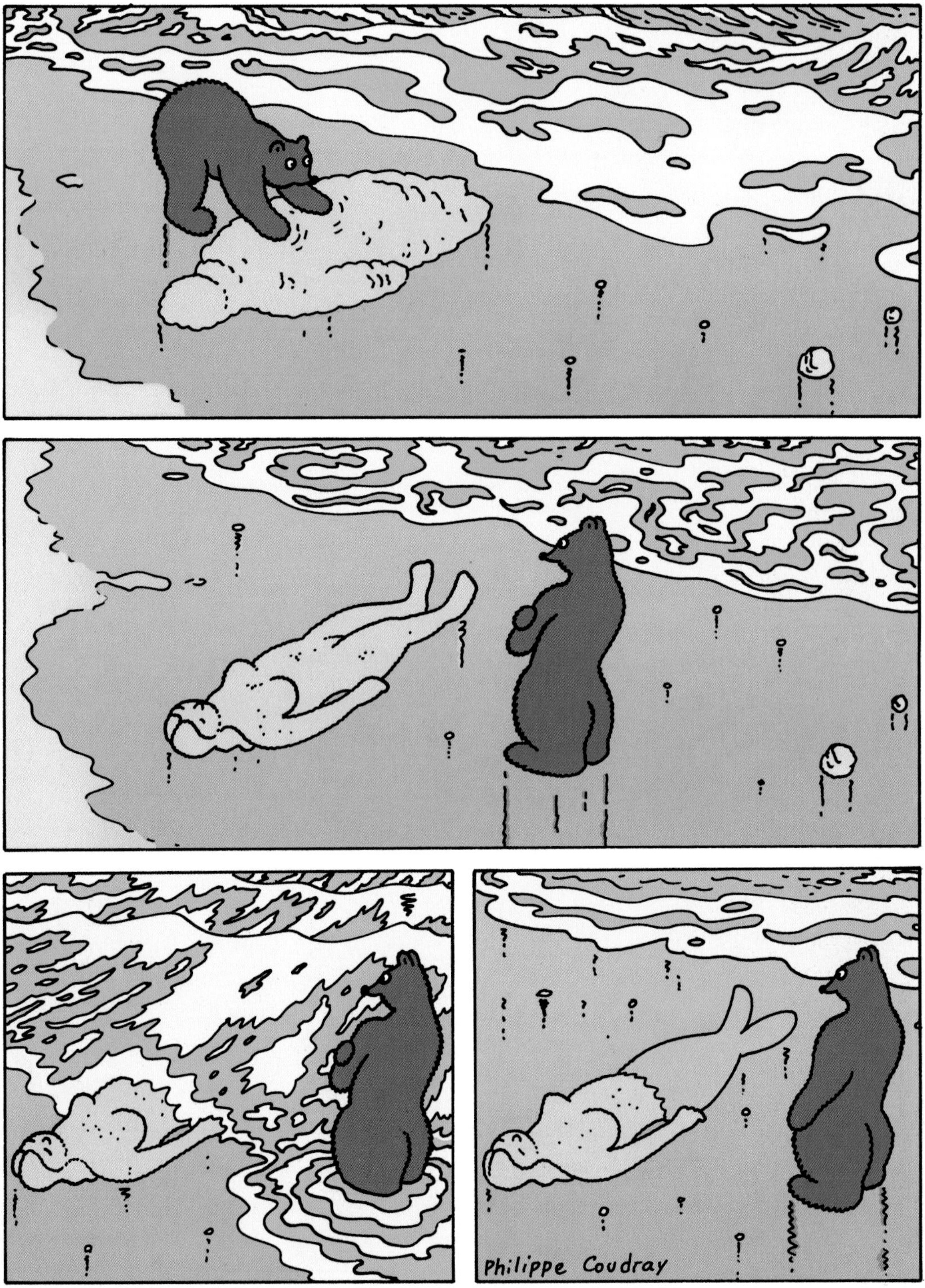
Philippe Coudray

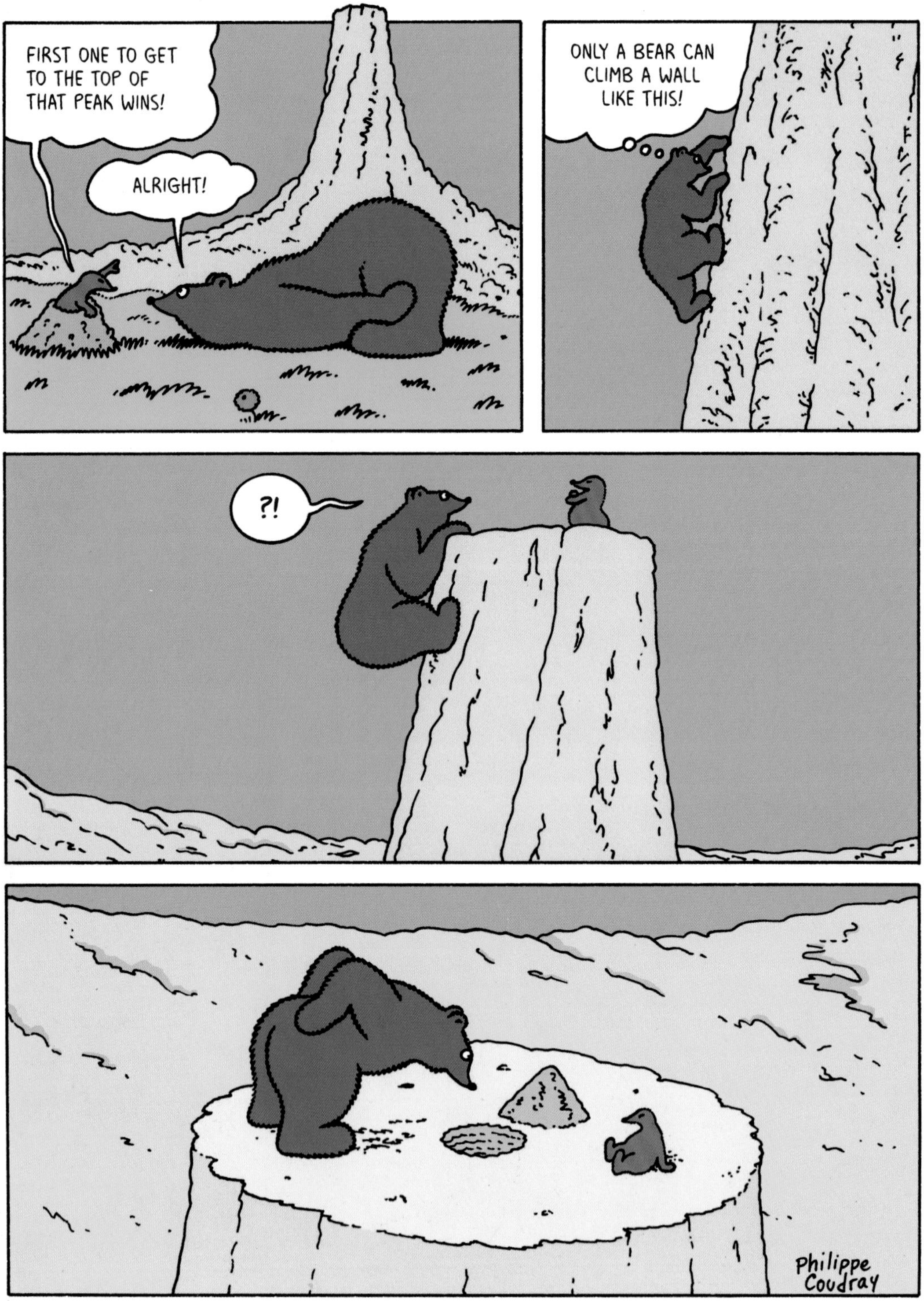
FIRST ONE TO GET TO THE TOP OF THAT PEAK WINS!
ALRIGHT!
ONLY A BEAR CAN CLIMB A WALL LIKE THIS!
?!
Philippe Coudray

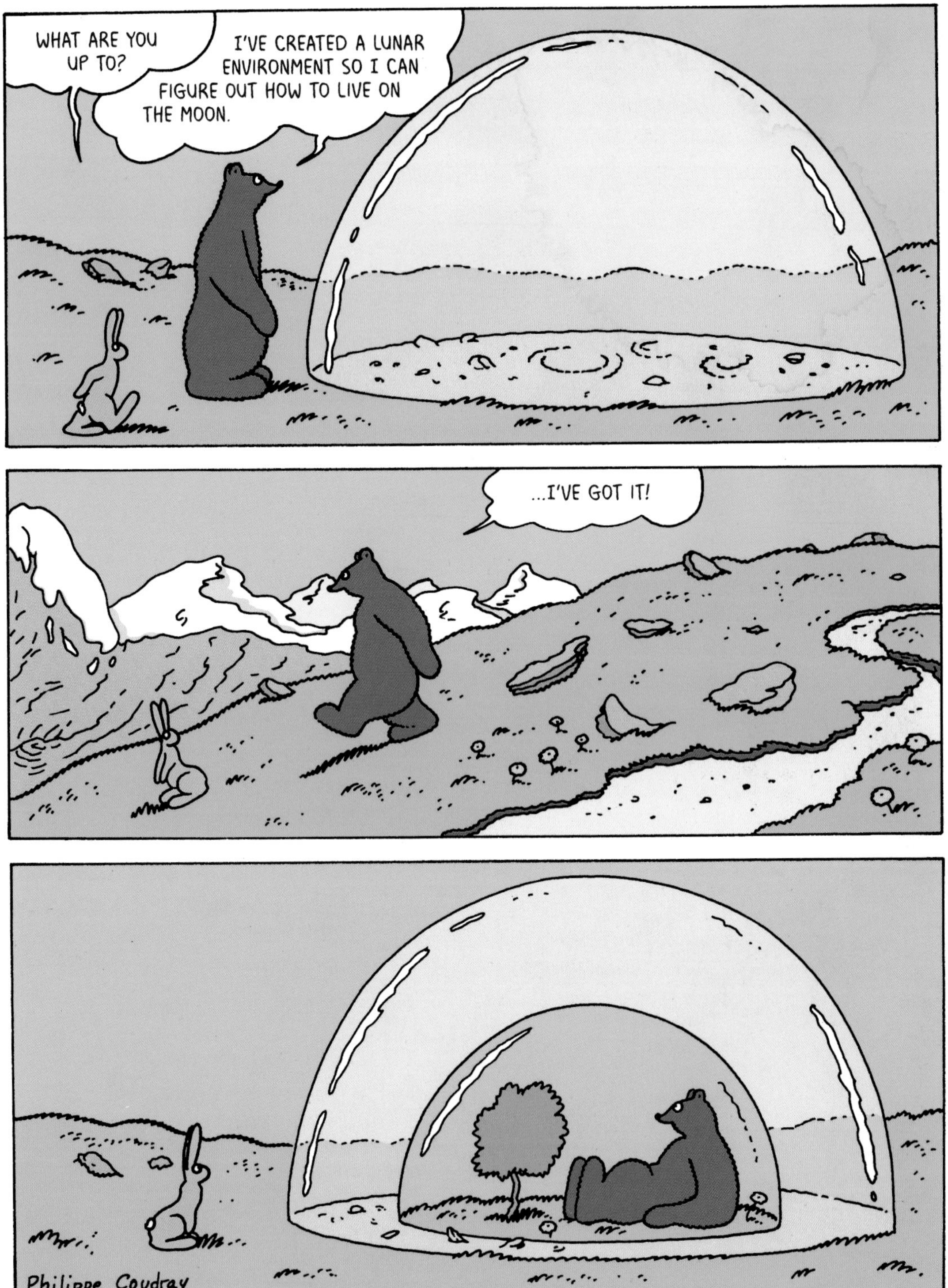
WHAT ARE YOU UP TO?
I'VE CREATED A LUNAR ENVIRONMENT SO I CAN FIGURE OUT HOW TO LIVE ON THE MOON.
...I'VE GOT IT!
Philippe Coudray

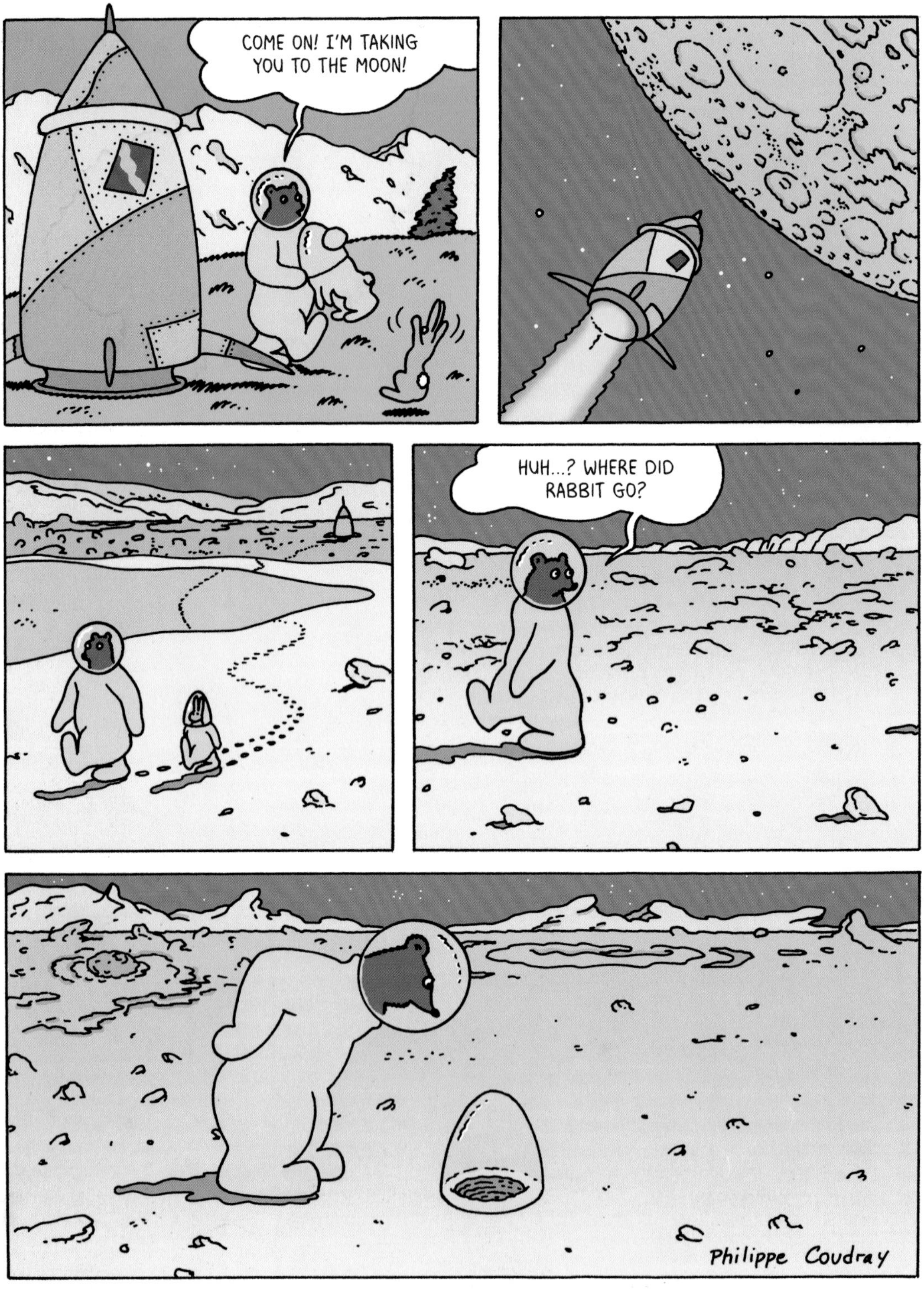
COME ON! I'M TAKING YOU TO THE MOON!
HUH...? WHERE DID RABBIT GO?
Philippe Coudray

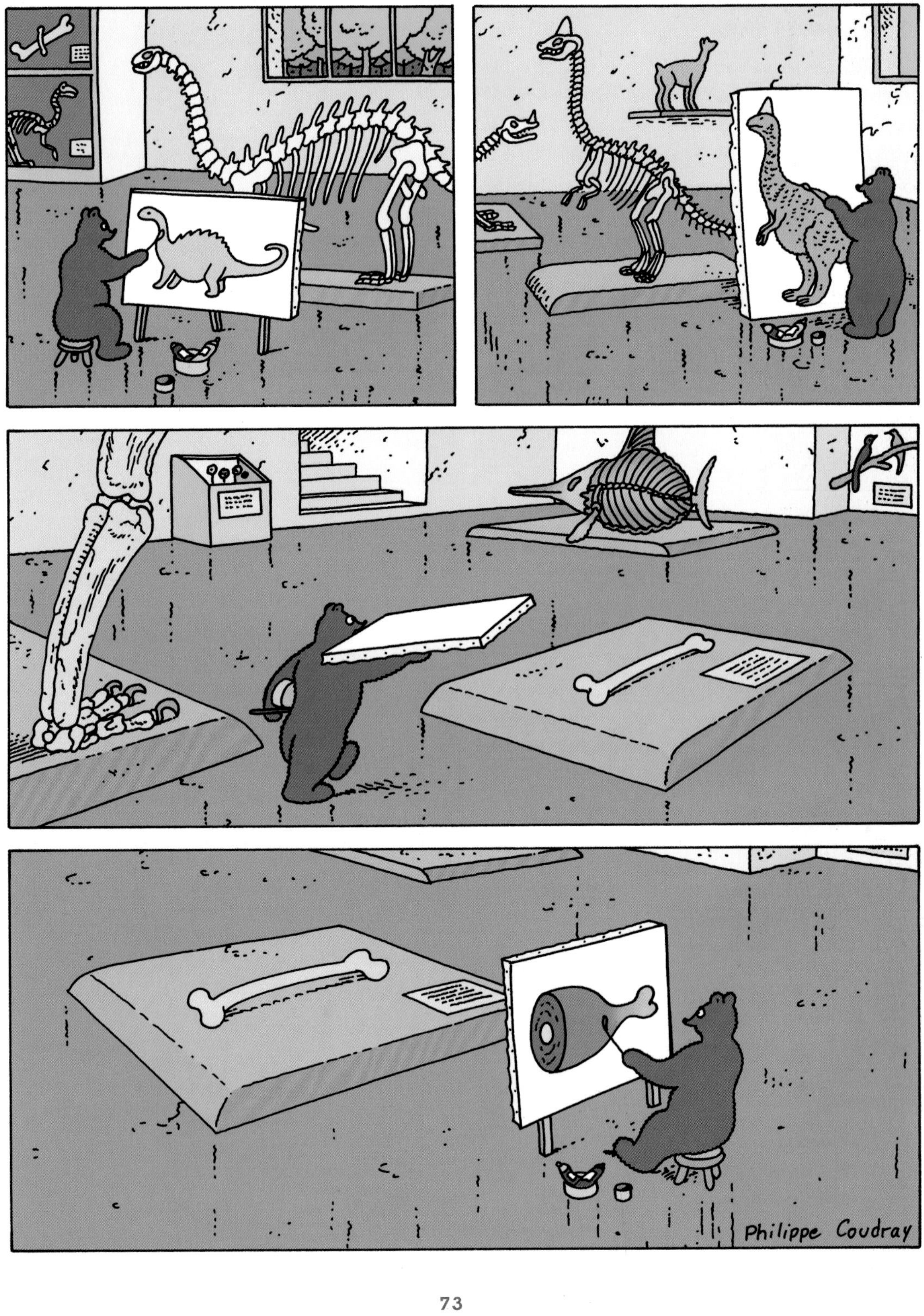
Philippe Coudray

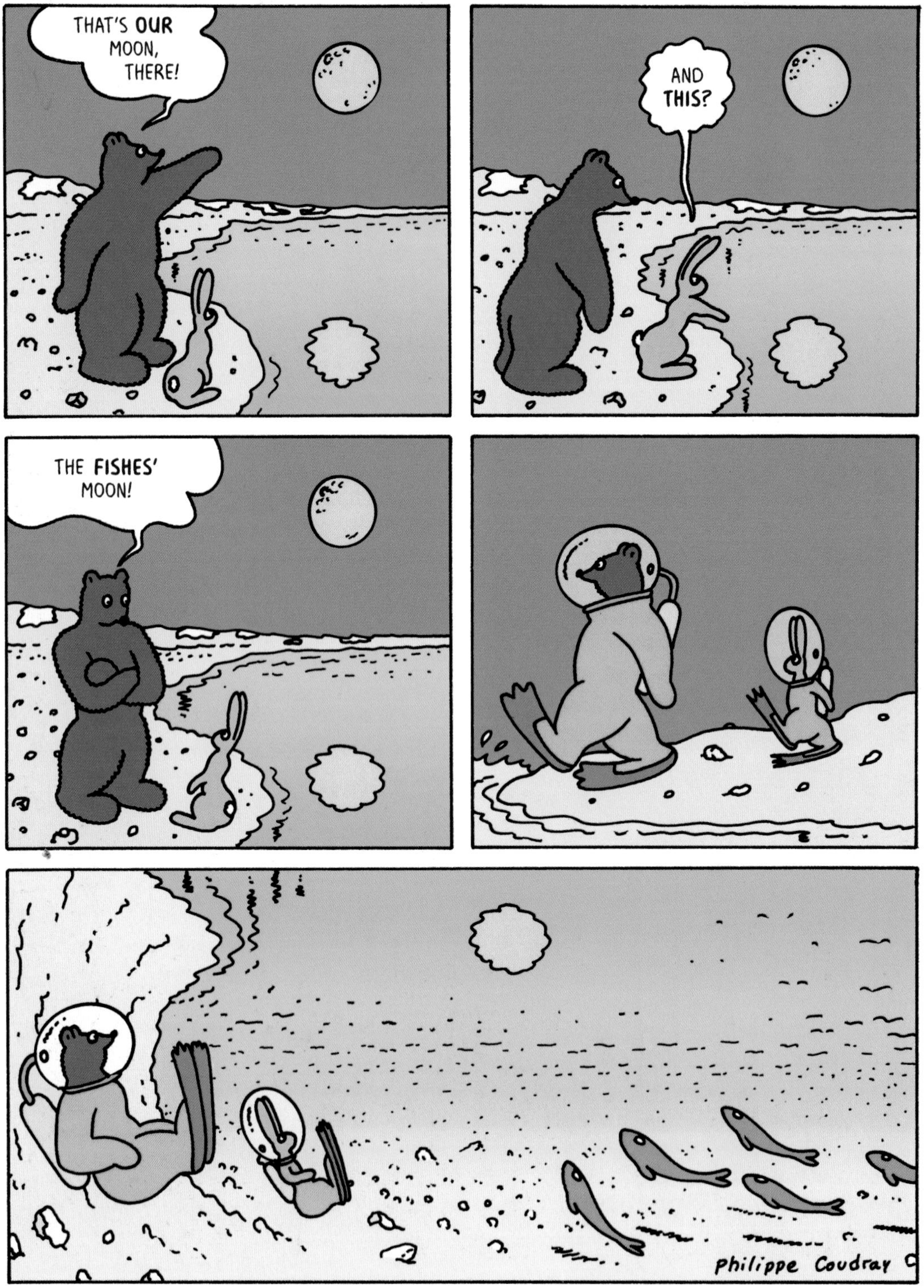
THAT'S **OUR** MOON, THERE!
AND **THIS?**
THE **FISHES'** MOON!
Philippe Coudray

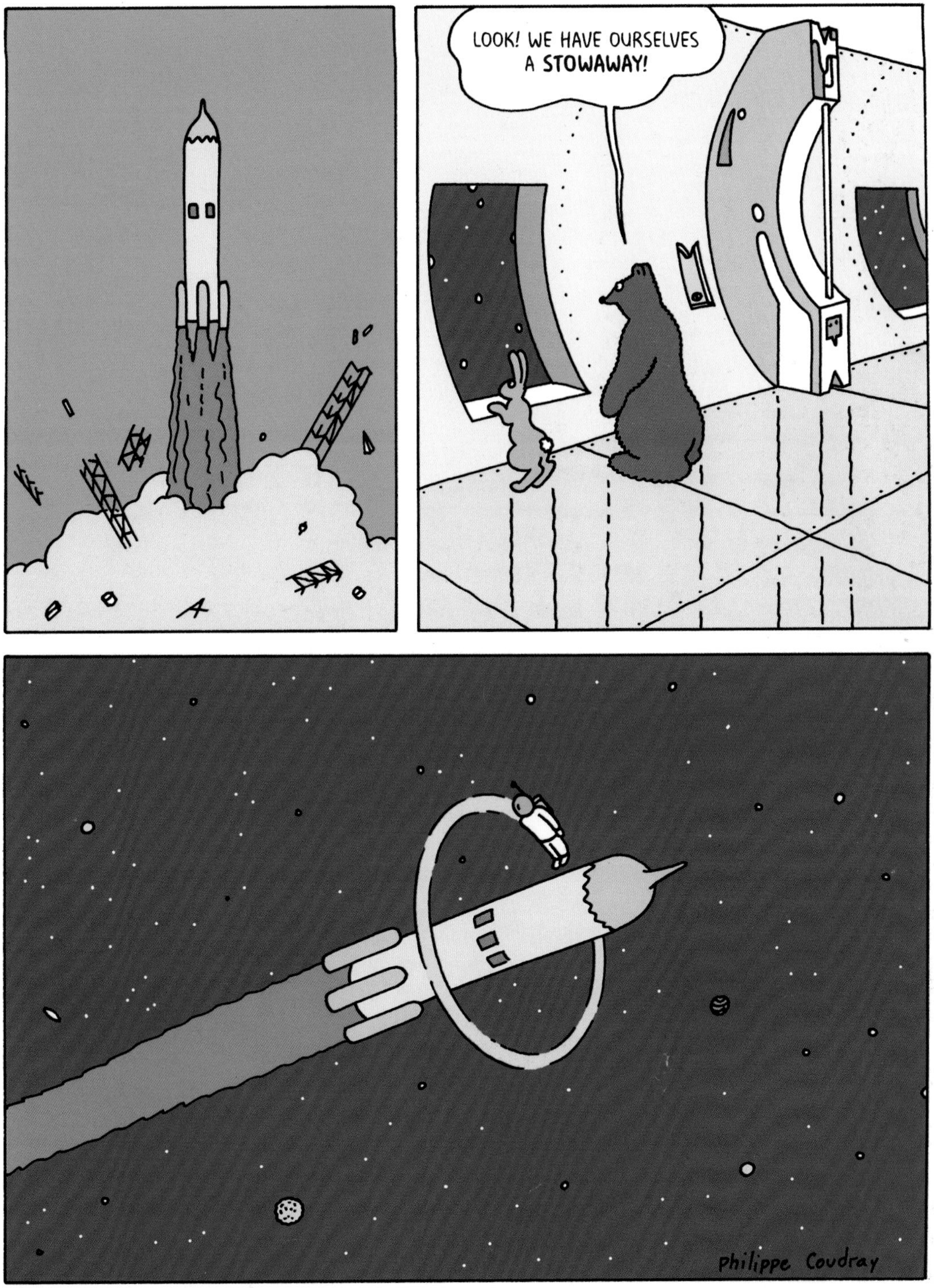
LOOK! WE HAVE OURSELVES A STOWAWAY!
philippe Coudray

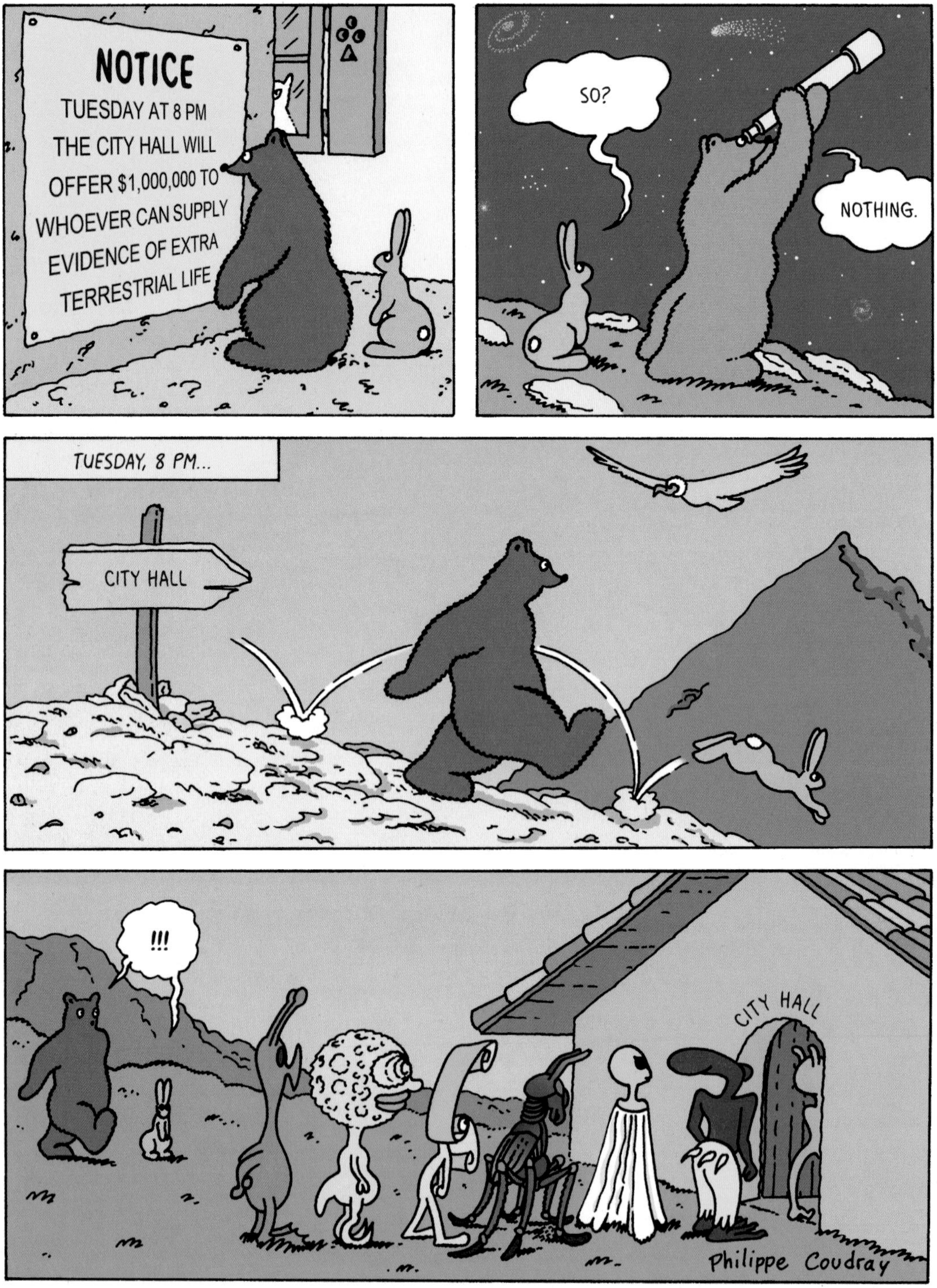
NOTICE
TUESDAY AT 8 PM
THE CITY HALL WILL
OFFER $1,000,000 TO
WHOEVER CAN SUPPLY
EVIDENCE OF EXTRA
TERRESTRIAL LIFE
SO?
NOTHING.
TUESDAY, 8 PM...
CITY HALL
!!!
CITY HALL
Philippe Coudray

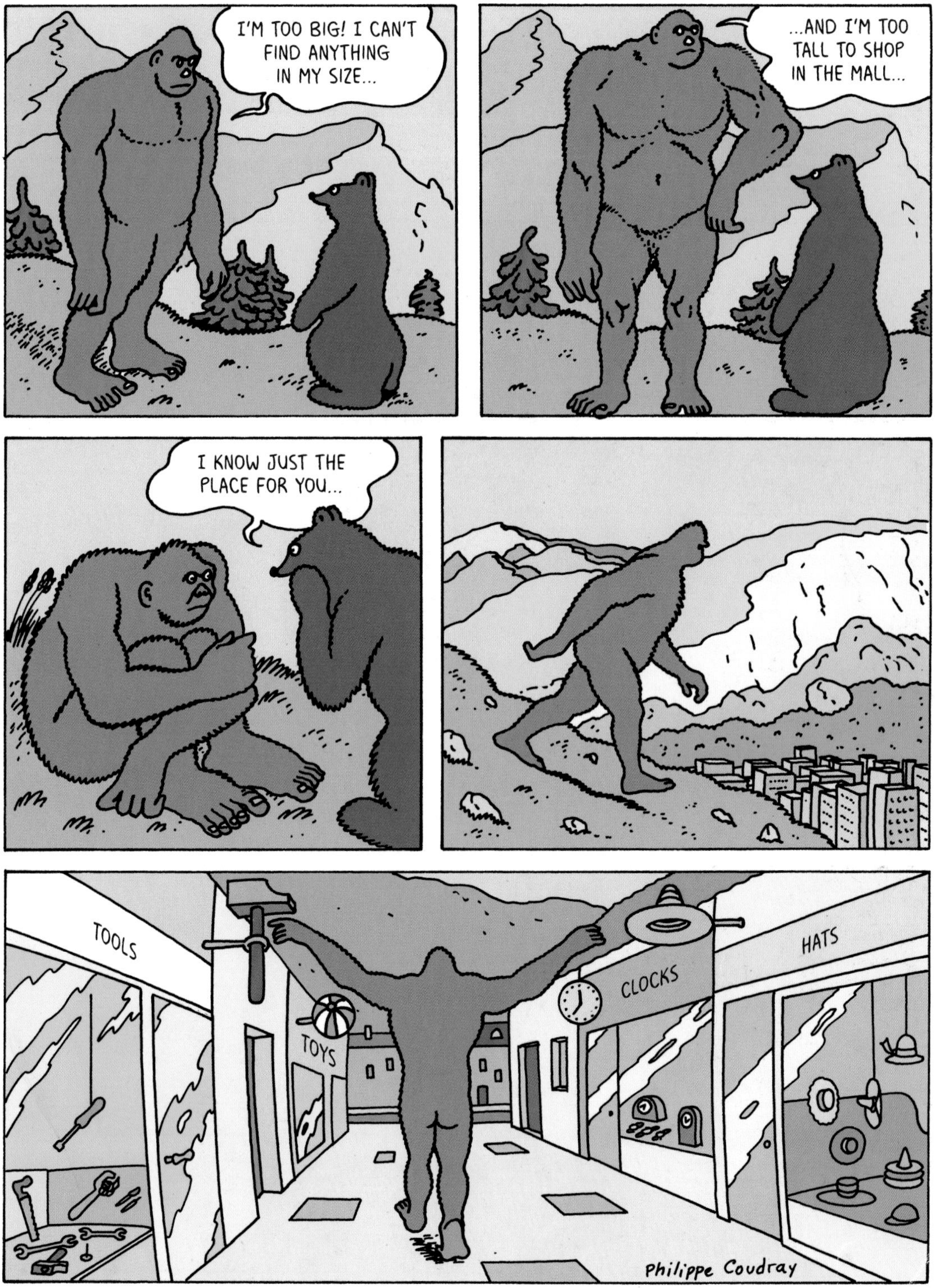
I'M TOO BIG! I CAN'T FIND ANYTHING IN MY SIZE...
...AND I'M TOO TALL TO SHOP IN THE MALL...
I KNOW JUST THE PLACE FOR YOU...
TOOLS
TOYS
CLOCKS
HATS
Philippe Coudray

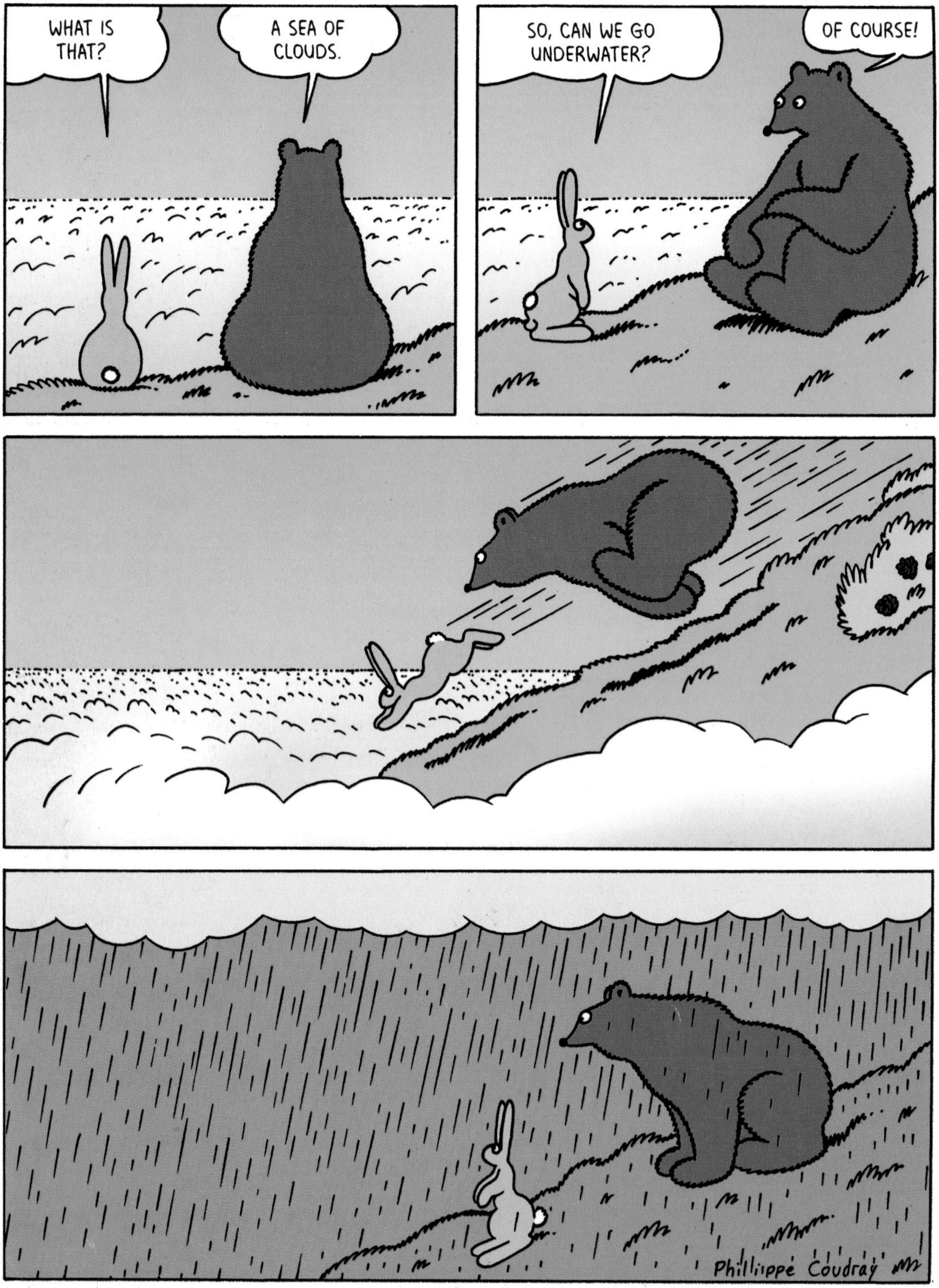
WHAT IS THAT?
A SEA OF CLOUDS.
SO, CAN WE GO UNDERWATER?
OF COURSE!
Phillippe Coudray

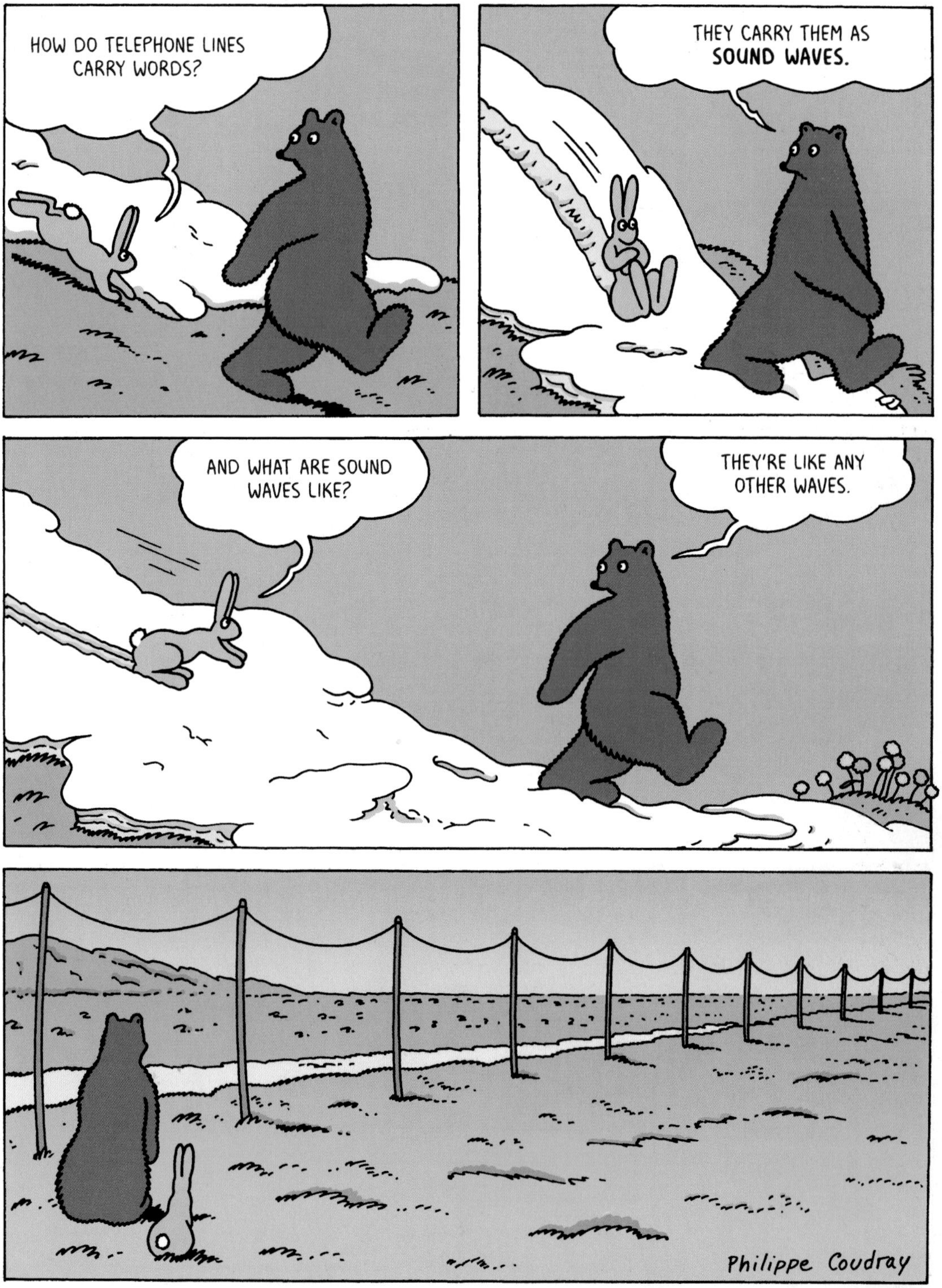

HOW DO TELEPHONE LINES CARRY WORDS?
THEY CARRY THEM AS **SOUND WAVES.**
AND WHAT ARE SOUND WAVES LIKE?
THEY'RE LIKE ANY OTHER WAVES.
Philippe Coudray

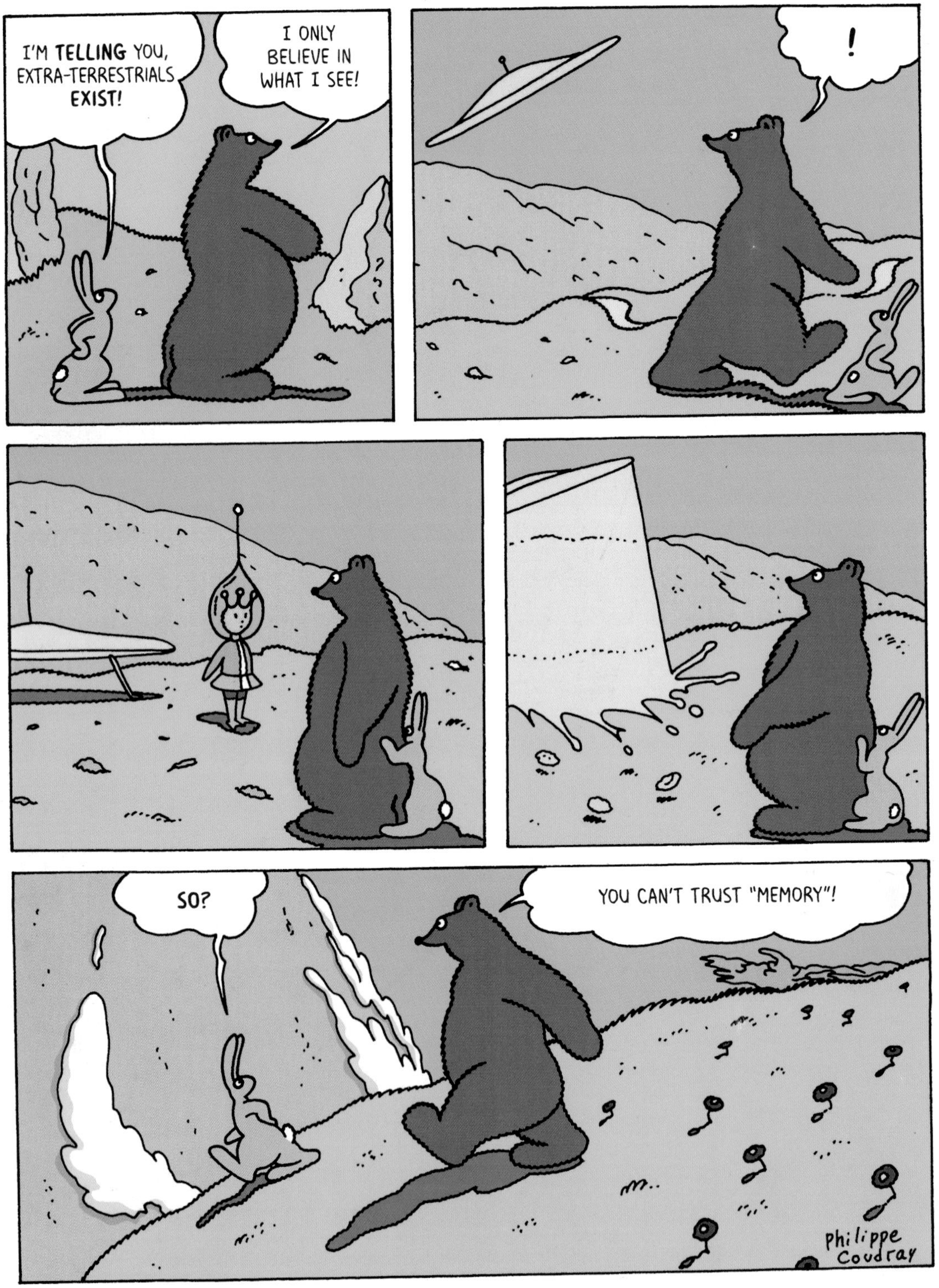
I'M **TELLING** YOU, EXTRA-TERRESTRIALS **EXIST**!
I ONLY BELIEVE IN WHAT I SEE!
!
SO?
YOU CAN'T TRUST "MEMORY"!
Philippe Coudray

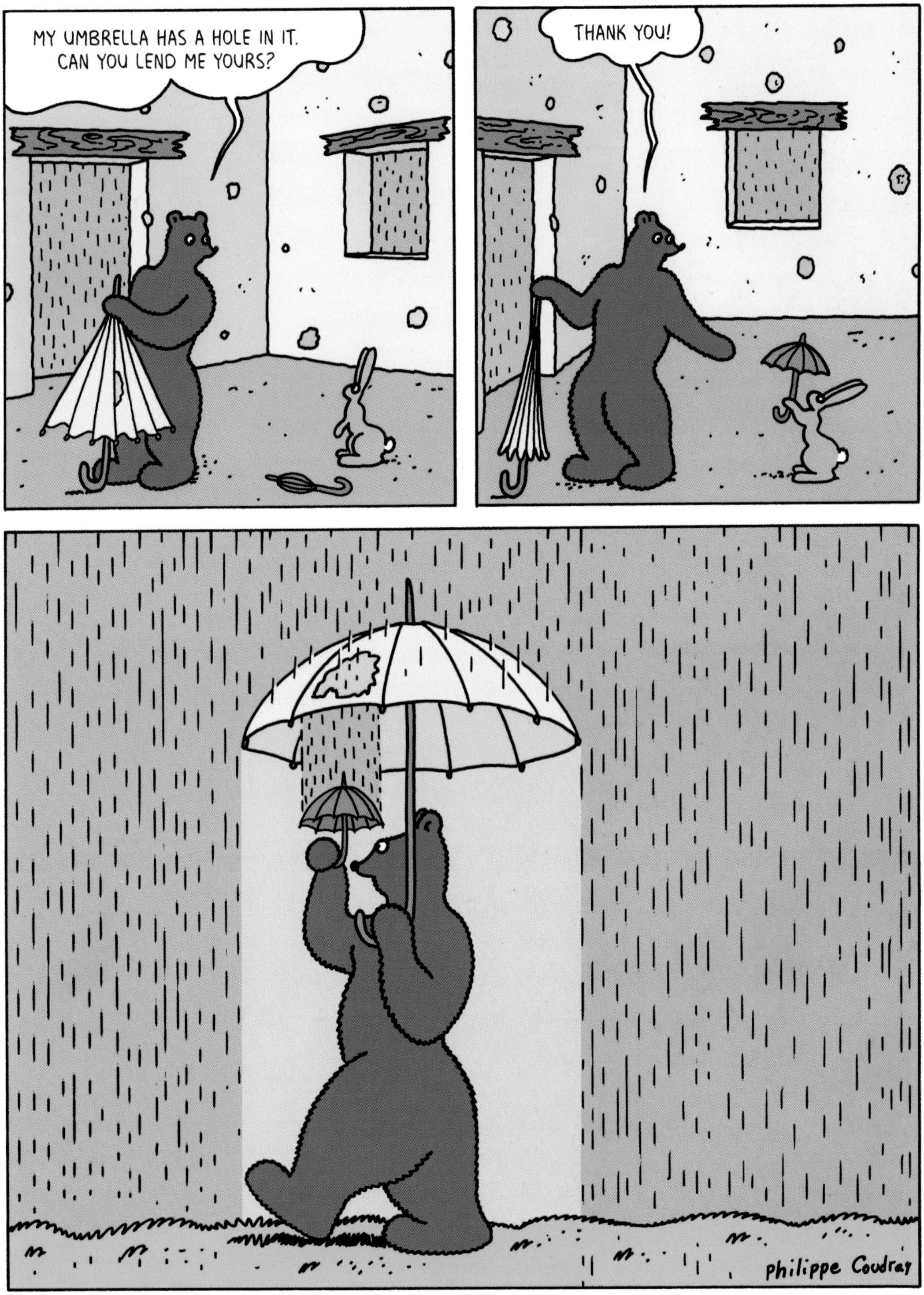
MY UMBRELLA HAS A HOLE IN IT. CAN YOU LEND ME YOURS?
THANK YOU!
Philippe Coudray

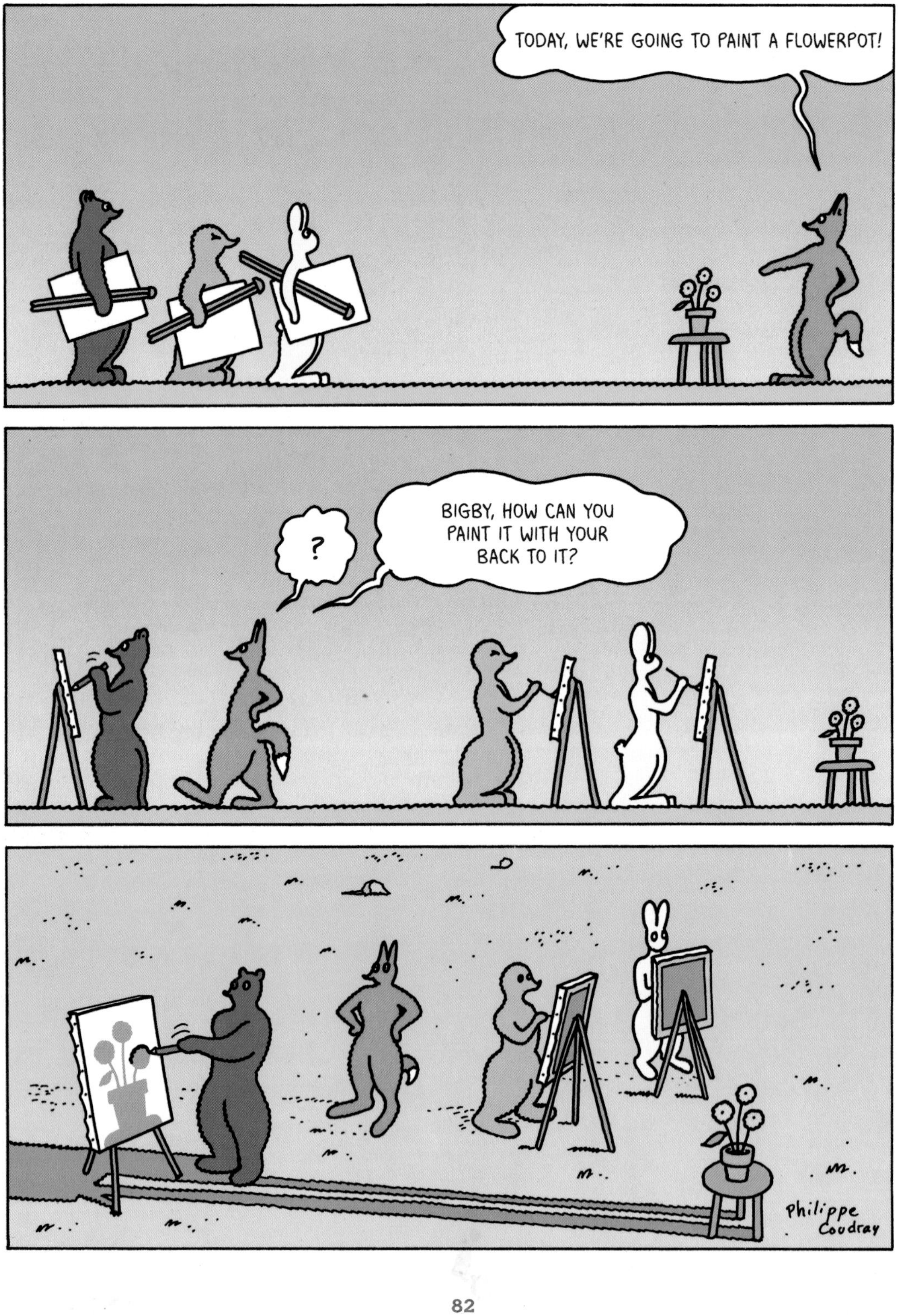
TODAY, WE'RE GOING TO PAINT A FLOWERPOT!
?
BIGBY, HOW CAN YOU PAINT IT WITH YOUR BACK TO IT?
Philippe Coudray

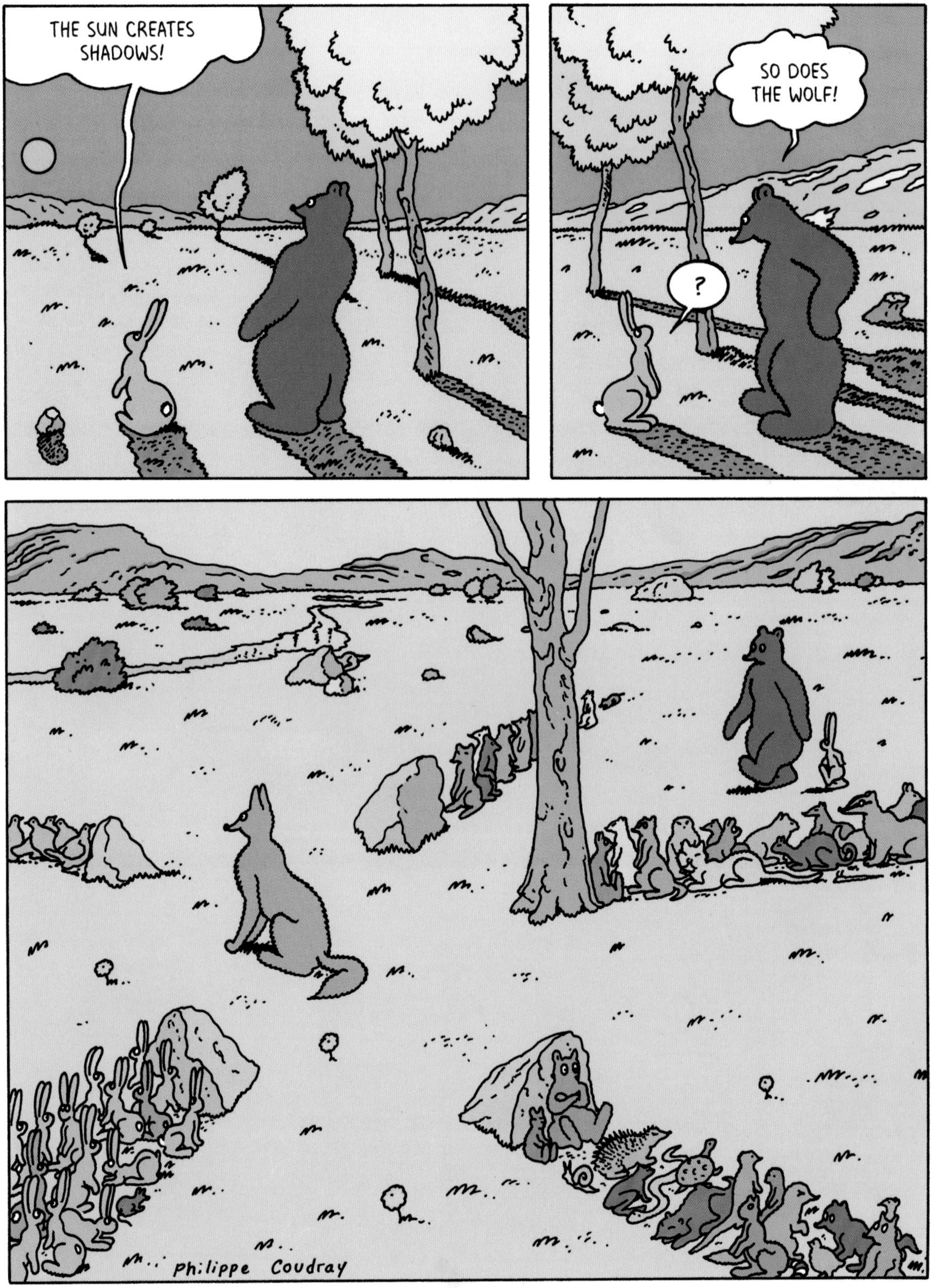
THE SUN CREATES SHADOWS!
SO DOES THE WOLF!
?
philippe Coudray

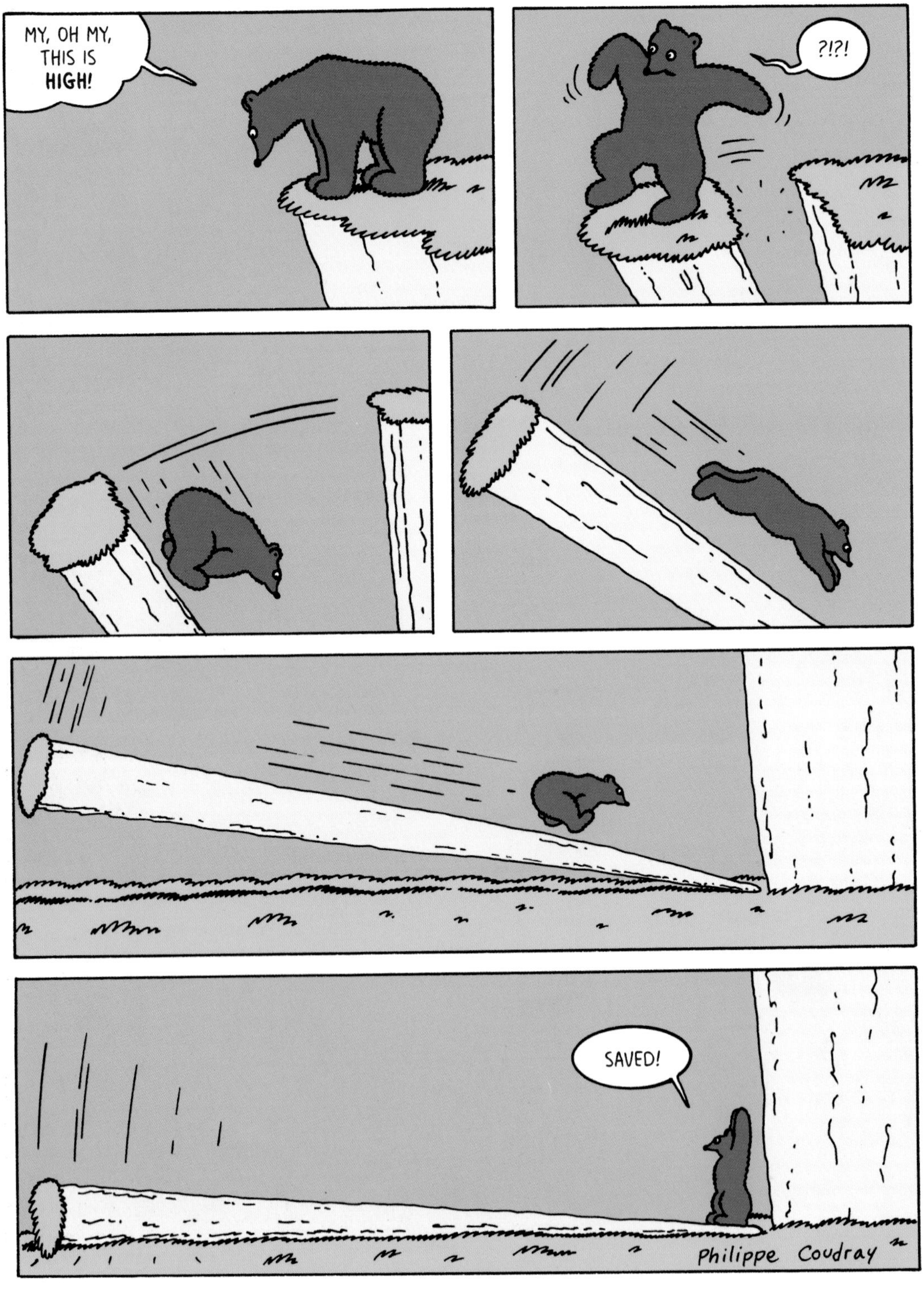
MY, OH MY, THIS IS **HIGH!**
?!?!
SAVED!
Philippe Coudray

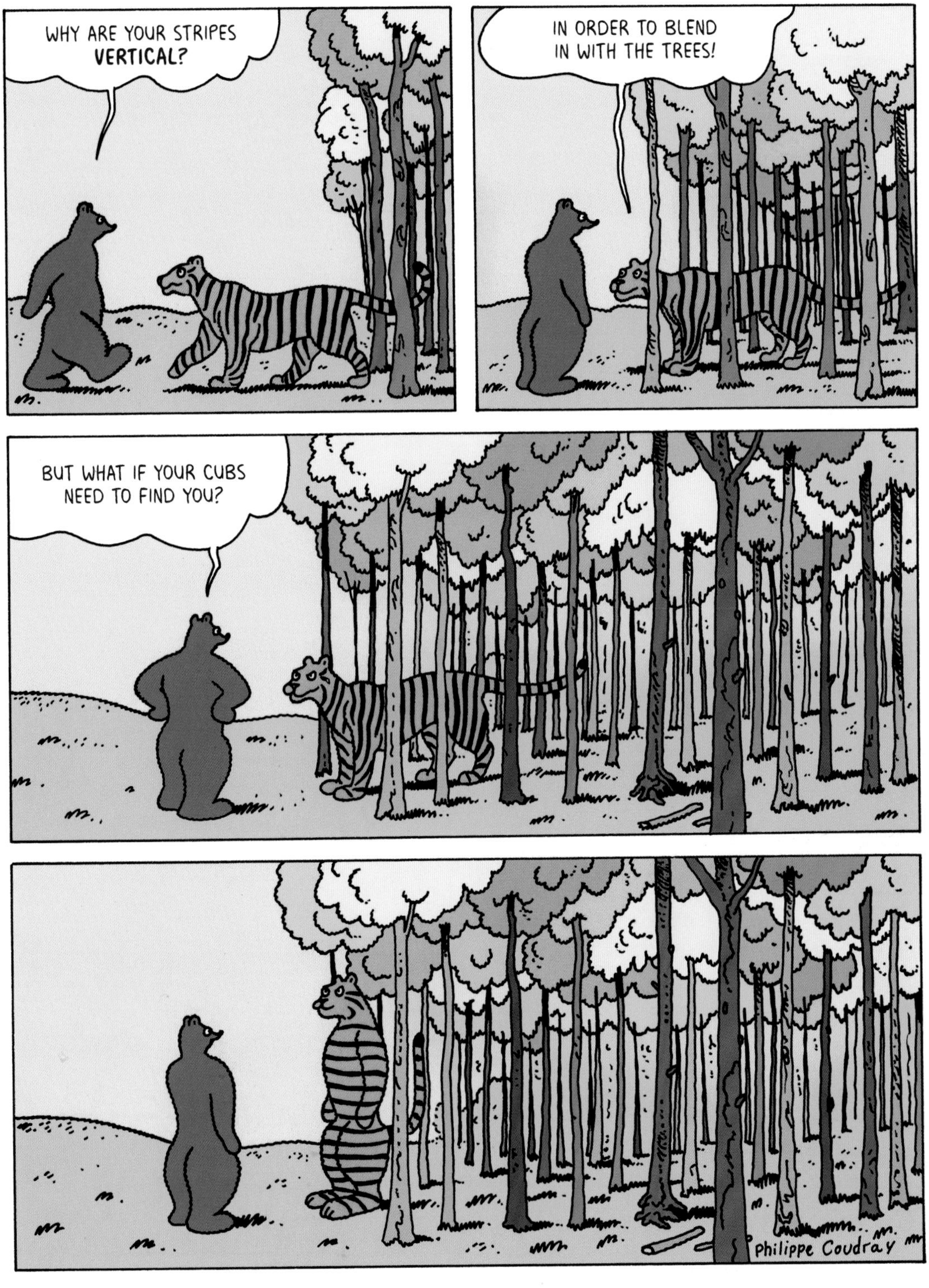
WHY ARE YOUR STRIPES **VERTICAL?**
IN ORDER TO BLEND IN WITH THE TREES!
BUT WHAT IF YOUR CUBS NEED TO FIND YOU?
Philippe Coudray

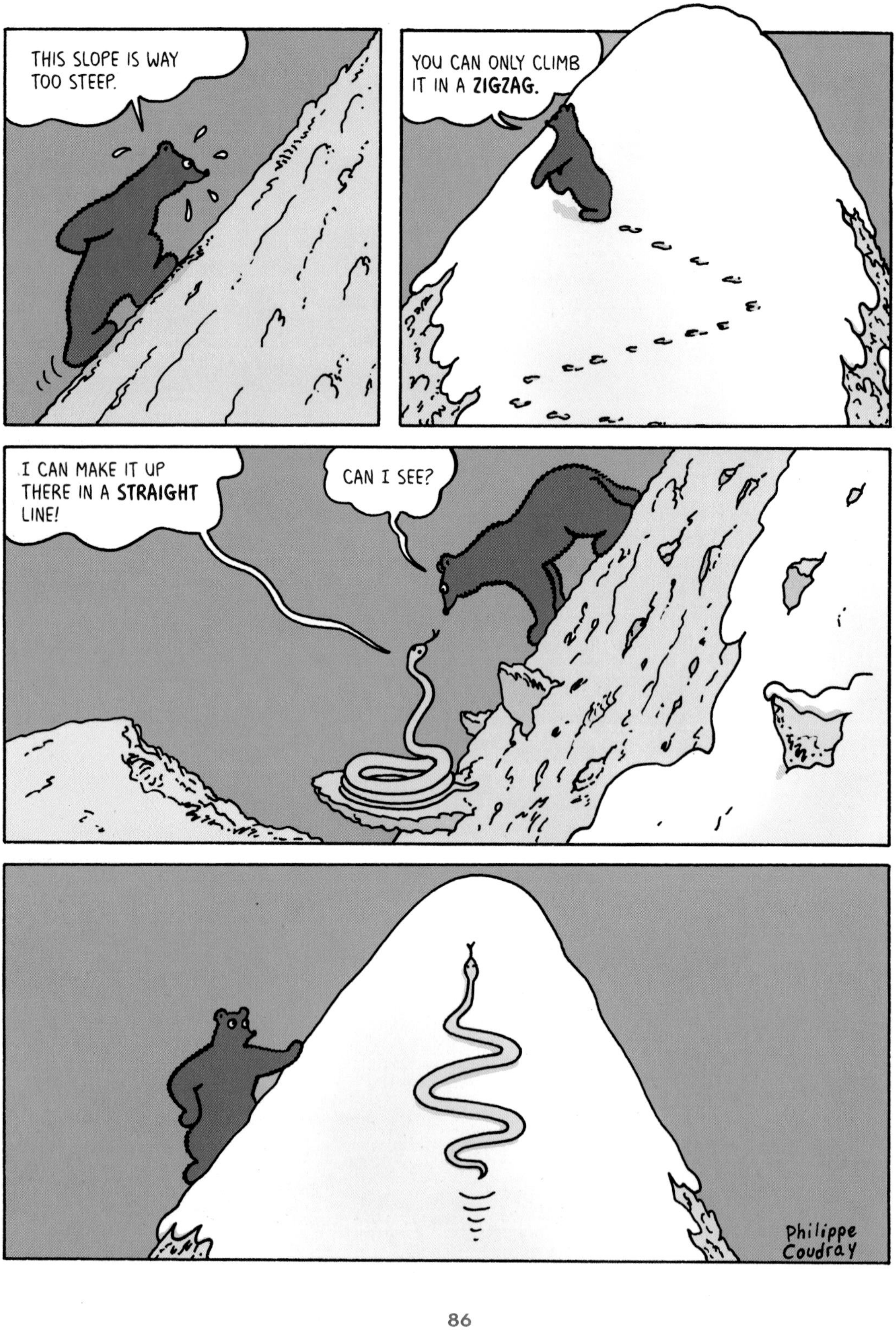
THIS SLOPE IS WAY TOO STEEP.
YOU CAN ONLY CLIMB IT IN A **ZIGZAG.**
I CAN MAKE IT UP THERE IN A **STRAIGHT** LINE!
CAN I SEE?
Philippe Coudray

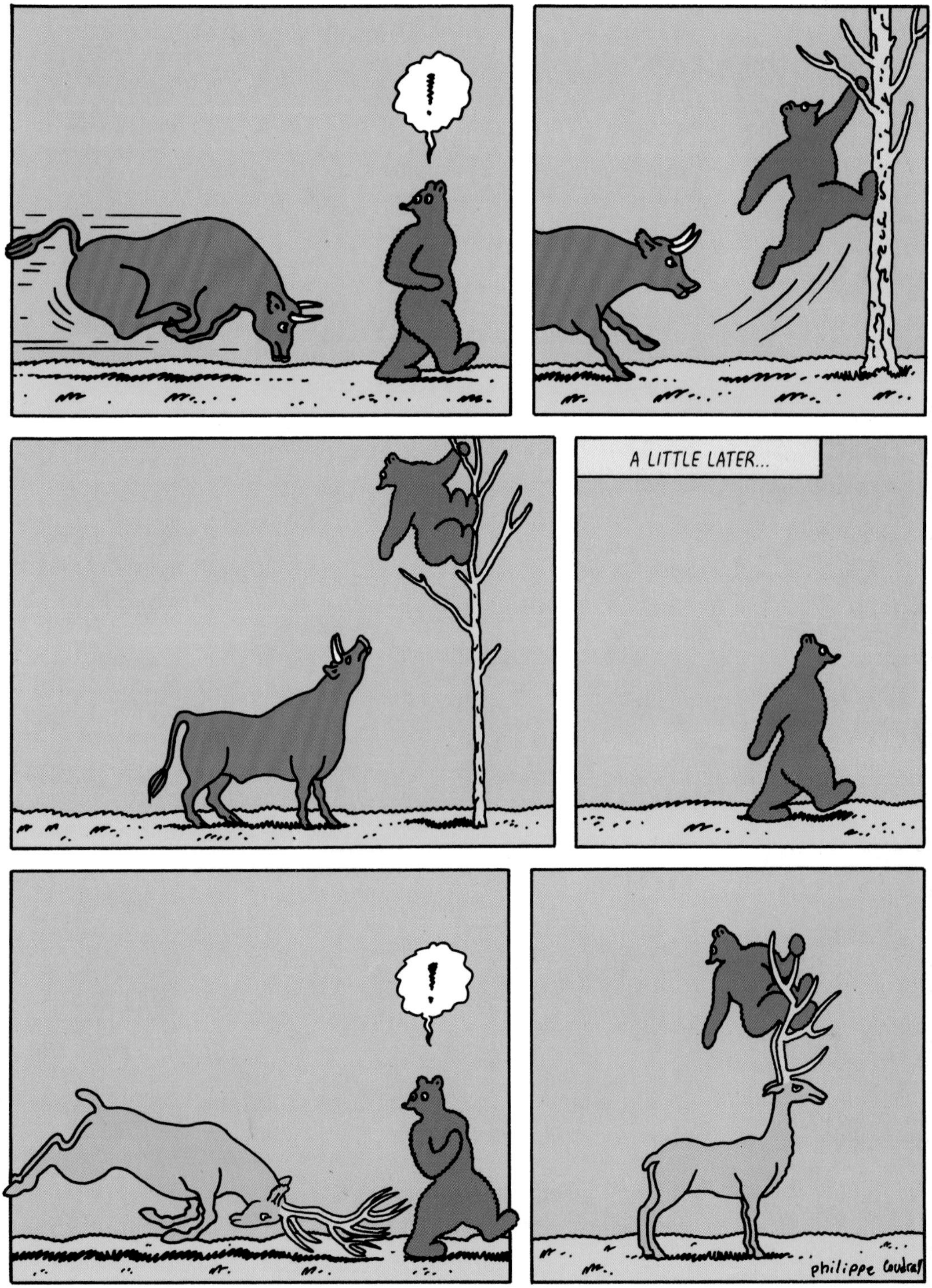
!
A LITTLE LATER...
!
philippe Coudray

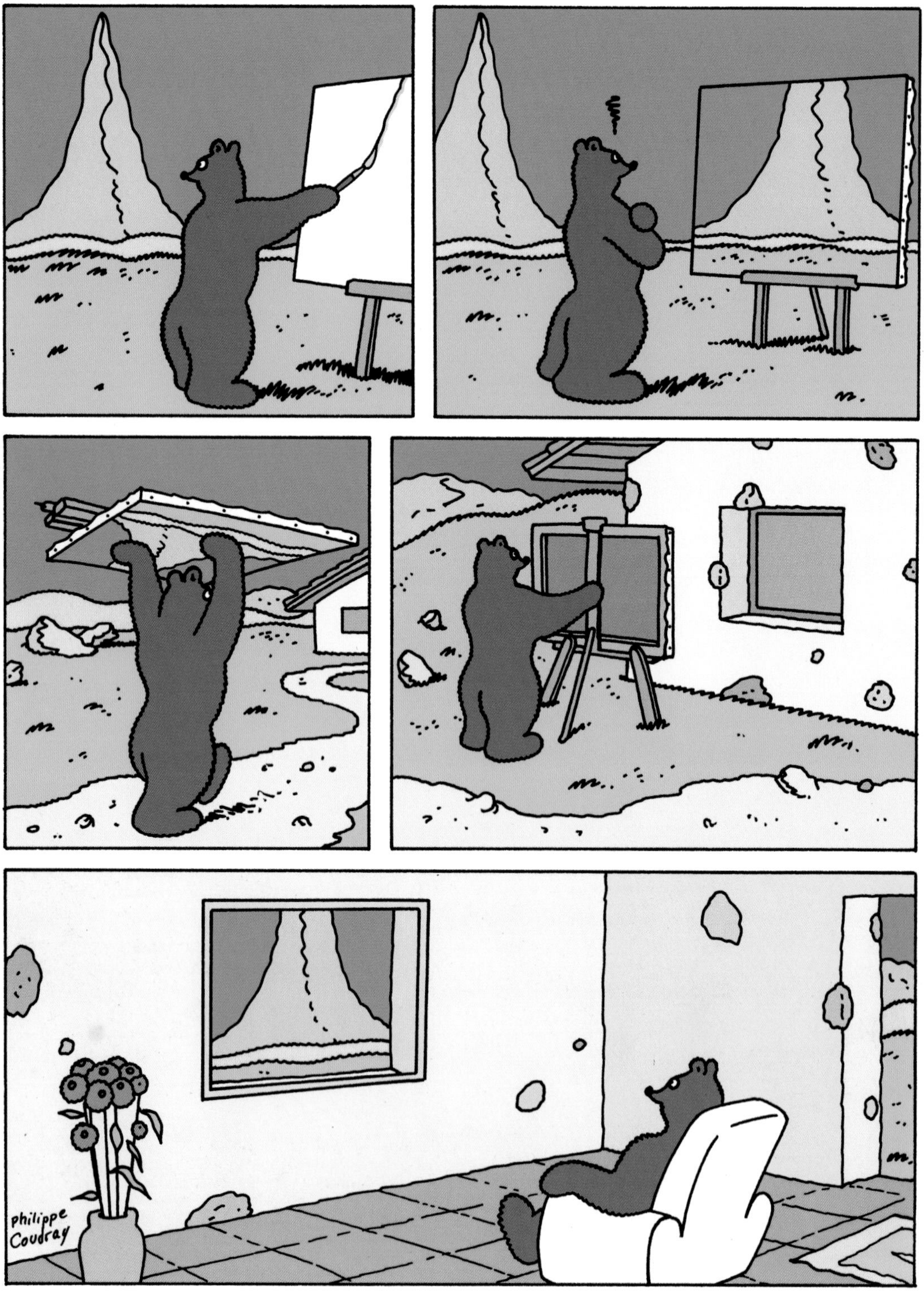
philippe
Coudray

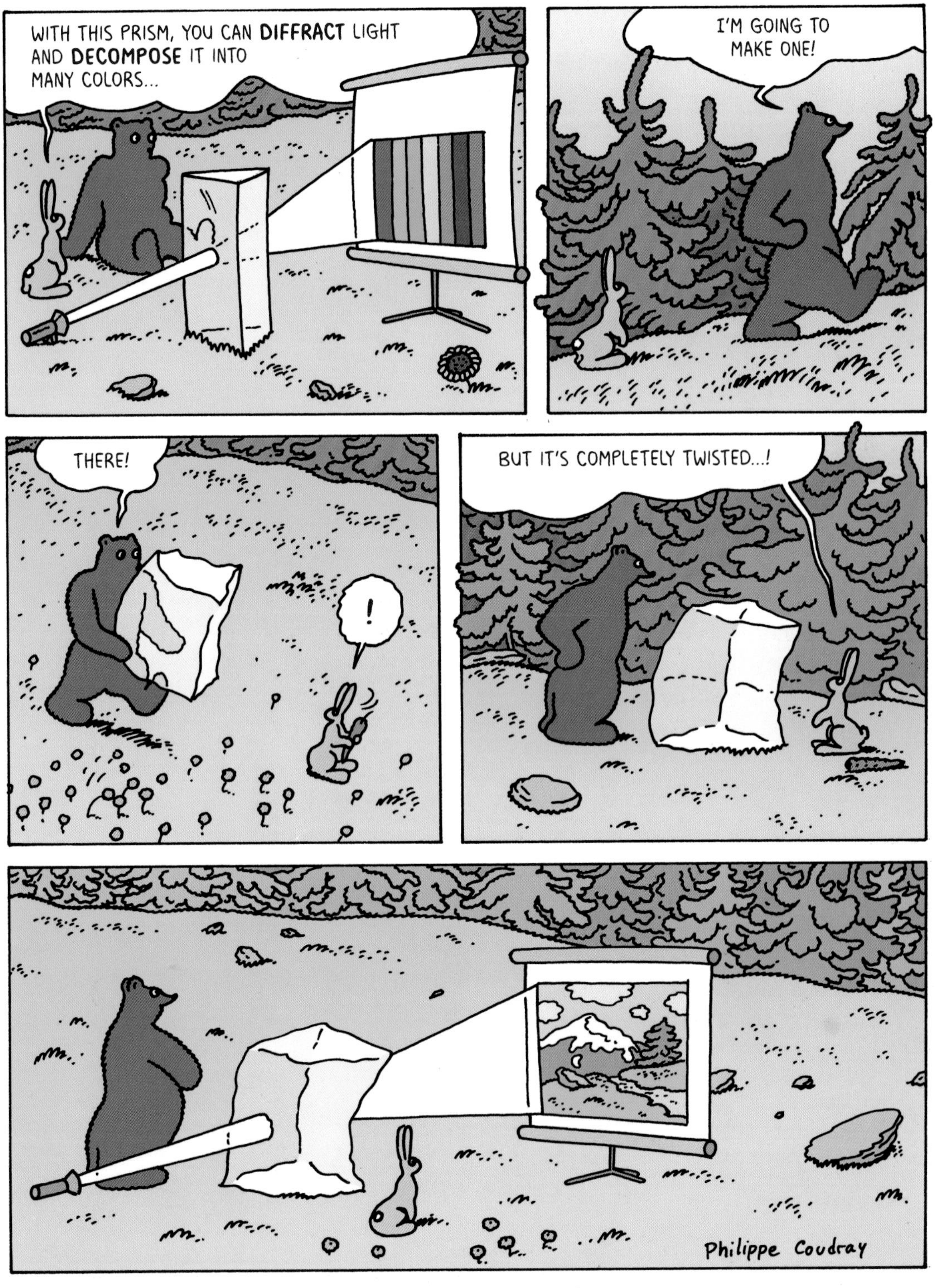
WITH THIS PRISM, YOU CAN **DIFFRACT** LIGHT AND **DECOMPOSE** IT INTO MANY COLORS...
I'M GOING TO MAKE ONE!
THERE!
!
BUT IT'S COMPLETELY TWISTED...!
Philippe Coudray

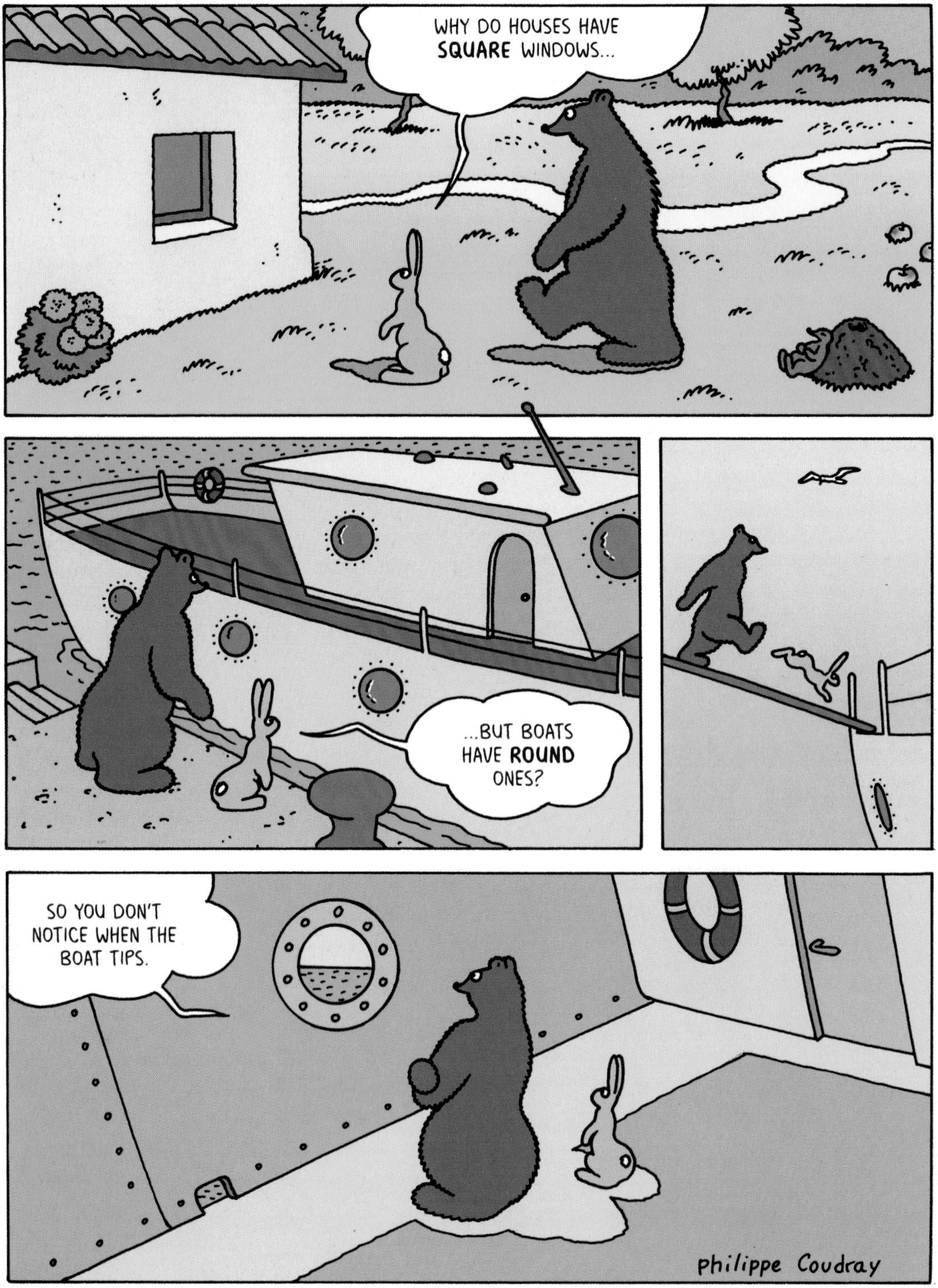
WHY DO HOUSES HAVE **SQUARE** WINDOWS...
...BUT BOATS HAVE **ROUND** ONES?
SO YOU DON'T NOTICE WHEN THE BOAT TIPS.
Philippe Coudray

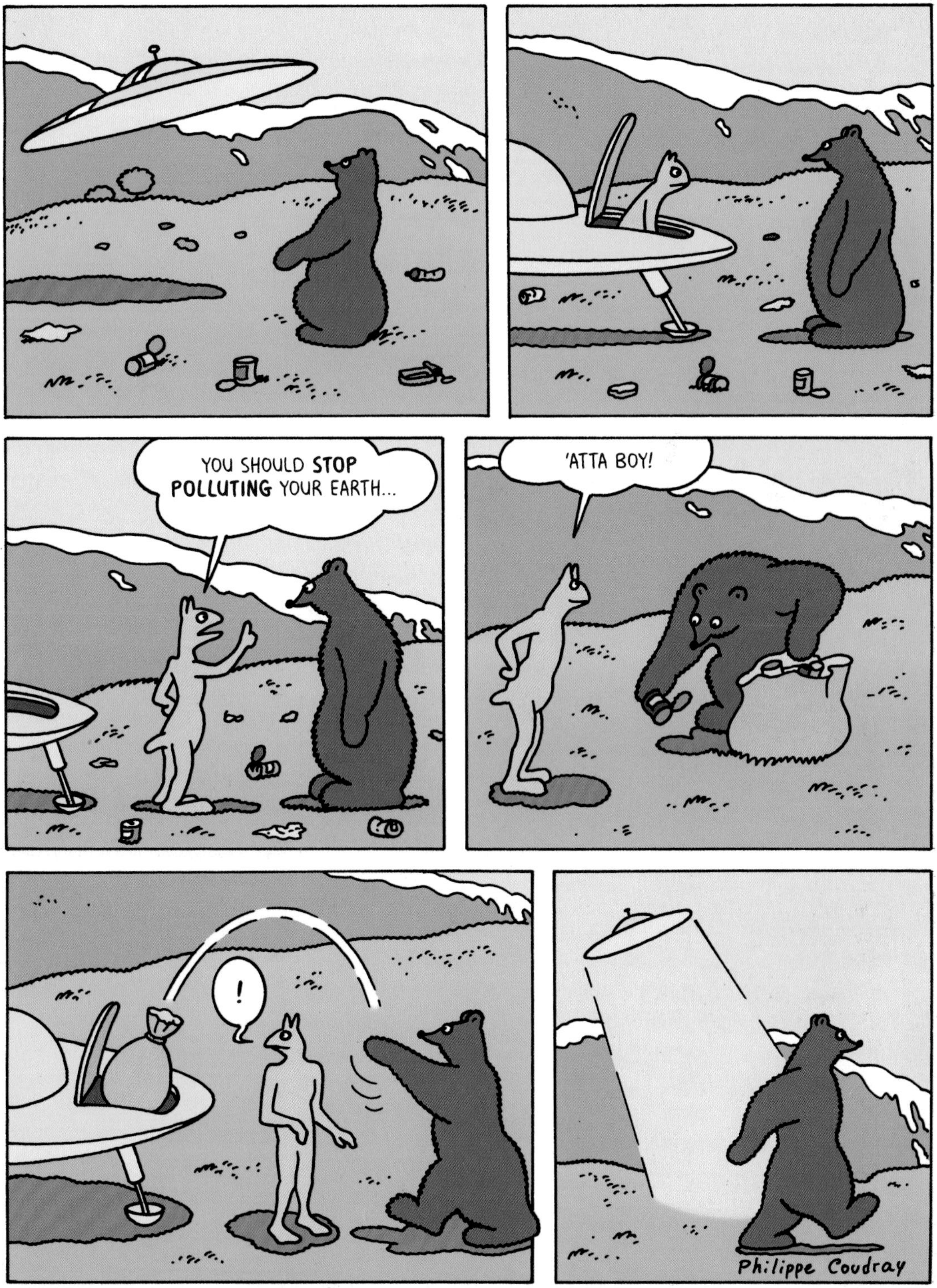
YOU SHOULD **STOP POLLUTING** YOUR EARTH...
'ATTA BOY!
!
Philippe Coudray

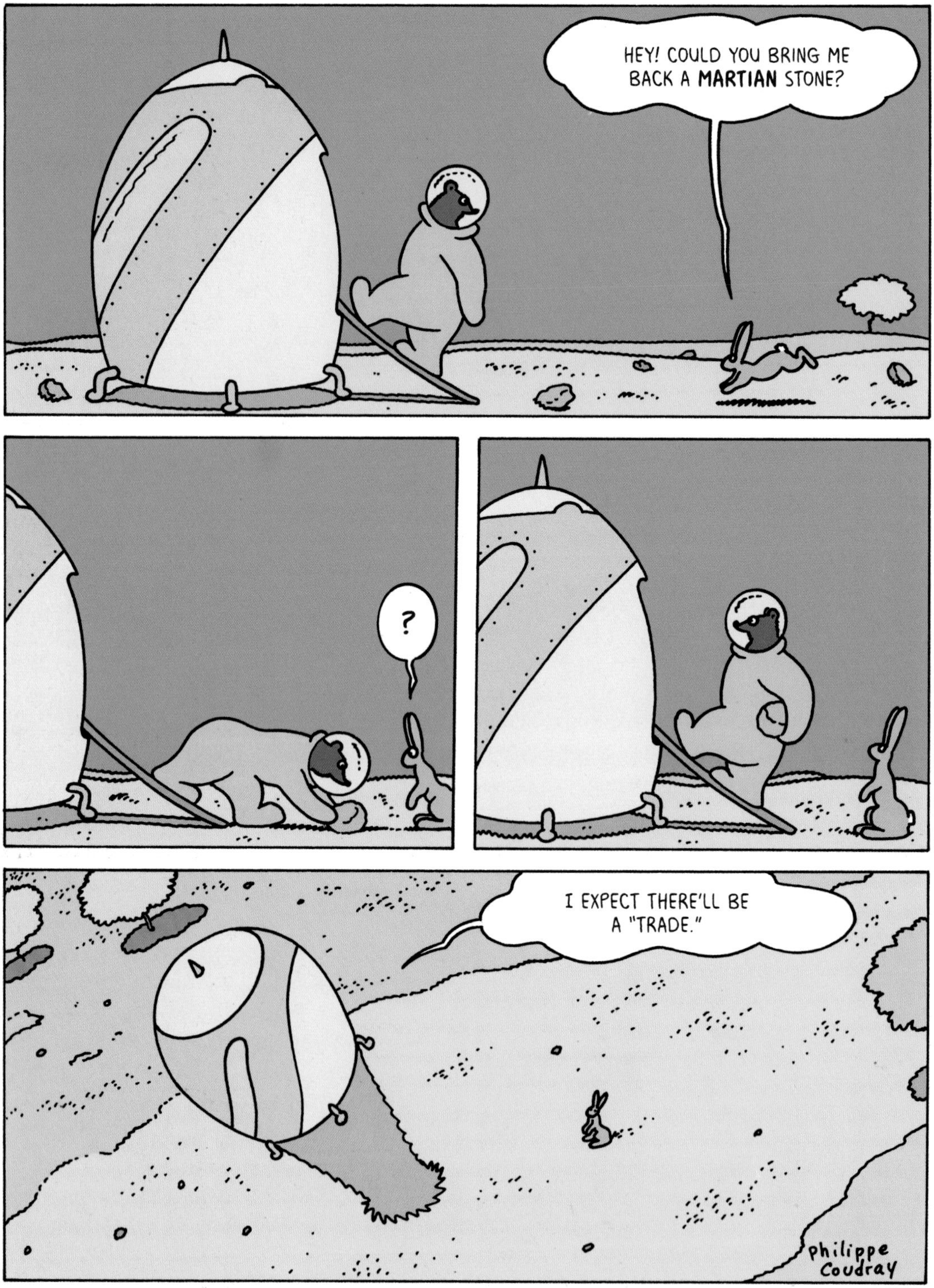
HEY! COULD YOU BRING ME BACK A **MARTIAN** STONE?
?
I EXPECT THERE'LL BE A "TRADE."
philippe Coudray

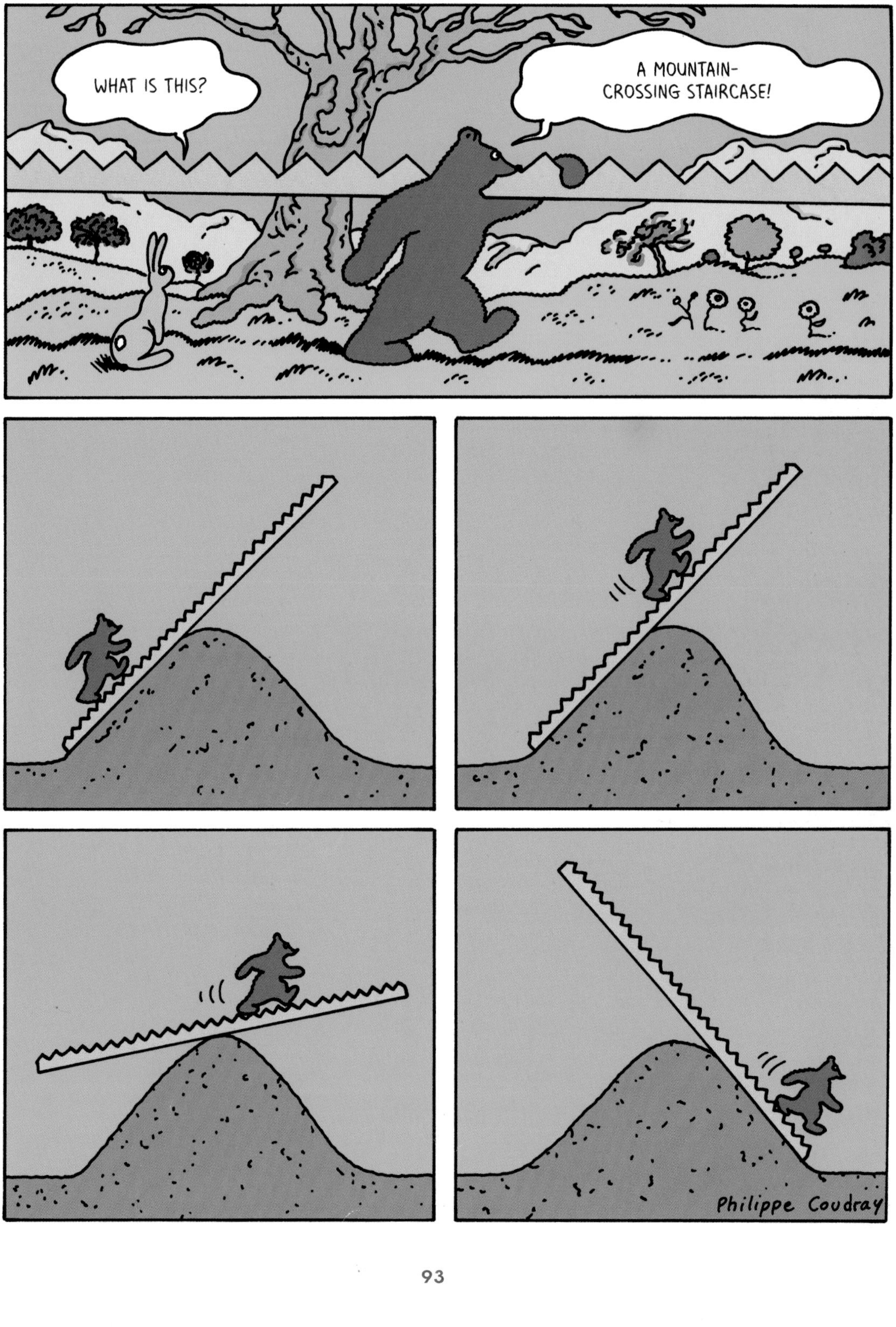
WHAT IS THIS?
A MOUNTAIN-CROSSING STAIRCASE!
Philippe Coudray

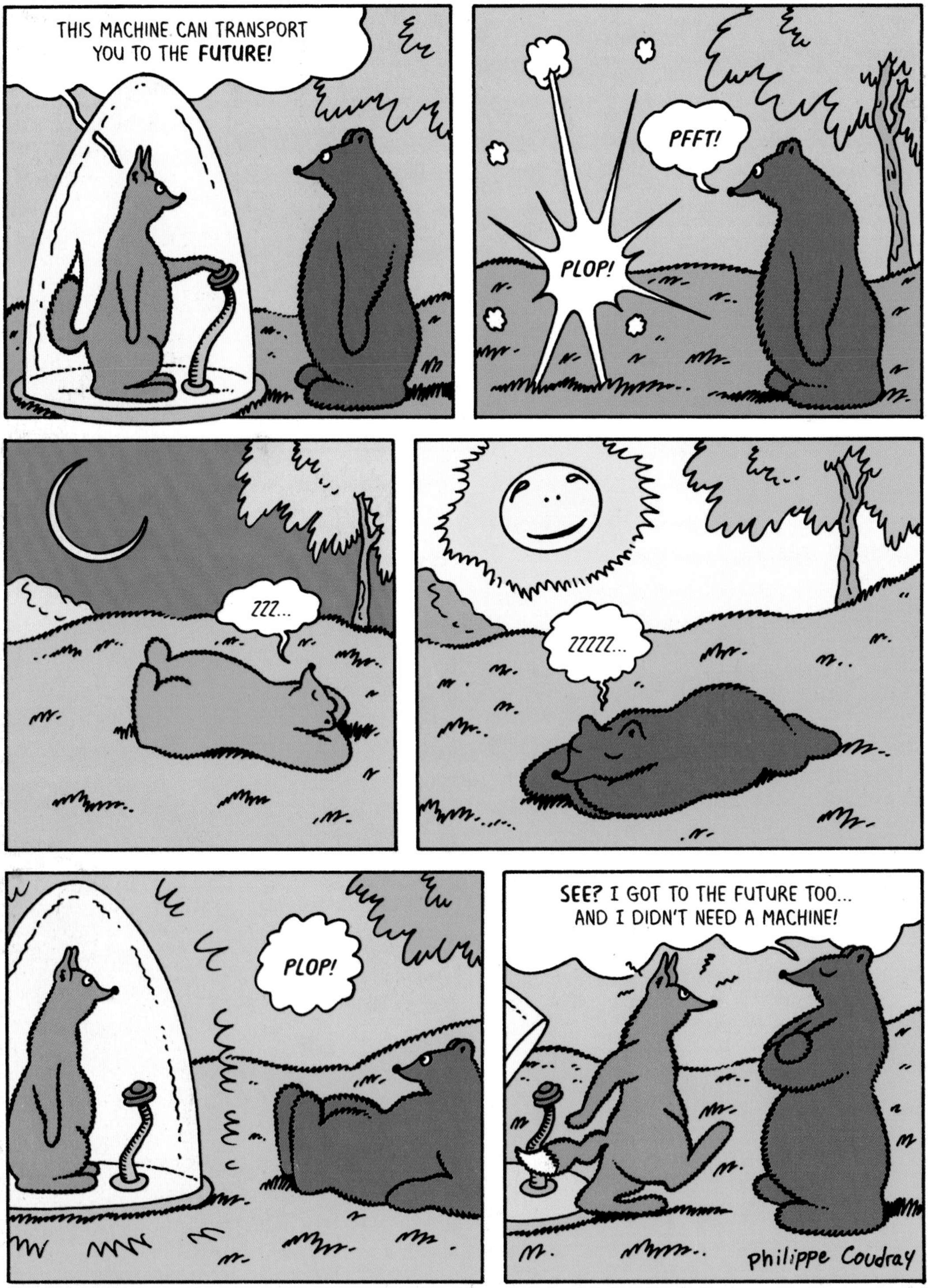

THIS MACHINE CAN TRANSPORT YOU TO THE **FUTURE!**
PLOP!
PFFT!
ZZZ...
ZZZZZ...
PLOP!
SEE? I GOT TO THE FUTURE TOO... AND I DIDN'T NEED A MACHINE!
Philippe Coudray

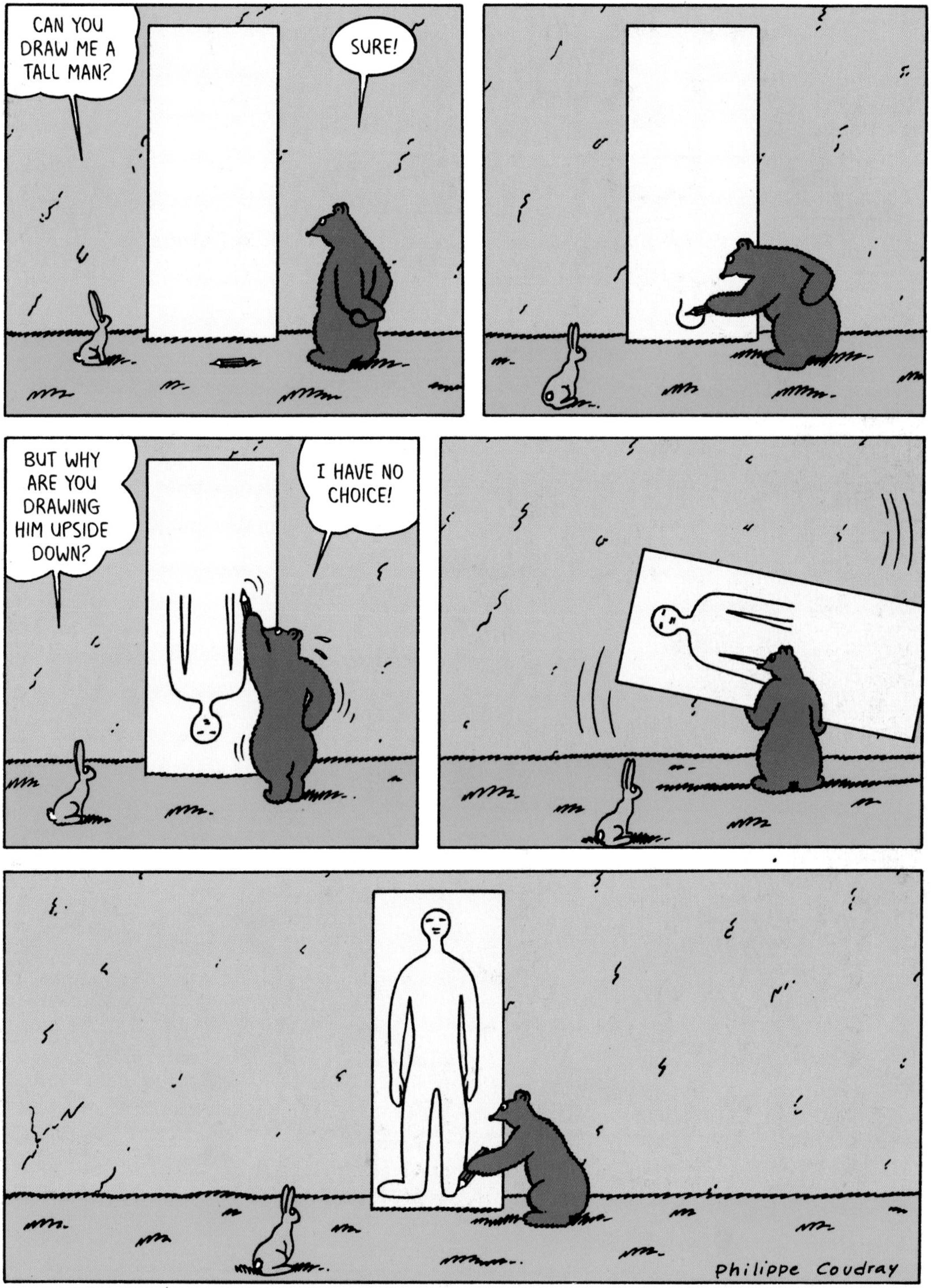
CAN YOU DRAW ME A TALL MAN?
SURE!
BUT WHY ARE YOU DRAWING HIM UPSIDE DOWN?
I HAVE NO CHOICE!
Philippe Coudray

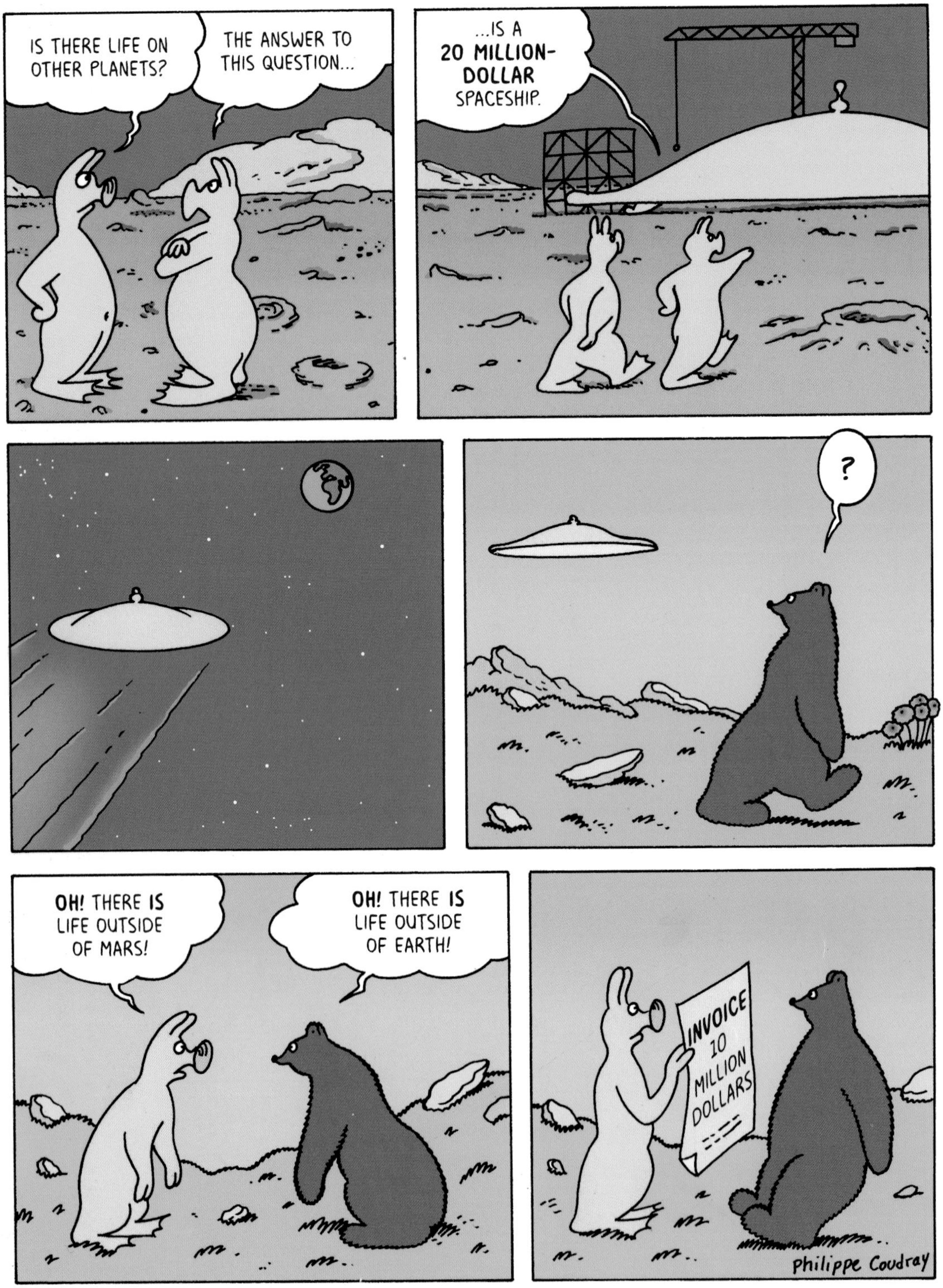
IS THERE LIFE ON OTHER PLANETS?
THE ANSWER TO THIS QUESTION...
...IS A **20 MILLION-DOLLAR** SPACESHIP.
?
OH! THERE **IS** LIFE OUTSIDE OF MARS!
OH! THERE **IS** LIFE OUTSIDE OF EARTH!
INVOICE 10 MILLION DOLLARS
Philippe Coudray

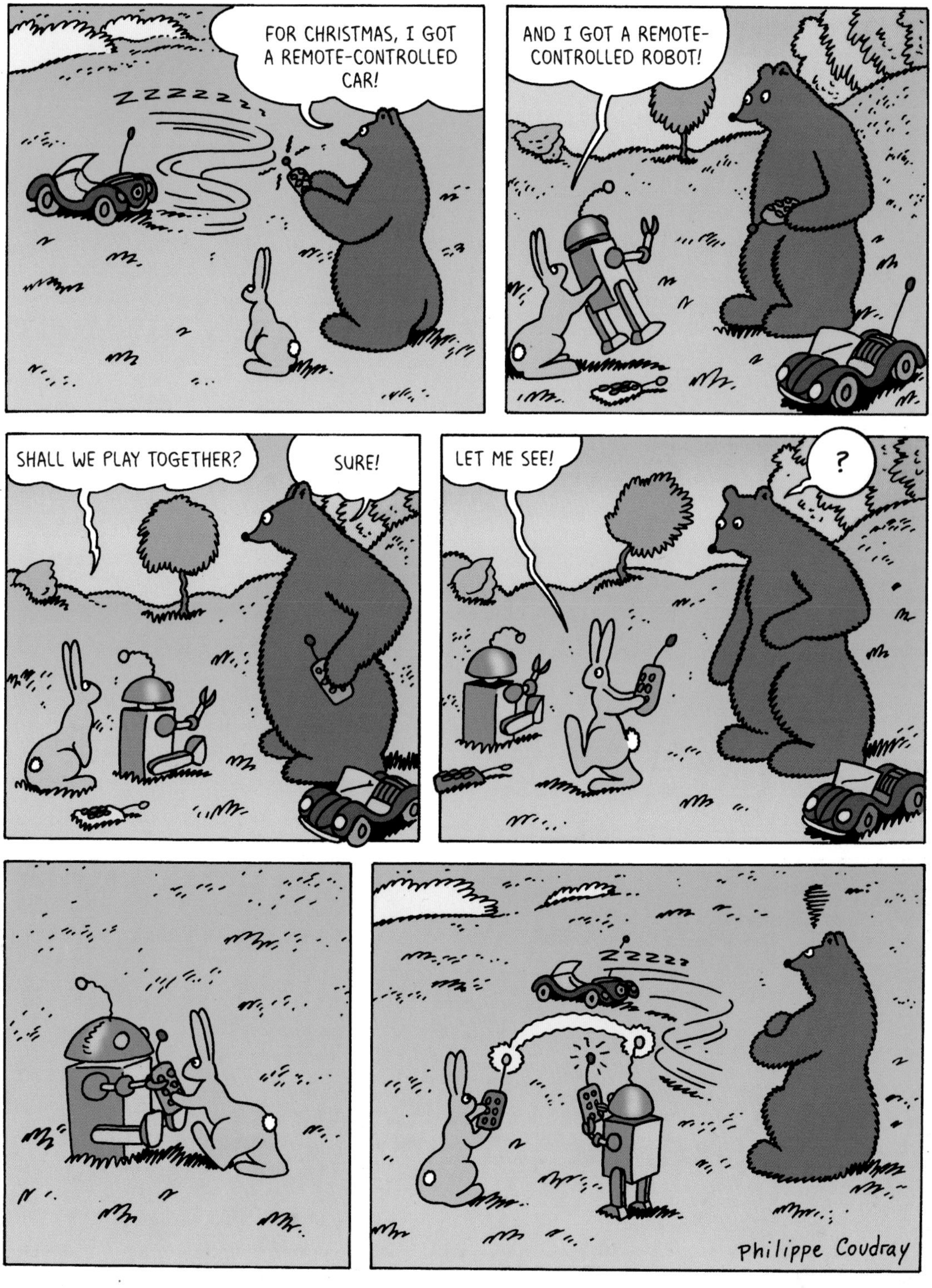

FOR CHRISTMAS, I GOT A REMOTE-CONTROLLED CAR!
ZZZZZZZZ
AND I GOT A REMOTE-CONTROLLED ROBOT!
SHALL WE PLAY TOGETHER?
SURE!
LET ME SEE!
?
ZZZZZ
Philippe Coudray

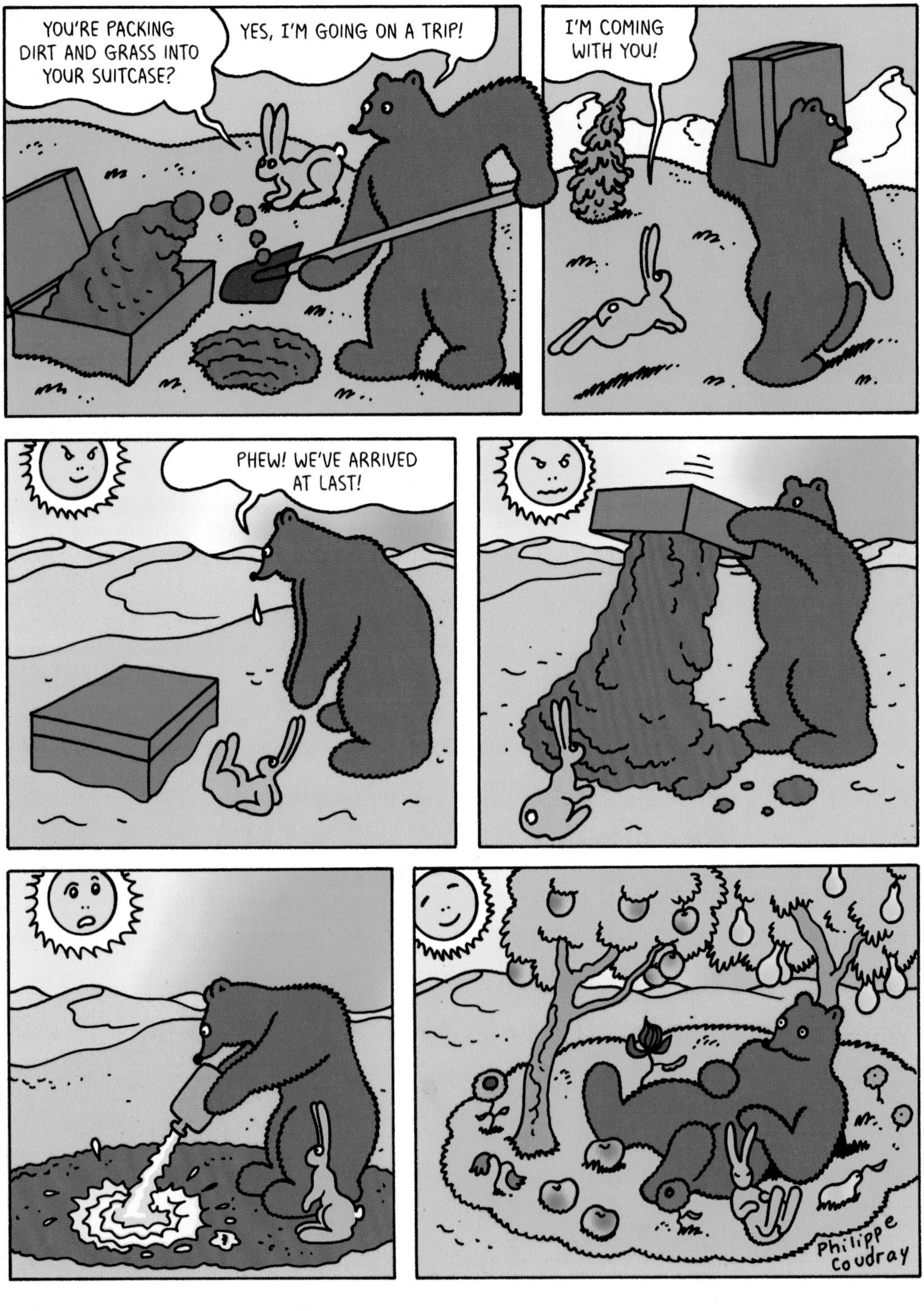
YOU'RE PACKING DIRT AND GRASS INTO YOUR SUITCASE?
YES, I'M GOING ON A TRIP!
I'M COMING WITH YOU!
PHEW! WE'VE ARRIVED AT LAST!
Philippe Coudray

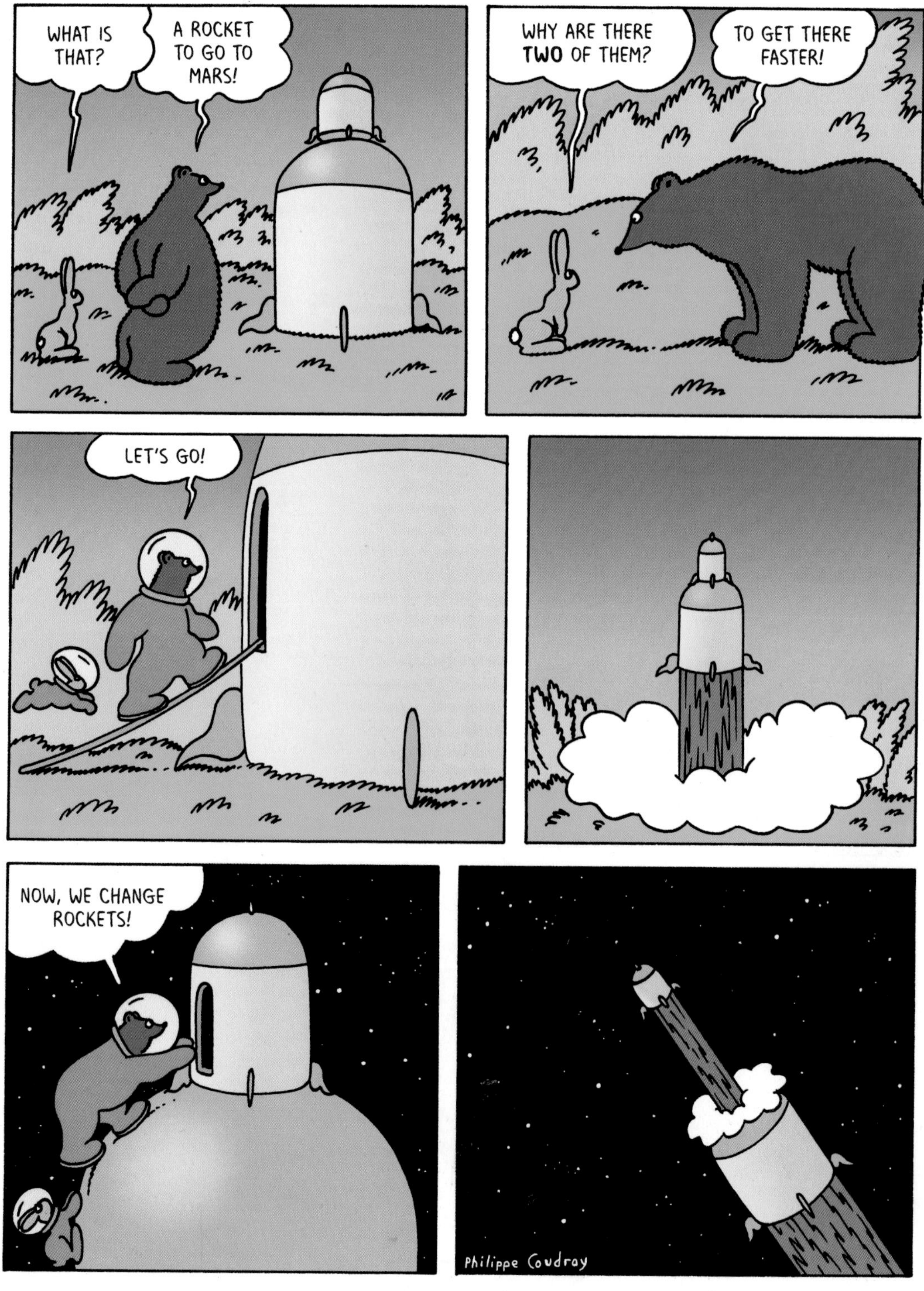
WHAT IS THAT?
A ROCKET TO GO TO MARS!
WHY ARE THERE **TWO** OF THEM?
TO GET THERE FASTER!
LET'S GO!
NOW, WE CHANGE ROCKETS!
Philippe Coudray

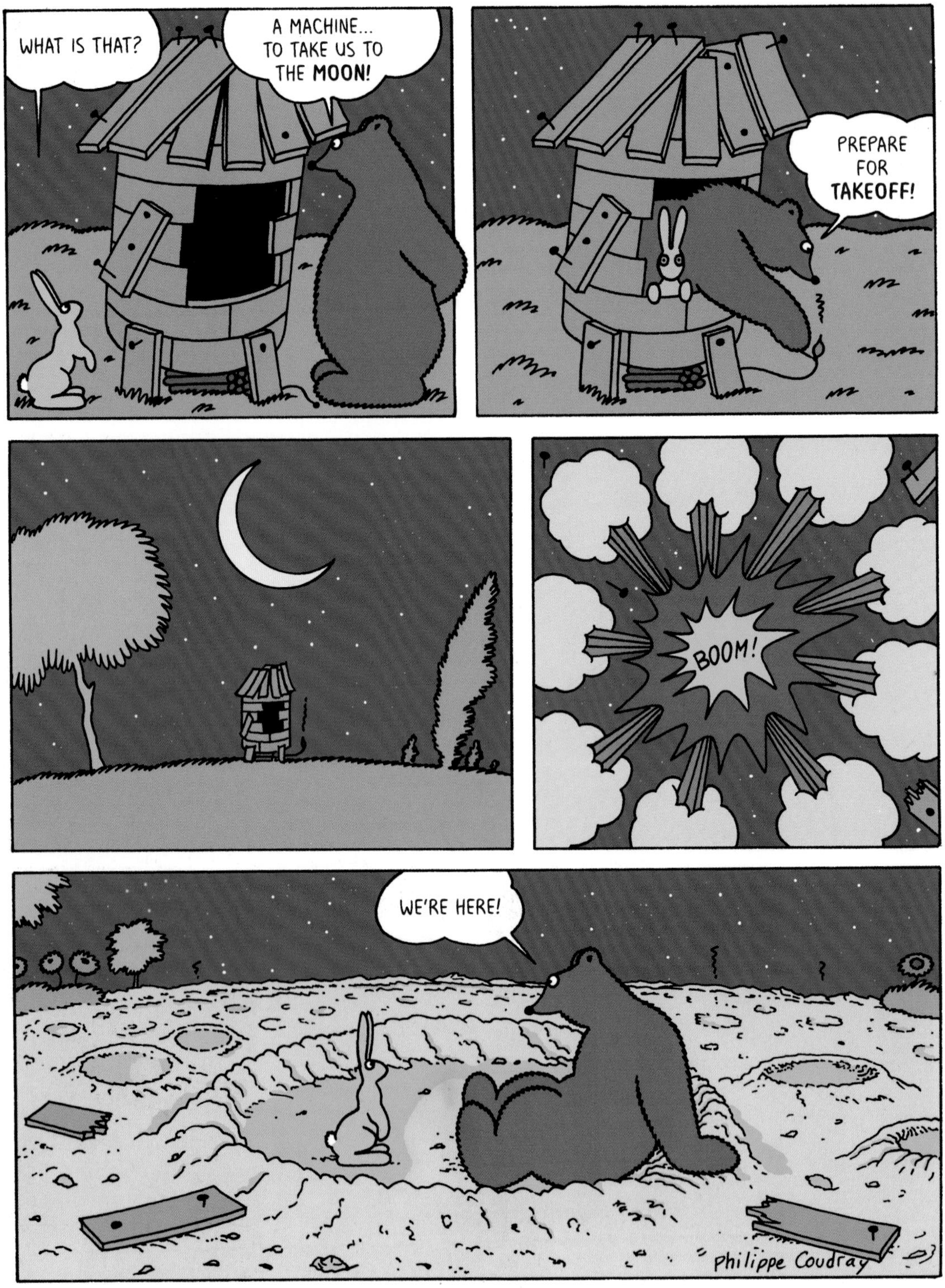
WHAT IS THAT?
A MACHINE... TO TAKE US TO THE **MOON!**
PREPARE FOR **TAKEOFF!**
BOOM!
WE'RE HERE!
Philippe Coudray

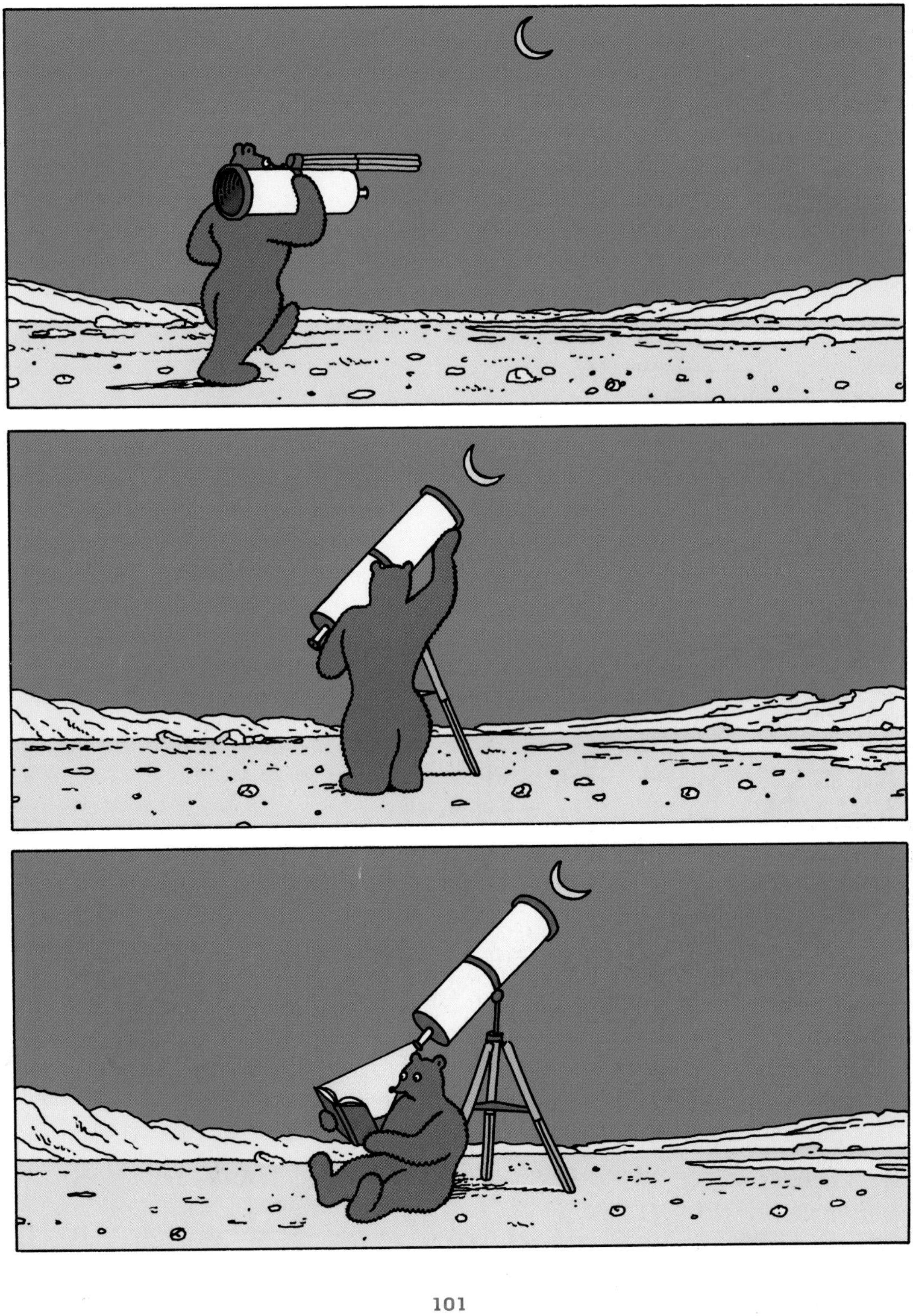